The DOUBLE-D

vs.

The Super Nudists

William Winckler

CHAPTER ONE

It was a sunny afternoon in Driftwood Valley, when a golf cart suddenly appeared from out of nowhere. It was illegally driving down busy Humdingers Highway from the nearby golf course, zooming erratically towards the town's bank, Liberty Bells Savings. Behind the wheel of the electric-powered cart was city councilman Max Phuckter, a sweaty, intoxicated, burly man in his forties, downing his sixth can of beer! It was nearly four-o'clock, as Phuckter, dressed in golf clothes, pulled into the bank's driveway.

The bank building itself was one of Driftwood Valley's most magnificent achievements in mid-century novelty architecture, built in the shape of a giant, two-story piggy bank! The entire pink pig structure looked like a child's toy bank, with the drive-up teller window strategically placed under the building's curly tail . . . exactly where the gigantic hog's posterior exit for its digestive tract would be! A separate sign out front read *LIBERTY BELLS SAVINGS & LOAN*.

As the golf cart abruptly jerked to a halt in front of the drive-up teller window, the bag of clubs in back nearly fell out. A sexy female teller with huge knockers appeared in the kiosk's window.

"Good afternoon, welcome to Liberty Bells Savings. How may I assist you today?" she cheerfully asked.

The loaded councilman let out a long, loud belch in reply. *"Buuuurrr-aaaah-aaaaaapppp!"*

"Pardon?" stuttered the shocked teller. She was lucky to be behind protective glass, so she didn't have to smell his bad breath and terrible body odor!

"Ha, ha, ha," he chuckled, while lustfully gazing at the young beauty in the window. "No wonder they call this place Liberty Bells . . . you got some king-sized *liberty bells* yourself! Nice jugs!" he drunkenly joked. "Listen sugar-tits, I need'ta cash this check!" he added, while digging around in his pockets to find it. "I just played a round a' golf,

1

and need a few more bucks before hitting the clubhouse lounge again."
He finally pulled out the wrinkled check and waved it in front of her
window.

"Certainly," she replied, struggling to maintain her professional
composure. "I'll just need two forms of identification. Do you have
your driver's license and Liberty Bells Savings ATM or credit card with
you?"

"*What?!*" barked the shocked drunk. "Why do you need *that?!*
Don't you know who *I am*?!"

"Well, I'm afraid not sir," she answered.

"What do you mean *you* don't know me? The whole f'en town
knows me!" he roared in indignation. "I'm *the* Max Phuckter, city
councilman! Now open that money door below your window and cash
this thing, or else I'll call the president this f'en bank! You know how
much dough I got tied up in this place?!"

"Just one moment," she quickly replied, before leaving the window
to check with her lead teller.

The belligerent, obnoxious, sleaze ball had no idea what was about
to happen to him next! High above the bank . . . eight-thousand feet in
the sunny sky to be exact . . . appeared a group of ten skydivers! These
weren't any normal group of skydivers . . . they were *nude skydivers* . . .
or nearly nude skydivers!

Five women and five men, all in their late twenties and early to
mid-thirties, were free-falling down towards the bank, each wearing
unusual bits of light-green and yellow-colored clothing. These super
fit, athletic nudists all wore motorcycle helmets with black goggles,
which completely disguised their eyes. Each light-green and yellow
colored helmet also had ornamental identification symbols or markers
painted on the front forehead areas, just above the goggles. These were
individual, one-of-a-kind *fruit* or *nut* helmet symbols for each nudist,
which included; a lemon, a banana, a walnut, a papaya, a peanut, a
coconut, a kiwi, a macadamia nut, a guava fruit, and a pecan. Matching

light-green and yellow colored gloves, boots, utility belts and waving capes (beneath their parachutes) completed these nudists minimal attire.

The ten skydivers were topless and bottomless . . . their tanned chests, bare behinds, and the females' large breasts were disrobed for the whole world to see. However, every man and woman did wear a metallic green *fig leaf*, covering their front private parts. These unusual jockstraps and Jillstraps protected their exposed pickles and beavers, and were attached by small chains leading up to the front buckles of their utility belts.

Down, down, down, they went! *Za-Zoom!* The moment they descended to four-hundred feet above the giant piggy bank, the male nudist wearing the banana symbolled helmet . . . and the *largest* metallic green fig leaf . . . gave a 'thumbs-up' sign. He pulled his rip cord and his parachute quickly popped open, instantly slowing his descent. *Pop! Whooosshh!* The other nine skydiving nudists did the same thing, opening their parachutes one by one.

Back down at the drive-up teller window, councilman Phuckter was still waiting impatiently for his money. He was alarmed when the buxom teller's loud voice was heard over the speaker.

"You're all set councilman. Here you go."

The teller window's cash door automatically opened, and the pig . . . not to be confused with the piggy bank shaped building . . . took his several hundred dollars in cash.

"Thanks, sweetie!" he smiled, while thumbing through the bills. "Sorry about losin' my temper a second ago. Hey, is it hot out here, or is just you?"

She reacted bug-eyed.

"I ain't no photographer, but I sure as hell can see *us* together" he added, winking. "Treat me like a pirate and give me that booty! *Ha, ha, ha!*"

"Have a nice day," she spat, while quickly leaving her window.

"Wait, when I text you later, what number should I use? We'll grab a couple 'a drinky-poos!"

The hammered sleazebag stuck the bills in his wallet, but then something caught his drunken eye. The ten skydiving nudists all touched down, landing right in front of him! *Zap! Zap! Zap! Zap! Zap! Zap! Zap! Zap! Zap! Zap!* In fact, they surrounded his golf cart! Although mysteriously disguised behind helmets and dark goggles, these nudists were clearly specimens of physical perfection . . . the men were handsome, tanned and muscular, and the women were spectacularly gorgeous, with marvelous bodies featuring perky, oversized breasts! Most of them were ethnically white, but one beauty was Asian, another babe was black, and one of the guys was Hispanic.

In a flash, they threw off their spent parachutes and attacked, swiftly moving like synchronized Chinese acrobats.

"What the hell?!"

Phuckter didn't have time to say anything else, as the sexy lady nudist in the guava symbolled helmet shot him in the face with some kind of knock-out gas from a can in the shape of a guava fruit! *Ssssssss!* He didn't see the weapon, because his wide eyes were fixated on her big, beautiful, rubbery boobies! The unique guava gas weapon was then snapped back onto her utility belt, while the man in the banana helmet, along with another young man in a walnut helmet, pulled the unconscious Phuckter out of his golf cart and physically carried him away.

"Super Streakers, go!" commanded their leader in the banana helmet.

As the busty young teller returned to her window, she looked up and was quickly *mooned!* Yes, her eyes nearly popped out, as she was mooned for a few fleeting seconds by twenty shiny, tanned buns! The nudists took off running at incredible speed . . . *streaking* away from the bank . . . at close to *fifty miles per hour!* Their light-green and yellow colored capes waved behind them! Banana held Phuckter's arms, while

Walnut held his legs. No normal human beings could ever have run so fast! They were incredible! *Unbelievable!* These helmeted, super-human streakers were *Super Nudists* and they were kidnapping the councilman! Within seconds, the shadowlike villains vanished with their captive!

Several hours later across town, another city councilman, Harry Bottoms, was getting a much needed massage at Driftwood Valley's infamous Asian massage parlor, *Happy Ho-Ho Massage*. The sleazy, Chinese body rub establishment was located in a small, mid-century strip mall. The mall itself was built on the edge of the valley's biggest body of water, Lake Tittykookoo.

From the outside, the public could not see through the massage parlor's front windows, since they were covered by white curtains and full-sized poster art of relaxing men getting massaged by delicate female hands. A big sign above the front glass door read *Happy Ho-Ho Massage*. A smaller, flashing neon sign below it blinked *'OPEN'* in fluorescent red light.

Inside was a small reception room with a front desk, a cash register, and musical wind chimes hanging above the entrance/exit door. These chimes would go off, making noise, whenever male customers walked in or out. A Chinese lantern hanging from the ceiling illuminated the lobby in soft red light, and Asian paintings lined the walls. A long, beaded string curtain hung over the inside doorway, which led to a hall with eight private massage rooms.

Councilman Bottoms was in one of these small rooms, lying face down on a toweled massage table, with his face sunk into a cushioned hole cut out of the end of the table. The politician was skinny and middle-aged, with sandy blond hair. He was, of course, naked as a jaybird, while relaxing Chinese music played softly in the background. The smell of sweet burning incense was in the air too.

A pretty Chinese woman in her thirties, Hoo Ha, was massaging him with oil, delicately rubbing her soft, warm fingers all over his shoulders, back, legs and rear end.

"Mmmm," he happily moaned.

"You rike, honey?" she sweetly asked in her rough Chinese accent.

"Oh, yes, Hoo Ha, I like!"

Her fingers then reached down between his legs and gently began playing the piano on his man berries!

"Holy Sheee . . . yeah, keep tickling the boys! Love it!" he cried, slightly lifting his caboose off the table.

"You know, back in Beijing, I had rittle doggie with no back regs and *metal barrs* the vet gave him," confessed the sexy masseuse. "He used to run on cement sidewalk."

"Your dog had no back legs, metal balls, and he ran on cement sidewalks?" he panted.

"That right," she answered.

"What was your dog's name?"

"Sparky!"

The little devil reached further and started stroking his trouser monkey with one slippery, oiled hand, while massaging his snow globes with her other.

"Aaaaaahhhh," he whimpered in ecstasy, while lifting his rump a bit higher.

"Okay, turn over!" she ordered.

The councilman quickly did as requested and faced her. He was *very happy* to see the Asian beauty, *in more ways than one!*

"Ooo . . . that big egg rorr!" she declared, widening her pretty brown almond eyes. "That no rittle spring rorr, that New York style *jumbo* egg rorr!"

"Thanks, honey!" he grinned.

Hoo Ha lifted his head and placed a soft pillow under it, covering the table hole he'd previously stuck his face into. She then grabbed her bottle of massage oil and squeezed it hard into her open palm . . . but nothing happened! No oil squirted out. Nada! Zip! Zero!

"*Oh, damn it!*"

"What's wrong?"

"No mo' oi-errl! I be right back."

"Okay."

Bottoms grinned, as she disappeared out of the room.

"Money can't buy you happiness, but it *can* buy you a happy ending! *Ha, ha!*" he chuckled to himself.

The rascal was all excited thinking about the exhilarating, mind-blowing, oriental 'hand job' he was about to receive! However, the cocky councilman, in his wildest dreams, never could have ever imagined what was about to happen next! It wasn't the rip-roaring 'happy ending' he was expecting!

The sun was setting outside the Happy Ho-Ho Massage parlor, and on nearby Lake Tittykookoo, a powerful speedboat towing ten nude water-skiers was quickly approaching. The *Super Nudists* were back! The classic speedboat was a light-green and yellow-colored fiberglass beauty from the 1960's . . . aerodynamic and sleek.

The dastardly water-skiers looked exactly as they did during their bank kidnapping. Each athletic nudist wore black goggles and a signature light-green and yellow colored helmet with a fruit or nut symbol painted on the front forehead area. The five women and five men were; Lemon, Banana, Walnut, Papaya, Peanut, Coconut, Kiwi, Macadamia, Guava, and Pecan. Their minimal uniforms, once again, included light-green and yellow colored gloves, boots, utility belts, waving capes and metallic green *fig leaf* jockstraps and Jillstraps.

The front of the speedboat was lifted up in the air a bit, as it zoomed towards shore, leaving a white foamy wake in the choppy water. The boat's driver, a man in his forties with a 'regal air' about him, was wearing a similar light-green and yellow colored helmet, except his had an ornamental identification symbol of a gold *fig leaf* painted on the front . . . just above his black goggles.

The Super Nudists were excellent on waterskies, rocketing over the lake in perfect formation. Their shiny wet bodies were sprinkled by cool water flying up from the front of their skis and from the rear of the speedboat towing them. They all kept their hands and arms straight while holding onto their tow lines, and their knees were slightly bent. Big bare tits and buck naked booties were exposed for the whole world to see, as ten trails of wavy, white, foamy water jetted behind them. Their light-green and yellow colored capes waved in the fast wind!

The helmeted skiers sped along at lightning velocity, and when the speedboat's driver made a sharp turn towards shore, they followed. Banana gave a thumb's up signal, and one by one, in perfect synchronization, the unclad skiers let go of their tow lines and coasted to shore. Like magic, they glided onto the dry sand, and when they came to a complete stop, they slipped their boots out of their skis.

Banana, their leader, pointed towards the strip mall where the Happy Ho-Ho Massage parlor was located. They all nodded in agreement and followed him, streaking off in that direction.

Back in the councilman's massage room, the front door chimes could be heard dinging. *Ding-ding-ding!* Bottoms thought it was another customer out in the lobby.

Hoo Ha was in the supply room, still frantically searching for that other bottle of massage oil.

"Where the he-rl is it?! Don't terr me we run out!" she told herself.

When she heard the door chimes, she poked her head out of the room and yelled down the hall.

"I be right with you! One moment prease."

From inside the supply room, Hoo Ha never saw the swift and silent Super Nudists creeping down the hall, searching for the naughty politician. Five of the wet kidnappers were inside, while the other five remained outside, guarding the massage parlor's front door.

Female Super Nudist Coconut and male Super Nudist Peanut spotted the massage room the skinny councilman was resting in! They motioned back to the other three to grab him!

The small helmeted group quietly filed inside and busty Guava gave him a blast of her knockout guava gas! *Sssssss!* Dazed councilman Bottoms never knew what hit him! Hispanic male Super Nudist Macadamia, along with his buddy Pecan, carefully picked up the disrobed fool and carried him out. Coconut and Peanut collected his clothes, socks and shoes. The Super Nudists, with their unconscious captive, then streaked out as fast as they snuck in.

A second later, Hoo Ha strolled into the empty massage room with a new bottle of oil she finally found. She quickly gazed around the small space, and then went bug-eyed, realizing the councilman was gone!

"Harro?!" she called out. "Harro? Where you go? Bathroom?"

Dashing back out into the hall, she knocked on the bathroom door. There was no response, so she opened it. He wasn't there! Dropping the plastic oil bottle, she ran out to the front lobby. The long, hanging, beaded string curtains flew wildly around, swinging all over the place, as she quickly passed through them. Hoo Ha then noticed the front door was ajar!

"That son of bitch!" she howled.

Another sexy Chinese masseuse rushed out to the front lobby.

"What wrong?" she asked, holding chopsticks in her hands. "I was eating dinner in break room and hear you yell."

"Customer run out without reaving me my *big* tip!" growled Hoo Ha.

"Oh no," frowned her co-worker. "No happy ending for Hoo Ha!"

Hoo Ha shook her fist and rattled off the filthiest Chinese profanity ever spoken, to describe what she thought of city councilman Harry Bottoms! She then switched back to English.

"I hate this job! I hate it! Hate it! Hate it!" she roared.

"Why don't you quit and go work for famous fast-food hamburger chain down street? They always hiring," said her co-worker.

"Because famous fast-food hamburger chain down street no pay two-hundred an fifty-dolla per hour to Hoo Ha!" she snapped back. *"That why!"*

Outside the Happy Ho-Ho Massage parlor, on Lake Tittykookoo, the powerful green and yellow speedboat raced off into the moonlit night, pulling the mooning Super Nudist water-skiers behind it. Bottoms was out cold, stretched out on the back seat of the speedboat, as the boat's regal driver in the fig leaf helmet delightfully smiled.

CHAPTER TWO

Meanwhile, across town, business was booming . . . as usual . . . at Chastity Knott's English Pub. The pub was located on the corner of a busy street . . . the main boulevard running from one end of Driftwood Valley to the other. It was a white, one story restaurant and bar, with dark wood trim around the front entrance. British and American flags flew outside, and the front patio had hanging Italian lights illuminating several tables.

Most of Chastity Knott's customers were inside having drinks at the long, beautifully carved, wooden bar. Next to it were several more bar stools and tall tables. The restaurant section was across from the bar, looking like the interior of a cozy British cottage. It had a fireplace and ten dining tables.

Behind the building was a large, free parking lot with spots for twenty cars. The pub also had a back entrance that Chastity, her cousin Billy, and the customers often used.

Cousin Billy was a clean cut, all American guy with a friendly face, who had been a Boy Scout when he was young. He was in his mid-thirties, with a medium build and dark hair. He graduated from culinary school, and after graduation went straight to work for his wonderfully kind cousin Chastity. Billy helped her run the British pub and restaurant as chef and sometimes bartender. He was the only person who knew Chastity Knott was secretly *the Double-D Avenger*, busty, costumed crime-fighter!

Billy, in his white apron, was cooking in the kitchen, while Chastity was busy working behind the bar. She was a beautiful young woman, about twenty-five years old, with wavy blond hair that had curls at the ends. Chastity's sexy figure was like an hourglass, and her cute face had a button nose. There was a slight Hispanic look to her, but her most astounding physical attributes were her great big boobs! Chastity Knott possessed *incredibly large breasts!* Her face was friendly, just like

Billy's, but few men ever noticed it. The first thing everyone saw when they laid eyes on Chastity was her humongous hooters.

Chastity's majestic melons were actually bigger than a DD bra-cup size, but she always referred to them as her 'double-ds.' The tits were absolutely perfect in every way, shape and form.

She wore a black low-cut blouse, and had on the tightest pair of jeans ever made. They showed off her perfectly round behind and were so tight, even people looking at them had trouble breathing. Chastity didn't wear much jewelry, and both she and her cousin Billy stood around five foot seven.

She was having a friendly chat with Driftwood Valley's recently elected leader, Mayor Artie Phishel, who was finishing his dinner. The slightly overweight politician was in his early sixties, with a comical face, sleepy eyes, dark hair, and a sneaky smile . . . a smile like that of a cat who had just swallowed the canary!

It was a bit noisy in the restaurant/pub, with many happy customers enjoying themselves.

"So, you were a farmer before becoming mayor?" asked a surprised Chastity.

"That's right. The Driftwood community found me *outstanding* in my field," Phishel slowly replied with a big grin. "Get it . . . *outstanding* in my field?"

"*Ha, ha,* yes, very funny," she chuckled, rolling her eyes.

The mayor looked at his empty dinner plate while wiping his mouth with a napkin.

"Chastity, I must say, that was the one of the best meals I've ever had! Just like Mother tried to make, but couldn't."

"Thank you," she smiled.

"That roast beef, mashed potatoes, and Yorkshire pudding were superb!" he applauded. " . . . and the vegetables . . . broccoli, carrots, parsnips and peas . . . all perfect!"

"I'm glad you liked them. Billy and I are proud our pub was voted 'best restaurant' in Driftwood Valley."

"Well, you certainly deserve it!"

"Thanks!"

She then took his empty plate.

"Any dessert?"

"Now do you think I'd turn down dessert?" he said, while patting his big sloping belly. "Of course I'll have dessert . . . I'll try your sticky toffee pudding."

"Great choice . . . we make it from scratch using finely chopped dates, fresh sponge cake mix and toffee sauce. Would you like homemade vanilla custard or vanilla ice-cream with it?"

"Both!"

Suddenly the mayor's cell phone went off, and he took the call immediately.

"Hello?"

He listened intently for a few seconds, with a concerned look on his face. He then turned to Chastity.

"Chastity, I'm going to have to take this call outside . . . it's a bit noisy in here . . . city business. It's my brother Soupy."

"Your brother?"

"Yeah, he ran for city council three years ago," he replied, covering his phone with one hand.

"What does he do now?" she asked.

"Nothing . . . he got elected."

"No problem mayor, I understand. We'll keep your dessert warm."

"Thanks," he added, while quickly walking to the back exit.

Out in the pub's rear parking lot, Billy was tossing a big plastic bag full of garbage into a dumpster. Mayor Phishel exited the pub, closing the rear door behind him, to carefully listen to his brother on the other end of the phone.

Suddenly, from out of nowhere, the Super Nudists appeared in the pub's lit parking lot! Lemon, Banana, Walnut, Papaya, Peanut, Coconut, Kiwi, Macadamia, Guava, and Pecan, in their black goggles and a signature light-green and yellow colored helmets with fruit or nut symbols painted on them, popped up from behind the many parked cars . . . just like sprung jack-in-the-box toys! *Boing! Boing! Boing! Boing! Boing! Boing! Boing! Boing! Boing! Boing!*

Mayor Phishel looked up, startled! He couldn't believe what he was seeing! His jaw dropped and he lowered his phone, as the bandits ambushed him in their light-green and yellow colored gloves, boots, utility belts, waving capes and metallic green *fig leaf* jockstraps and Jillstraps! Of course, what drew his attention the most, were the female Super Nudists supersized, unclad, *kalamazoos!*

Banana pulled out a boomerang in the shape of a banana from his utility belt. The Super Nudist threw it, and it clobbered the shocked politician, knocking him out cold! *Zoo-zoo-zoo-Boom!*

"*Errgh!*" moaned the mayor, as he fell unconscious to the asphalt.

Hispanic male Super Nudist Macadamia and Korean female Super Nudist Kiwi picked him up, as Billy turned and spotted them!

"*Super Streakers, go!*" commanded Banana.

They mooned Billy, for a few fleeting seconds, with their twenty buns!

"*Hey! What the . . . ?*" sputtered surprised Billy.

The nudists took off running at incredible speed . . . *streaking* away from the pub into the night . . . at close to *fifty miles per hour!* Macadamia and Kiwi disappeared with the rest of the group, holding Mayor Phishel's lifeless arms and legs in their gloved hands. Their light-green and yellow colored capes waved behind them!

Back inside the pub, Billy dashed up to Chastity.

"*Chastity!*"

"What's wrong?" she asked, realizing something was the matter.

Billy answered in a hushed voice, so as not to alarm the pub's customers.

"*The Mayor!* He was just kidnapped . . . by a bunch of . . . a bunch of. . . "

He struggled to find the right words to describe the culprits.

"*A bunch of what?*" she demanded.

"They wore helmets . . . goggles . . . so I couldn't see their faces . . . but I saw their bodies . . . they were all *nude!*"

"*Nude?!*" she exclaimed, bug-eyed.

"Yeah, mostly nude . . . like a bunch of weird nudists!" he stuttered.

"This is a job for you-know-who!" she declared.

"Right!" he agreed.

"Watch the pub, I'll be back!"

"Be careful!" he warned.

"You know me!"

Chastity made her way to the pub's back exit, without running, so none of her customers would become curious.

When she stepped out into the rear parking lot, she glanced around to make sure nobody was looking. She discreetly moved towards her parked car in the corner . . . a classic, metallic blue, 1970's Corvette Stingray. Seeing the nighttime coast was clear, Chastity quickly spun around in a circle . . . creating a dizzying blur of red, blue and yellow . . . and instantly changed into her Double-D Avenger superhero costume! Within seconds, she was dressed as *the Double-D Avenger,* in her complete blue leotard costume and red bra-mask, red gloves, red boots, red cape and red belt with two upper-case white letter 'D's' on its buckle.

Once her transformation was completed, the busty, costumed crime-fighter took a running leap, and bounced up into the air!

"*Booby-Bounce!*" she cried, as she soared away, up into the night sky.

Boi-oing-oing-oing-oing-oing!

Using her incredible powers, Chastity was able to jump, propelling her massive melons upwards. This *dynamic momentum* of her super breasts actually *catapulted* the rest of her body hundreds or thousands of feet *into the air,* depending on how high or how far she needed to go.

Our super woman with super jugs could fly many city blocks with each bounce, before returning back to Earth, to safely land on her strong red boots. She could leap tall buildings and travel over great distances in a single 'Booby-Bounce.' The enormous, rubbery breasts even helped *soften* her landings, acting like *shock absorbers* when her boots hit the ground. The impact of her landing feet ran up her legs and was absorbed by her gigantic, super jiggly puffs.

From a couple hundred feet in the cool night air, Double-D quickly surveyed the town and main highway through the two eye-slits of her brassier mask. All of a sudden, her huge honkers felt funny.

"Oh, my *titties* are *tingling* . . . they sense danger down there!" she told herself.

A few seconds later, she spotted the fleeing Super Nudists with their capes waving behind them!

"Holy Hooters! There go some naked buns!" she exclaimed. "That's got to be them!"

Our hero quickly descended . . . down, down, down . . . and then landed on the sidewalk. *Zap!* She summoned her superhuman strength and powers to continue the pursuit on foot, running at incredible speed! She zoomed past many of Driftwood Valley's mid-century modern, *'novelty architecture'* buildings; a liquor store with a huge neon sign of a circus clown out front, a donut shop with a giant fiberglass donut on its roof, and a steak house resembling a log cabin topped by artificial snow. There were even two life-like, full-sized dinosaur statues . . . a tyrannosaurus rex battling a triceratops . . . displayed outside the natural history museum.

As Double-D dashed past each strange structure, nighttime pedestrians walking down sidewalks or driving by in cars did *double-takes* staring at her! The over-endowed, bra-busting superhero was just as unusual as the mid-century modern 'novelty architecture.'

She finally caught up to the helmeted Super-Nudists and saw Mayor Phishel being carried away by Macadamia and Kiwi.

"Stop right where you are!" shouted the Double-D Avenger in a loud, commanding voice.

Banana and the rest of the Super Nudists looked back and were surprised! They immediately recognized the famous, big balconied superhero.

"It's the Double-D Avenger!" cried female Super Nudist Coconut.

"The Double-D Avenger?!" gasped male Super Nudist Walnut.

The fleeing kidnappers slowed down.

"Kiwi . . . get the mayor back to headquarters!" ordered Banana. "We'll take care of the Double-D Avenger!"

"Right!" nodded the Asian villainess.

Macadamia let go of the mayor, and super strong Kiwi took over, throwing the politician's limp body over her shoulder. She then disappeared in a flash with her captive, while Super Nudists Banana, Lemon, Guava, Pecan, Papaya, Walnut, Coconut, Macadamia and Peanut surrounded Double-D.

"Too bad you stuck your big boobs into our business, Double-D!" threatened Banana.

"We won't allow anyone to interfere with our plans!" added female Super Nudist Lemon.

"Bring the mayor back this instant!" demanded Double-D. ". . . and put some real clothes on while you're at it! Parading around like that in your birthday suits . . . in public . . . is utterly disgraceful! *It's indecent!*"

"Super Nudists . . . attack!" ordered Banana.

The birthday suit bandits moved in to stop our hero . . . by using marital arts on her!

Chastity, as the Double-D Avenger, noticed how each one of the strange nudist kidnappers all looked physically perfect! They were just like supermodels hidden beneath their dark goggles . . . with the strong, handsome, masculine men possessing square jaws and tanned, muscular bodies . . . and the fit, topless, big breasted women all drop-dead gorgeous with beautiful faces and luscious lips!

Each Super Nudist was an expert in *Nude-jitsu*, a nudist version of Jiu-jitsu! Big breasted female Super Nudist Lemon flew at Double-D at lightning speed, chopping and kicking at her!

"*Key-Yah!*" cried Lemon.

Our hero bravely blocked each fight move with her red gloved hands and arms, and then used some judo action of her own.

"Two can play at Jubblie Judo!" declared Double-D. "Time to give you a little *Tit-for-Tat!*"

Double-D fought Lemon off using several '*Booby-Punches.*' These fight moves consisted of Chastity turning, twisting and throwing one powerful breast at her opponent after another.

Ba-Bap! Ba-Bap!

"*Waaaahhh!*" hollered Lemon, as she was clobbered.

Double-D's indestructible tom-toms knocked Lemon down the block faster than a speeding fart!

"How's *that* for a *Ta-Ta trick?!*" laughed Double-D.

Nighttime spectators . . . sidewalk pedestrians and drivers . . . were dumfounded by what they saw! The wild street brawl stretched out over several city blocks!

Female Super Nudist Guava and male Super Nudists Pecan and Walnut closed in with more punching, chopping and kicking!

"*Whoo-Wah!*"

"*Hoo-Raahh!*"

"*Eeerr-aaahh!*"

Our hero quickly blocked most of their moves, and those she missed were absorbed by her indestructible honkers. Chastity, as Double-D, suddenly realized something was very wrong! These weird, practically nude kidnappers seemed to have super human powers similar to hers! Chastity's mind raced as she thought to herself . . . *Whoa, wait a second here! What the heck's going on? These indecent crooks . . . have super strength too! Just like me! But how . . . ?*

CHAPTER THREE

Male Super Nudist Macadamia pulled a whip from his utility belt and lashed it at the Double-D Avenger! *Za-Whap!*

It whipped around our hero's neck, stinging her terribly!

"Aaaahhh!" she sputtered.

Chastity, as Double-D, struggled to breath! *Gasp!* The whip felt like a mighty anaconda had wound its long snake body around her neck! She reached up to grab it.

Macadamia pulled the tightly wrapped whip using his super strength! He then flung the Double-D Avenger by her neck . . . up and away . . . into a giant, twenty-foot tall fiberglass statue standing in front of a tire store! The big advertising statue was of a smiling, bearded man holding a huge tire.

Wha-Whoooosshh! Ka-Bang!

Dazed but not seriously injured, Double-D ripped the whip off! *Eeerrr-rriiipp!* She got back onto her feet and dusted herself off.

"Time for a *Booby-Lightning Bolt!*" she declared, massaging her colossal Dairy Pillows! "I've got to generate enough *static electricity* between my big bra and costume," she told herself. Her eyes grew wider, as she began to feel some powerful static electricity building up. *Zit-zit-zit-zit-zit!* "Ah, here we go . . . *Booby-Bolt!*" she loudly echoed.

The busty costumed crime-fighter *threw out* her arms and a bright lightning bolt *shot off* her giant Bra Buddies! *Za-Zapp!!* There was an instant *thunderclap* that sounded like *'Va-Voom!'*

The electrical bolt *nailed* Macadamia right on his metallic-green fig leaf! *Zoom! Ouch!* He was *absolutely shocked*, literally and figuratively, and hollered in *all-out agony!*

Waaaaa-haaaa-haaaa-haaaa-hoooo-hooo-hooo!

Macadamia held his burning crotch with both hands!

20

"Thank goodness for my indestructible tits!" said Double-D, congratulating herself. She grabbed one blue costumed boob of hers at a time and kissed them. *"Mmm-waah! Mmm-wah!"*

Guava dashed up to our hero and pulled out her Guava gas weapon! She tried to spray the fruit can of knock out gas at Double-D, but wasn't quick enough, as our hero booby-bounced away!

"Booby-Bounce!"

Double-D flew up into the air . . . *Ba-Boing* . . . completely missing the jet of knock-out gas!

Seconds later, our hero was back on the sidewalk again! Double-D twisted her torso and whacked Guava with a powerful booby-punch! *Ba-Boom!* The villainess was knocked past the Dutch bakery with a rotating neon sign of a windmill on its roof! She then flung smack into the front door of the famous trashy lingerie store, the Booby Trap! *Ka-Crash! Bang!*

Banana whipped out his banana shaped boomerang and threw it from his gloved hand! *Whoosh-whoosh-whoosh-whoosh-whoosh!*

Seeing it coming at her, Double-D cartwheeled out of the way just in time! She then dashed over to Banana, and grabbed him *under* his green metallic fig leaf! She squeezed his balls . . . *Honk* . . . and he howled in pain!

Looking up fast, our hero saw Banana's boomerang flying back towards them! She let go of his cojones, and rolled out of the way. *Wham!* The returning boomerang nailed Banana right on the head, and then it ricocheted off his helmet! He cried out again!

"Aaahh!"

"Good thing you wore your helmet!" chuckled Double-D, while waving a finger at him.

The Double-D Avenger then did a *double-take!* Banana had spun around, mooning her, as he leaned forward to recover from being clobbered and zapped! Chastity, as Double-D, found Banana 'very interesting,' and her romantic heart fluttered in delight! His bare bubble butt was tight, perfect, and muscular, and our hero couldn't resist giving it a quick pinch!

"Ooo . . . nice buns!" she smiled. Her eyes grew wide open beneath her red bra mask!

She playfully pinched his right bubble-like butt cheek with her red gloved hand, and he instantly straightened back up! Banana couldn't believe what she just did, and was pleasantly surprised! The handsome young man behind the black goggles and helmet took a closer look at Double-D. He was taken away by her beauty and sex appeal . . . *it was love at first sight!* Banana didn't know whether to fight her, or start making love to her! He was totally *smitten* with the Double-D Avenger and wanted to *kiss* her!

While Double-D and Banana were preoccupied, male Super Nudist Pecan carefully removed the pecan slingshot from his utility belt. He started firing some rock hard, unshelled nuts at her! *Ka-pow! Ka-pow! Ka-pow!* These little rock hard projectiles were *deadly!*

Our hero saw them coming, so she used her powerful front bumpers again, to repel the dangerous, rocketing pecans! *Ting! Ting! Ting!*

Double-D cartwheeled over to Pecan, and snatched the slingshot away from him! In a flash, she pulled back the rubber band, stretching it as far as it could go, and then released it right on his nose! *Ssss-nap! Pop! Ouch!* Pecan fell over backwards, in stinging torture, as she tossed the weapon away!

"Waaarrghh!"

Female Super Nudist Coconut decided to throw her coconut bolas . . . a throwing weapon made of round weights, resembling coconuts, connected to each other by a long cord. The villainess's bolas flew through the air, spinning around and around by their cord, like an out of control helicopter propeller! A second later, they struck Double-D . . . *Woo-Woo-Woo Zap* . . . and wrapped around her sexy body! However, our hero only needed to expand her strong lungs . . . and big blorps . .

. to tear the connecting cord apart! *Riiipppp!* The useless coconut bolas fell to the ground, making loud clanking sounds. *Ka-Klung! Ka-Klung!*

The black female Super Nudist Papaya, and male Super Nudist Peanut, then attacked Double-D at the same time, chopping, punching and kicking!

"*Ho!*"

"*Yah!*"

"*Zaa!*"

Our hero blocked their martial arts moves, as new confirming thoughts raced through her head . . . *No doubt about it! They definitely do have super human strength and powers, just like my own! Bless my 'over-the-shoulder-boulder-holder!' It's unbelievable!*

Double-D grabbed both Super Nudists by the backs of their necks and knocked their two helmets together! *Ka-Klang!*

The disrobed attackers cried out in pain and nearly passed out from their head concussions!

"*Aaah!*"

"*Argh!*"

"Like my *Jiggler Judo?!*" teased Double-D.

The helmeted villains quickly regrouped, huddling together in front of the valley's iconic tiki bar and restaurant, The Tiki's Tom-Toms. A huge *female* tiki totem pole, with humongous *coconut-like breasts*, stood out front! The Polynesian tiki goddess was actually an illuminated sign, not an actual wooden sculpture. She was holding a flashing neon sign above her head which read *The Tiki's Tom-Toms.*

The outside of the restaurant/bar looked like a large bamboo house with a thatch roof on top. Tiki statues, tropical plants, flaming gas torches, and wooden war masks decorated the exterior. A multi-colored, illuminated waterfall constantly recycled chlorinated water into a little pond near the front doors.

Before the nefarious nudists could strike again, the Double-D Avenger inhaled . . . taking a deep breath . . . and then used her *super breath* to blow them all away!

"*Whooooosssshhh!!!*"

This incredibly strong wind the super-woman blew knocked all nine Super Nudists into the tiki bar's front pond and waterfall! *Splish! Splash! Ka-Crash! Bang! Boom! Ker-Plunk! Sploosh!*

The tiki bar's valet parkers, dressed in their red vests, came running over to see what all the commotion was about!

"*It's the Double-D Avenger!*" shouted one of the surprised, young male valets.

"Who are those naked chicks with the nice titties?!" asked another wide-eyed male valet.

Our hero chuckled at the soggy, bare-assed baddies, flailing around in the pond's illuminated, four foot deep water. The female Super Nudists bare *tom-toms, u-boats* and *mau-maus* dangled, bobbed, jiggled and quivered in the chlorinated waves.

"*Ha, ha, ha!*" boasted Double-D. She stuck her chest out, placing both hands defiantly on her hips! "You'll have to be a lot cleverer, if you want to nail these double-d's!"

Male Super Nudist Walnut pulled a smoke bomb out of his wet utility belt, and ignited it by pushing a small button. It miraculously lit up! He instantly tossed it at Double-D . . . and the walnut-shaped bomb landed right in front of her and exploded! *Boom!*

A blinding cloud of purple smoke mushroomed up all around her! *Ssssssssss!* The valet parkers and sidewalk pedestrians panicked!

"*Super Nudists, retreat!*" yelled Banana. He was still confused over his mixed feelings for the enchanting super woman with super tits.

The Super Nudists obeyed Banana's orders and dashed out of the tiki bar's front pond and waterfall.

Chastity, as the Double-D Avenger, coughed her lungs out and was blinded by all the purple smoke. *Cough! Cough! Cough!* She couldn't see a thing, so she tried her super breath again!

"Whooosssshhh!"

Seconds later, the smoke cleared, but the Super Nudists were gone! They completely vanished.

"I can't let them escape!" Double-D told herself! *"Booby-Bounce!"* she cried, as she rocketed up to the stars. *Boi-oing-oing-oing-oing-oing!*

All the parking valets and onlookers jaws dropped, as they watched Double-D take off!

"There she goes!" exclaimed one of the valets.

Flying through the nighttime sky thanks to the centrifugal force of her catapulted tits, Double-D quickly looked down at the passing ground below. She saw the drive-in movie theater, the bowling alley, and the infamous Chinese restaurant, Flung Dung's Number-Two House. The old restaurant was in the shape of a towering Chinese pagoda, with bright neon lights and colorful lanterns decorating it . . . but no fleeing fannies were spotted. The Super Nudists had escaped.

"They got away! My Ta-Ta's were tricked!" she complained to herself.

Chastity, as Double-D, couldn't stop thinking . . . *Who were those crazy nudists? They had super powers and strength too! How on Earth did they get them? Why did they kidnap Mayor Artie Phishel? Was he all right?* These questions and others bombarded our hero's brain, as she Booby-Bounced back to the pub.

The moment our hero returned to her restaurant/bar's parking lot, she looked around to make sure the coast was clear . . . and quickly spun in a tight circle to transform back into her normal civilian clothes as Chastity Knott. She then bolted for the pub's rear entrance door and raced inside to phone the Sheriff. There were still a few hours left before closing, and Cousin Billy was serving some draft beers to a couple bar customers.

Once she was off the call, Chastity motioned Billy over and the two of them moved to the now empty and quiet dining room area. They spoke in whispered tones, and she told him everything.

"So like I said . . . I left a message with the Sheriff, as Chastity Knott, explaining to him what happened, as told to me by the Double-D Avenger," she explained.

"I see. What's he going to do?"

"I don't know, he and the Deputy were out on patrol. Buxom policewoman Officer Peaks took my message."

"I see," replied Billy. "Chastity, I'm still amazed by everything you've told me. Thank goodness you weren't hurt! Those nudist kidnappers possessed super-human powers, just like the Double-D Avenger's!"

"I know," she grimly replied. "I wonder how those semi-costumed super-criminals got their extraordinary strength and speed? It's unimaginable! I'm completely flabbergasted!"

"The Crockozilla fruit? That rare, magical South American plant you sucked on, which gave you your super-powers and made you young again?" questioned Billy.

"Perhaps . . . or perhaps not. I'll see the Sheriff first thing tomorrow morning."

" . . . as the Double-D Avenger?" he asked.

"Of course!" she told him, while thinking carefully. "I suddenly have a *'breasted interest'* in this Super Nudist matter!" Chastity, with a look of determination on her face, cupped the bottoms of her two titanic torpedoes and slightly shook them, as she uttered the words 'breasted interest.'

"Right!" agreed Billy. *"Super Nudist?"*

"That's what I heard their leader call them! They're the Super Nudists."

"Oh wow!" declared Billy. "I have a feeling the Double-D Avenger is about to get very busy handling this Super Nudist case for our

bumbling Sheriff . . . as usual. I'll phone busty Connie Cans to come in and help waitress for us, while you're out tracking down those bare-assed criminals."

"Oh, thank you, Billy!" she said, giving him a hug.

Her giant boobs nearly smothered him.

"Hey watch it, you trying to kill me?"

"Whoops . . . sorry," she chuckled. "It's so hard fighting crime as a superhero, while trying to run a restaurant and bar at the same time."

"I know. Don't worry about it. Protuberant Connie and I will have the pub covered. You just bring those evil nudists to justice and rescue the mayor!"

"Will do!"

About two hours later that same night, yet another political scandal was happening at one of Driftwood Valley's most unique motels. The flashing neon sign out front read, *Chief Talkingbull's No Tell Motel*. The motor lodge was comprised of a dozen little rooms, all separate and apart from each other, in the shapes of Native American *teepees!* However, the twelve tents were made of concrete, wood and drywall, not animal skins. Each teepee had its own electricity, running water, and heating and air conditioning. The entire crazy motel resembled a Native American teepee village. A smaller flashing neon sign out front read *'Make Whoopee in a TeePee!'* . . . and that sign wasn't kidding!

Recently divorced city councilwoman Helga Hoodwink was having secret rendezvous in one of the teepee motel rooms with her young male intern, Rod Long! Councilwoman Hoodwink was an incredibly busty, middle-aged goddess in sexy dark lingerie. Her hair was flaming red, and she wore red lipstick to match. The horny vamp totally exuded sex! In fact, her wondrously ripe, chesty charms were outrageous in size!

The lustful politician, in her skimpy bedroom attire, teasingly posed and pranced around, showing off her hot body to the smiling intern. The lingerie barely covered anything! Rod was lying in his underwear on the motel bed. He was a recent college graduate . . . good looking, with an athletic build and short blond hair. His whole future career in politics was now laid out in front of him . . . figuratively and literally!

Councilwoman Hoodwink seductively teased him, while playing with her long red hair.

"Now Rod darling, as I explained, if you treat me right, your intern days are over!" she grinned. "I can fix it so you'll be our new city treasurer at a handsome salary, if you play ball with me!"

"I'm game, Ms. Hoodwink," replied the excited intern.

"Call me Helga," she corrected.

"Oh right, sorry Helga!" he grinned.

Standing in front of him, Hoodwink continued to prance around at the foot of the bed. She lifted her right leg up and began to sensuously rub her naked, beautifully tanned rear end!

"Like what you see, Baby?" she cooed.

"I sure as hell do, Ms. Hoodwink . . . I mean, Helga!"

Rod's eyes bugged out, as the vixen turned around and started wiggling her gorgeous butt at him! His eyes grew even wider, when she started to playfully spank herself! *Slap! Slap! Slap!*

The temptress then rubbed her hands all over her French brassier, while batting eyes at him! A second later, she undid the brassier and swung it around, tossing it against the fake teepee's wall. The bra hit a painting of a buffalo.

"Bullseye!" she chuckled.

She rubbed her bare breasts and teasingly squeezed her nipples, all while smiling.

"You sure took that top off fast!" the young man told her, grinning from ear to ear. "It took me half an hour trying to take off my ex-girlfriend's bra!" He paused for a second, then added, "I never should have tried it on in the first place!"

Hoodwink raised an eyebrow.

"I don't understand why guys think it's so hard to take off a lady's brassiere," she purred. "I can do it with both hands behind my back!"

The excited intern was aroused beyond belief! Rod's hot rod was up and ready to race away beneath his boxer shorts . . . making a teepee of its own! There was a teepee inside the teepee!

Hoodwink slowly whipped of her lacey thong panties and unsnapped her garter belt. Once the enchantress's panties were removed, she twerked her tempting fanny at him again. In a flash, she hopped onto the bed and crawled over to him on all fours.

To his shock, the sexpot hovered over his eager *face,* and then she slowly sat down! *Sploop!* Her pink taco was now firmly planted in Rod's hungry mouth!

"Do you like eating pink tacos?" she playfully asked.

"*Mmmm . . . Mmm!*" he positively mumbled back. He turned his head to the side for a split second to add, ". . . and *red snappers* too!" His face instantly returned to its important business.

"*Oh yes! Yes!* I see you do! *You do!*" she pleasantly murmured. "Don't bother speaking darling, just keep doing what you're doing . . . besides, it's not polite to speak with your mouth full!"

The councilwoman slowly gyrated all over Rod's face, and he loved every lustful second of it! In fact, he couldn't get enough of it! He gently stimulated her camel toe using his flickering wet tongue and lips, in a long, red-hot, 'yodeling in the canyon' session! The horny femme fatale went wild and so did her swollen ding-ding!

"*Oh yeah!*" she bellowed. "Oh! *Ha-ha-ha-ha . . .* oh, yes! *Yeah! Oh, yes-yes-yes!* You naughty boy! Love it!"

She began to ride waves of pure, multi-orgasmic ecstasy!

"Oh, yes please!" she called out. "Ah . . . *ha-ha-ha . . .* oh, that's good!" She then declared in a high-pitched, opera singer's falsetto voice . . . "*Oh yes!* Someone's getting that *pro-mo-tion!*"

Rod stopped licking and sucking her front door buzzer, in order to offer her a compliment.

"*Mmm. . . .*your panty hamster smells like Rose's!" he blissfully muttered while turning his head.

"Thank you!"

". . . but Rose's is a little tighter," he added.

She reacted bug-eyed, then looked down at him.

"Rod darling, my furburger's like the weather . . . once it's wet, it's time to go inside!" she ordered.

"Yes, Ms. Hoodwink . . . I mean, Helga!"

The femme fatale hopped off his face . . . *Sploop* . . . and then scooted back to lie down at the foot of the bed. Like a proud peacock spreading its tail to display its colorful plumage, Hoodwink slowly and seductively spread her legs wide apart for him.

"Watch my honey pot! I'll make it blow you a *kiss!*"

Rod eagerly watched, wide-eyed, and was shocked to see her cooter actually blow him a kiss! *Mmm-waah!*

"*That's amazing!*" he cried out in astonishment. "*Wow!*"

"I can also make it wink! Watch!"

When the sexy siren made her poontang wink at him, the horny-as-hell intern was even more surprised! *Va-Voop!*

"It *did* wink! I can't believe it!" he stuttered.

She then raised an eyebrow and stared at him with a serious look on her face. The woman was in total heat!

"Now I want you to stick two fingers in it," she urgently gasped.

"You gotta be kiddin' me! It can *whistle* too?!"

CHAPTER FOUR

Three blocks away from Chief Talkingbull's No Tell Motel, the Super Nudists were back, about to strike again! The five women and five men . . . Lemon, Banana, Walnut, Papaya, Peanut, Coconut, Kiwi, Macadamia, Guava, and Pecan . . . in their minimal light-green and yellow costumes, streaked to a halt in the middle of an empty street. There wasn't any traffic on either side of the road that late at night, and the entire surrounding area seemed deserted. The only sound the topless and bottomless bandits could hear was the chirping of crickets.

Leader Banana turned his banana symbolled helmet around to face the team behind him!

"We've got to be close! Let's get a bird's-eye view to make sure!" calculated Banana. *"Super Nudists Pyramid Formation!"* he cried!

The rest of the Super Nudists quickly followed Banana's order! Like amazing Chinese acrobats, they instantly took up their positions to form a human pyramid! The men . . . Banana, Pecan, Walnut, Peanut and Macadamia . . . lined up side by side, throwing their arms over each other's shoulders, to form the pyramid's strong base. They stood still in a perfectly straight line. Next, three of the women . . . Lemon, Guava, and Papaya . . . super jumped up into the air, to stand on top of the men's shoulders! *Zoop! Zoop! Zoop!* The near naked ladies did it, and then threw their arms over each other's shoulders to form the pyramid's second level.

Finally, the last two female Super Nudists . . . Coconut and Kiwi . . . super hopped up, to stand on top of the ladies shoulders forming the third and final level of the human tower! *Zoop! Zoop!* The two placed an arm over each other's shoulders for support, just like the others below them had done.

This incredible, three-storied human pyramid demonstrated the Super Nudists superb skills at stabilizing themselves and retaining their balance! It was an amazing feat!

Banana looked up and smiled . . . getting a wonderful eyeful of several gorgeous 'Bermuda Triangles' under the ladies Jillstraps!

"Coconut, Kiwi, you spot the motel?" he asked.

The top two Super Nudists, with their short capes blowing in the nighttime breeze, scanned the surrounding landscape through their goggled helmets. They were about sixteen feet up in the air! Coconut then saw the top part of the motor lodge's flashing neon sign which read, *'Chief Talkingbull's No Tell Motel.'* The motor lodge was hidden behind some bushes and tall trees.

"Yes! I see it!" exclaimed Coconut, as her bare breasts jiggled.

"I do too!" agreed Kiwi, as her bare knockers quivered. "It's down the road and to the left!"

"Great! Let's go!" declared Banana. *"Super Nudists Pyramid, disassemble!"*

The Super Nudists demonstrated their astounding Chinese acrobatic abilities once again, only this time in reverse. Coconut and Kiwi, on the top level, lifted their arms off each other's shoulders and super jumped back down to the street. *Zoop! Zoop!* The other topless and bottomless ladies on the second level followed, doing exactly the same thing. *Zoop! Zoop! Zoop!* Once all five women were safely down, the men slipped their arms off each other's shoulders and stepped apart.

"Super Streakers, go!" commanded Banana.

Off the helmeted Super Nudists ran, with their light-green and yellow colored capes waving behind them!

Back at Hoodwink's teepee motel room, the naughty councilwoman was literally 'having a ball' with her young intern! The redheaded sexpot was positioned on the bed, kneeling on all fours, while pushing her tail end up against her soon-to-be city treasurer Rod Long and his long shlong! She was humping him, more than he was humping her, thrusting and slamming her overheated rear end against his lower abdomen! She still had her sexy high-heeled stripper shoes on, and the sound of skin slapping against each other filled the room

. . . along with the couple's moans and groans of ecstasy, their heavy panting, and the squeaking of the old bed springs!

Ba-Boom! Ba-Boom! Ba-Boom! Ba-Boom! Ba-Boom! Squeak! Squeak! Squeak! Squeak!

"*Mmmm . . . oooo! Yeah . . . ahhh . . . mmm . . . ahh . . . oh!*" she sputtered, as her big dairy pillows and long red hair swung back and forth. "*Yes . . . I think I'm going to . . . I think I'm going to . . .* " she trembled, before completing her sentence.

All of a sudden, Rod's rod accidentally slipped out of her pink canoe. *Ker-Plop!*

"Whoopsie, *he* slipped out," Rod grinned.

"Slipped out?! What are you tryin' to do?! Blow that promotion of yours?!" she snarled. "Put '*him*' back in, or else!"

"Yes, Ms. Hoodwink . . . I mean, Helga."

"Never mind, I'll do it! If a woman wants a job done right, she's gotta do it herself!"

In a flash, she reached back with her right hand and *grabbed it!*

"*Ouch!*" he gasped, as she squeezed his magic wand.

She then shoved the joystick back in . . . *sploop* . . . and the clam jamming continued! *Ba-Boom! Ba-Boom! Ba-Boom! Ba-Boom! Ba-Boom! Squeak! Squeak! Squeak! Squeak!*

"*That feels so good! Oh yes! Harder! Harder!*" she demanded.

Rod picked up the tempo! His buns flew so fast, they appeared as a blur of swift motion!

"*Aahhh!*" he mumbled, closing his eyes.

"*Yes!* Jackhammer me like a jackrabbit!" she commanded.

He obeyed, balling her even harder . . . 'feeding her kitty' as fast as he could!

"I heard . . . you can't hear . . . jackrabbits . . . while they're making love," he muttered, practically out of breath.

"You can't hear jackrabbits while they're making love?! How come?"

"Cause they have . . . cotton balls," he breathily replied.

Knock-Knock!

An unexpected knock at the door brought everything to a premature halt!

"What the hell?!" she furiously spat.

The sweaty couple de-coupled, and Hoodwink grabbed her lingerie. She quickly put it back on.

"Who's there?" shouted Rod, hopping up and down on the carpet while slipping back into his underwear. "We don't want to be disturbed!"

"Pizza delivery," responded a woman's voice.

"Pizza?! We didn't order any pizza!" snapped the frustrated councilwoman.

"You have the wrong room!" grumbled Rod.

The young man dashed over to the door and opened it.

"Listen, I told you, you've got the wrong . . . "

He was rudely interrupted by a powerful jet of knock-out gas, shot from Super Nudist Guava's weapon can! *Sssssss!* The last thing Rod saw were Guava's big, beautiful, rubbery boobies . . . before he fell unconscious to the carpeted floor!

"Whaaaaah!" screamed Hoodwink, witnessing the attack! *"Rod! Rod darling!"*

She looked up at Guava!

"What are you doing?! Get out!" she yelled.

Before the shocked councilwoman could say a thing more, Guava gave her a shot of the gas too! *Sssssss!*

"Oohh!"

Within a few seconds, Hoodwink was out like a light, collapsing back onto the bed.

Banana popped into the room with Guava and a few other Super Nudists. "We'll take them both!" he explained. "That guy works with the councilwoman. He's her intern."

"Right," replied Walnut.

Female Super Nudists Lemon and Papaya grabbed Hoodwink by her arms and legs, and carried her out. Macadamia and Walnut lifted Rod away.

The birthday suit bandits, with their latest kidnapped victims, quickly filed out of the teepee and gathered in the motel parking lot.

"*Super Streakers, go!*" ordered Banana.

The nudists took off running at incredible speed . . . *streaking* away into the night. As they did this, the eighty-one year old manager of the teepee village motel heard the commotion! He was wearing a flannel shirt and a pair of pants held up by suspenders. Curiously peeking out of his office window, he saw the Super Nudists fleeing tushies! The geezer's eyes nearly popped out!

"*What the heck?!*" stuttered the surprised old man in his hillbilly accent. "Can't believe it! What in tarnation do them naked folks think their doin'?"

He noticed the city councilwoman and her intern being carried away by the strange, nearly naked kidnappers! Grabbing his cell phone, he immediately called the cops.

"Hello, Driftwood Valley police? I think we just had a naked kidnappin' here at Chief Talkingbull's No Tell Motel. This is the motel manager speakin.'"

He paused for a second to listen to the dispatcher on the other end.

"Yes, I said naked kidnappers! They was runnin' around, naked as jaybirds, and super- fast! Thank heavens my wife Edith wasn't here to see'em! Thems was the fastest things on two feet! Had nothin' on but smiles . . . and motorcycle helmets, gloves and capes . . . carryin' away the councilwoman . . . whats-her-name . . . and that young gentleman friend of hers!"

The lit cigarette hanging from his lips, just below his white moustache, nearly fell out of his mouth as he explained everything. He then paused a second time to listen to the dispatcher.

"How do I know they was naked?!" he fumed. "I just told ya, them S.O.B.'s *mooned* me!"

Blocks away, a patrolling squad car making its nightly rounds, received the emergency call. Behind the wheel of the police vehicle was the Sheriff of Driftwood Valley . . . a serious, solemn, African-American man in his mid-thirties. His deputy, a stupid, pretty Caucasian boy in his twenties, was seated in the passenger seat.

"All units assist, code three! Reported kidnapping at sixty-ninth street and Bonbons Boulevard," announced the police dispatcher over the squad car's radio. "Suspects are eastbound . . . and are nude, over."

"Ten-Four," replied the Sheriff, while holding the steering wheel with one hand, and the dashboard's corded microphone in his other. He then did a double-take at the dash radio.

"Station, come in. Can you repeat that? Did you say *nude* kidnappers?"

"Affirmative Sheriff! Suspects reported as naked."

"Responding now. The deputy and I are close."

The police car's flashing red roof lights were turned on, along with its blaring siren. As the Sheriff floored the vehicle's accelerator, all four tires squealed, burning rubber.

"Naked kidnappers?" said the shocked Deputy.

"Hang on," warned the Sheriff.

The squad car barreled around a street corner and nearly hit an oncoming pickup truck! The speeding driver blew his horn as he swerved out of the way. His pickup wobbled all over the street, nearly crashing into a street lamp! At the last second, the driver luckily managed to slow down to regain control of his vehicle.

"He ran that red," spat the Deputy from his passenger seat.

"No time to give him a ticket now," snapped back the Sheriff.

As the law officers turned another corner, they could see the fleeing Super Nudists running directly ahead of them . . . in their helmets and waving capes!

"Sheriff! You see what I see?"

"Yes," replied the bug-eyed Sheriff.

"There's a whole group of them . . . they don't have any pants on! Look at them buns! Some of them are women too! No skirts!"

"I can see that, Deputy."

The Sheriff gazed at his speedometer, and shook his head.

"Impossible . . . they must be running at close to fifty miles an hour!"

"You're right!" exclaimed the Deputy. "But how . . . I mean, how are they able to run so fast?!"

As Banana led his team of streaking Super Nudists, he noticed the flashing red lights behind them. The lights illuminated the nighttime street and reflected off shop windows. He turned his head and became alarmed.

"The police!" shouted Banana.

The rest of the Super Nudists looked back and became nervous too, seeing the police car closing in on them! Swift female Super Nudists Lemon and Papaya still had Hoodwink by her arms and legs, and Macadamia and Walnut were running while carrying Rod.

"Lemon, Papaya!" yelled Banana. "Take a side alley and get Hoodwink back to headquarters using a different route! We'll lure the cops away!"

"Right!" said Lemon and Papaya simultaneously.

"Walnut, hand the intern over to Macadamia, then join us! Macadamia, follow Lemon and Papaya back to base!" ordered Banana.

"Right!" obeyed Walnut.

The three kidnappers, with Hoodwink and Rod, raced off to the side, down a dark alley as instructed. They successfully ditched the Sheriff, while the remaining seven Super Nudists lured the squad car away as planned. A high speed pursuit began between the streaking villains and the Sheriff and Deputy's squad car.

The Super Nudists streaked past the famous Driftwood Valley Hotel with the Sheriff close on their naked tails! Being so late, the whole place was quiet. The mid-century modern hotel was a round-shaped tower with twenty-five floors. The hotel's *'revolving restaurant'* took up the entire top level. Huge glass windows covered the round restaurant, so that as diners automatically circled the room, they could see different, panoramic views of Driftwood Valley.

The wild chase continued to a railroad crossing in the middle of the street! Suddenly, the train guard rails began to lower, warning bells rang, and red lights flashed! *Ding! Ding! Ding! Ding! Ding!* A huge, long freight train was approaching.

Banana and the rest of the Super Nudists saw it coming!

"Everyone pick up the pace! We've got to move faster!" declared Banana.

The Super Nudists nodded their helmets in agreement with their leader, and increased their running speeds. Like flashes of naked lightning, the villains and villainesses sped over the train tracks before guard railings came down.

Inside the squad car, the Sheriff hit the accelerator for what seemed like the fiftieth time.

"Sheriff, the train!" cried the Deputy. "It's coming!"

"We'll make it! We can't let those nudnik kidnappers escape!"

The squad car zoomed over the tracks, but the Sheriff wasn't fast enough! The guard railings came down on top of the squad car's roof, ripping off the flashing red lights and siren! A second later, one of the railings was snapped off too!

Crash! Riippp! Raaaapp!! Ka-Bang!

The police vehicle shook like hell as its top was scratched off, but somehow it made it over the tracks, beating the train just in time! As the freight train passed by, its angry engineer furiously blew his thunderous air horn!

Woooooaaaaammmmppppp!!!

"There went our lights and siren!" said the Deputy, while looking up at the squad car's crumpled roof.

The retreating Super Nudists turned another sharp corner, and as the Sheriff tried to follow, the accelerating squad car began to skid!

Eeeeee-eeeeee-eee-eeee!

"*Whoa!*" cried the Deputy.

The speeding police car's right side drove up onto the sidewalk and hit a vacant lot's white picket fence, smashing it into hundreds of pieces! Dozens of wooden planks were ripped, shattered and propelled high up into the nighttime sky.

Smash! Bang! Boom! Rii-iipppp!

"*Aaaahh!*" bellowed the Sheriff.

"*Waaaahh!*" cried the Deputy.

Miraculously, the Sheriff was able to regain control of the vehicle, and drive it back onto the street to continue the chase. Only the squad car's right side was damaged . . . the rest of the vehicle was still drivable.

"Hey, Sheriff . . . why do we always wreck squad cars whenever we're in high speed chases?"

"What do you mean?"

"I mean, during chases we always seem to crash into fruit stands, sending fruit flying all over the place . . . or we nearly hit a little old lady crossing the street, or a woman pushing a baby carriage . . . or we swipe a newsstand, scattering newspapers everywhere . . . or we roll the squad car . . ."

"Deputy, do I have to remind you to respect your senior officers again?"

"No, sir."

"One more crack about my driving and I'll request you be replaced by a police dog."

"Yes, sir. Sorry, sir."

The Sheriff glanced straight ahead to get a better look at the fleeing nudists.

"Hey, weren't they carrying *two people* a moment ago?"

"Yeah . . . you're right Sheriff . . . but they *aren't* carrying anyone now."

Further up the empty street, Banana turned to Walnut, who was running beside him.

"Walnut, your smoke bomb!"

"Right!"

Male Super Nudist Walnut pulled another one of his smoke bombs out from his utility belt. He ignited it by pushing a small button, and it lit up! He instantly tossed it behind him at the approaching squad car . . . and the walnut-shaped bomb landed right in front of the vehicle! It exploded! *Boom!*

A blinding cloud of purple smoke mushroomed up around the hood and front windshield of the car! *Sssssssss!* The Sheriff and Deputy panicked!

"What the . . . I can't see!" roared the Sheriff.

"Oh no! Look out!" pleaded the Deputy. "Here we go again . . . *.waaaaaaaa-aaahh!"*

"Aaaaaahhhhh!!!"

The police car barreled off the road, hitting a wooden billboard sign advertising the Driftwood Valley Drive-Thru Car Wash! The Sheriff, unable to see, actually crashed the squad car through the giant billboard's illustration of the car wash tunnel! It looked like the real vehicle actually drove through the wash tunnel picture itself!

Ka-Bang! Crash!

Billboard debris shattered and flew everywhere, as the police vehicle was airborne for a few moments, before crashing down into some muddy grass. The car's hubcaps soared off like flying saucers!

The Super Nudists turned around, seeing the disabled squad car. Banana then motioned them to stop running, and they carefully surveyed the scene, while panting for breath. Inside their police car, the

Sheriff and Deputy were dazed, moaning and groaning. Luckily, they were still strapped in their seats thanks to their safety belts.

"We'll take them too!" ordered Banana.

The Super Nudists nodded their heads in agreement. They raced over and pulled the injured Sheriff and Deputy from their damaged vehicle. Tossing the officers guns, they then streaked off into the night, carrying the two men with them!

CHAPTER FIVE

The next morning, the Double-D Avenger made her way to the Sheriff's office. Our hero flung her super-breasts upwards, as quickly as she could, bouncing up and down in the bright morning sky. *Boi-oing-oing-oing-oing-oing!* She covered long distances at great heights with each bounce, leaping like a rocket powered pogo-stick with boobs.

The Driftwood Valley Police Department building was a gorgeous Art Deco concrete and glass structure with stairs leading up to the front entrance. A huge American flag was displayed out front, proudly waving in the morning breeze. The moment she landed, Double-D raced up the steps and disappeared through the glass doors.

Inside the Sheriff's office, our hero noticed Officer Bob and busty policewoman Officer Peaks looking terribly stressed-out behind their reception desks.

"Double-D Avenger, thank goodness you're here!" declared Officer Bob.

"Don't tell me . . . you didn't find the Mayor?" asked our hero.

"It's worse than that Double-D," added sexy Officer Peaks.

"What do you mean Officer Peaks?"

On cue, the Sheriff and the Deputy waltzed out from a back office and into the front reception area . . . *totally nude!*

Chastity, as the Double-D Avenger, couldn't believe what she was seeing! She went bug-eyed!

"I'll watch the front doors," whispered Officer Peaks to Officer Bob.

In a flash, the policewoman dashed over to the doors to block them from anyone coming in.

"*Sheriff! Deputy!*" sputtered Double-D. "Where are your uniforms . . . *and why aren't you in them?*"

Our hero was so shocked she didn't know where to look! She was also astounded to see how well-endowed the handsome young Deputy was!

"Uniforms? Why would we need them?" smiled the nude Sheriff.

"The Sheriff's right Double-D," added the naked Deputy.

"See what I mean?" mumbled Officer Peaks to Double-D.

Our hero shot a look to Officer Peaks, and then turned her gaze back to the unclad officers.

"Sheriff, have you and the Deputy lost your minds, or have you been drinking or something?"

"Drinking Double-D? On the job?! Why never!" he sternly replied.

"Well, shouldn't you put on some clothes?!" she exclaimed. "Shame on the two of you! Don't you realize that parading around in your birthday suits is . . . is . . . going too far in the exhibition of intimate things?! After all, modesty is decency . . . and don't forget your badges! Where can you pin them without uniforms? Think of the Driftwood Valley Police Department's fine reputation you've got to uphold."

The Sheriff started pacing around the room, completely uninhibited, as the Double-D Avenger, the Deputy and Officers Bob and Peaks looked on. He had a strange look on his face, and began speak in 'flowery talk,' like some kind of *nudist guru*.

"Double-D . . . I've recently had a wondrous epiphany . . . or a 'eureka moment' you might say."

"Me too!" chimed in the Deputy.

"Deputy, don't interrupt while I'm explaining my wondrous epiphany," spat the Sheriff. "As I was saying before I was so rudely interrupted . . . I love the sun's rays . . . and a slight breeze . . . all over my nude body . . . *haa-haa-haa* . . . love it . . . without wearing a hot, sticky, confining pair of pants, or an itchy button down polyester shirt! It's a thrilling feeling of exposure without the bondage of a police uniform . .

. yes, an exhilarating sensation being freely exposed to the tingly air and warm sunlight."

"He's flipped" whispered Officer Peaks to Double-D. "Completely wacko!"

The Sheriff continued, with the Deputy nodding in agreement to his every spoken word.

"I believe that beneath this purely physical level of expression, is a subconscious rebellion against repression . . . repression of the need to be natural . . . to be naked . . . naked as a jaybird!"

"I couldn't have said it better myself Sheriff," added the Deputy.

"Of course you couldn't have," he snorted back.

"But . . . what about Mayor Phishel?" demanded Double-D.

"Oh, I'm sure he's fine and dandy. Don't worry about him!" the Sheriff calmly stated.

"He's probably back in his office by now," chimed in the Deputy.

Double-D shook her head in bewilderment.

Officer Bob pulled her aside. "We've called for some mental help for the two of them," he whispered. "They were found unconscious in their disabled squad car earlier this morning. No serious injuries . . . just this sudden crazy interest in nudism!"

"I see. Maybe they banged their heads on the police car's steering wheel and dashboard or something," Double-D softly calculated. "Officer Bob, where are their uniforms?"

"Who knows," he frankly said.

"We do have one clue that came in," Officer Peaks told her.

"What's that?"

"The nude skydivers who kidnapped Councilman Max Phuckter at the bank, were flown to their jump location by an outfit called Fly-By-Night Skydiving," she explained. "We just haven't had time to investigate, since the Sheriff and Deputy suddenly 'went nudist' on us."

"I didn't know councilman Phuckter was kidnapped too!" confessed Double-D. "Which bank was it?"

"Liberty Bells Savings. One of the bank tellers reported the incident."

Our hero thought carefully to herself . . . her mind racing a mile a minute. *"Hmmm . . .* Fly-By-Night Skydiving, huh? I think I'll check them out myself."

"We'd be grateful if you did."

"I'll keep you posted," declared Double-D. She then turned to the nude officers, "See you soon . . . Sheriff, Deputy."

"Bye."

"Later, Double-D."

Officer Peaks moved aside, opening the door for our hero as she exited.

Fly-By-Night Skydiving operated out of a small, private airport on the outskirts of Driftwood Valley. The airport only had an eight-thousand foot runway, a couple airplane and helicopter hangars, and a front office and control tower near its main gates. The airport's helicopters and small planes were used by the Driftwood Valley news, medical transport teams and aerial tour operators. No major commercial air services flew in or out of there since it was so small.

Inside the control tower, an air traffic controller's eyes suddenly widened.

"Unidentified aircraft, you are not cleared for landing . . . and you're descending too fast! What are you doing?!" he shouted into his headset's microphone.

A second controller, with a concerned look on his face, came over to check the same screen. He then shot a look out the tower's observation windows.

"A helicopter? No, it's too small," he broke in.

"I don't know what it is!" spat the first controller.

Up in the bright blue sky, the Double-D Avenger was descending from her last powerful Booby Bounce . . . heading down, down, down to the airport runway! In her blue leotard costume and red bra-mask, her red gloves, red boots, waving red cape and red belt with two upper-case white letter 'D's' on its buckle, she finally landed! *Za-Zap!* Her powerful super boobs absorbed the impact of her landing, and once recovered, she ran to the airport office.

Back up in the control tower, both air traffic controllers breathed sighs of relief.

"False alarm . . . it was only the Double-D Avenger landing!"

"Thanks goodness! That busty, costumed crime-fighter scared the fudge nuggets out of me!"

As Double-D neared the airport's main building, she noticed an outside ticket booth with a sign above it reading *Fly-By-Night Skydiving!* A heavy set British man with a comical face and bushy moustache was sitting in the window. His name was 'Bomb's Away' Plummet, and he was dressed like an old World War One bomber pilot . . . complete with long scarf, jacket, and leather helmet with goggles. The crazy character spoke in a heavy, old English accent.

"By George, if it ain't the Double-D Avenger! What a pleasant surprise," he declared through his booth's large open window.

"Hello sir, nice to meet you," she smiled back. "You work for Fly-By-Night Skydiving I assume?"

"Indeed I do, ma'am. In fact, I'm ticket-taker, telephone operator, reservations manager, skydiving instructor, and ace pilot, all wrapped up into one! The name's 'Bomb's Away' Plummet . . . at your service! Hang on a moment, I'll pop right out."

Plummet opened the ticket booth's side door and shuffled out to Double-D to shake her hand. She smiled again and shook . . . but as she did this *firm* hand shaking, her giant breasts jiggled up and down! *Ka-Bloop! Ka-Bloop! Ka-Bloop!* Naturally Plummet noticed, and a huge grin suddenly appeared on his funny face.

"You got some lovely thrupney bits there, ain't ya darlin'?" he sputtered, while staring at her shaking, gargantuan cleavage. "I've never seen such enormous 'Strawberry Creams,' as we lads used to say back in jolly old England! Who knew shaken' hands could be such fun! *Ha-Ha!*"

Chastity, as Double-D, withdrew her hand while clearing her throat, choosing to ignore his comments.

"Mr. Plummet, did you recently fly a group of skydiving nudists over the Liberty Bells bank?"

"Why yes, indeed I did . . . but I had no idea they'd land in the bank's car park. The head feller said they'd land on the nearby golf course for a nudist wedding. Judging by the size of his fig leaf, I'd say he was the best man. *Ha, ha!*"

"Who were those nudists?"

"Said they hailed from Adamite Acres."

"Adamite Acres? Where's that?"

"In Driftwood Valley . . . a nudists resort near Humdinger Hills."

"I see."

"I already explained all of this on the horn to the police, and to the big wigs here at the airport. Believe me miss, I had no idea those scoundrels were kidnappers!" he nervously confessed. "No, no, no! Fly-By-Night Skydiving follows strict rules and regulations! We always uphold the law and are completely aboveboard! For example, we never allow blind people to skydive."

"Why's that?"

"It scares the bloody hell out of their seeing eye dogs. *Ha, ha!*"

"I see. Well, thanks for your time Mr. Plummet. By the way, my good friend Chastity Knott runs a wonderful British pub and restaurant. Check it out sometime . . . I think you'd love it."

"I most certainly will! Thanks for the tip!"

"Don't mention it." She quickly waved goodbye, saying in her own lousy British accent, *"Tootle-pip!"*

"Ta-Tas!" Plummet waved back. He then corrected himself, "I mean, *ta-ta!* Feel free to drop in anytime for a free skydiving lesson!

It's rather simple really . . . the only hard thing about skydiving is the ground. *Ha,ha!*"

Our hero turned her head.

"Thank you, that's awfully sweet, but I don't need any skydiving lessons!"

She then took a running leap.

"Booby-Bounce!"

Off she flew back up into the sky, propelled by the centrifugal force of her catapulted super-tits! *Boi-oing-oing-oing-oing-oing!*

"Cor blimey!" sputtered Plummet, as he watched her bounce up to the clouds. "That was a smashing takeoff, if I do say so myself. *Ha, ha!*"

Flying through the sky, our hero pulled out her slim, tiny red cell phone secretly clipped behind her Double-D belt buckle. The phone was in the shape of a small brassiere, with a figure-eight screen in both bra cups. She had it custom made in Japan, through a third party, and it was totally secure and untraceable! This was to insure that Chastity Knott's true identity would never be revealed! She'd remain completely anonymous whenever using her bra phone to make calls as the Double-D Avenger.

She swiftly activated her customized GPS using a gloved finger.

"Directions to Adamite Acres nudist camp . . . or nudist colony?" she declared while soaring through the air.

"Directions to Adamite Acres nudist resort," replied the phone computer's female voice. "Starting Booby-Bounce directions now."

Off our hero catapulted, continuing her investigation into the bizarre naked kidnapping affair.

Adamite Acres was a three-hundred acre nudist resort, with high walls and large green bushes surrounding it, so no one could see inside. The main entrance had a large metal gate painted white, which would automatically slid open and shut for cars to drive through. A big fancy sign reading *Adamite Acres,* in cursive writing, appeared on the only wall free of manicured shrubs. Right next to it was a standalone two-way communication device, or intercom system, which allowed visitors and members to access the property.

The Double-D Avenger landed right in front of the place . . . *Zap* . . . then she walked up to the silver intercom and hit the buzzer. *Buzzz!* She was instantly greeted by a friendly woman, whose slim, wrinkled face appeared on a small screen. She was a lady in her sixties with white hair wildly sticking out in all directions. The video monitor only showed the woman's head and lower shoulders, but it was obvious she was not wearing a blouse or top.

"Hello, how can I help you?" she asked in her smoker's voice. A surprised look then flashed over her! She was startled seeing the famous superhero.

"Double-D Avenger?" she stuttered.

"Why yes, that's me!" our hero smiled. "I was wondering if I could take a quick tour of your resort today? Would that be possible, or do I have to make an appointment?"

"For you Double-D, most certainly! I'll open the gate, then meet me at the main office. It's straight ahead," she told her.

"Thank you. I'm double-dee-lighted!"

A second later, the elegant white gate slowly slid to one side, revealing a driveway. Our hero walked through, and when she was clear, the gate automatically reversed direction and closed behind her.

Chastity, as the Double-D Avenger, was so nervous she could feel her heart pounding under her blue leotard costume. Her palms began sweating inside her red gloves too. She was so embarrassed . . . ashamed of walking into such a place, full of stark naked people.

"This is so embarrassing, thank goodness I've got my bra-mask on," she mumbled to herself.

The woman with the crazy white hair walked out of a small bungalow, and sure enough, she was in her birthday suit! She was naked as naked could be! She waved and motioned for Double-D to come over to her.

"I have to say, this is a big surprise!" smiled the woman. "I had no idea you were a nudist or naturist! I'm Jeanie Jingle, membership director, pleased to meet you!"

The two of them shook hands.

"Nice to meet you Jeanie," stuttered Double-D. "I'm surprised too!"

"All the members here call me 'Jingle Bells'!" she laughed, while shaking her sagging boobs.

They both chuckled.

"I must say, I'm a bit nervous . . . Jingle Bells. I've never been to a nudist place before . . . where should I look?"

"Anywhere you like, just don't stare," Jingle chuckled. "Let me give you a tour. Relax and follow me."

"I don't have to take off my superhero costume for the tour, do I?"

"No, not for introductory tours, but if you do become a paid member, you must be nude at all times . . . except during the winter months when it's too cold outside."

"I understand," Double-D nodded in relief. "Thank you. Please lead the way."

The friendly nudist walked our hero around the lovely property, showing her all the different amenities. It was actually a very beautiful, well kept, mid-century modern resort . . . an enchanting oasis rivalling the finest world class vacation spots. The gardens, lawns and colorful flowers were all perfectly manicured, and the vacation villas were mid-century architectural masterpieces of steel and glass. As for the warm pleasant temperature, it was a perfect sunny day for nudist activities . . . not too hot, and not too cold.

"Adamite Acres is Driftwood Valley's original nude recreation community for adults. We've occupied the same gorgeous two-hundred acre site since 1940. We've got a full service restaurant and two lounges, and there are two beautiful heated swimming pools, a sauna, and a twenty-five person hot tub."

"Bless my over-the-shoulder-boulder-holder . . . how impressive!"

"Thanks. Our sports facilities include tennis, volleyball, horseshoes, shuffleboards, billiards, darts and ping-pong. As for our vacation villas, we have thirty two-bedroom cottages, each with HDTV, bathtub, desk, sleeper sofa, hair dryer, coffee and tea maker, microwave, mini refrigerator, and so on."

Chastity quickly scanned the entire place through her bra-mask, searching for the Super Nudist kidnappers and/or Mayor Artie Phishel. There wasn't a trace of any of them. Instead, she saw mostly middle-aged, average looking, naked people diving into stunning swimming pools and playing tennis and volleyball . . . the type of 'normal folks' she'd see at the grocery store or shopping mall. They came in all kinds of shapes, sizes and ethnicities.

"I'm a little surprised the gentlemen aren't sprouting any stiff 'love arrows' while participating in sports activities with the nude ladies," commented our hero.

"Our members are so used to the 'au naturel' lifestyle, it's no big deal."

"I see."

An all-female volley ball game on a sandbox court was going on between four attractive ladies in their thirties. Two nude women were playing one side of the court, and the other two were on the opposite side. They jumped around, some clasping theirs hands together as they struck the ball. Chastity was amazed they kept the volleyball flying back and forth in the air for so long! She also couldn't help but notice their naked bodies were oily and shiny from the all the sunscreen they had applied.

"They're excellent players!" she complimented.

"Yes, they sure are," replied Jingle.

"Argh!" cried one of the women as she spiked the ball. She instantly took a nosedive into the sand, landing on her stomach. When she got

up, her bare breasts had a light layer of white sand stuck all over them, thanks to the sticky sunscreen!

"Reminds me of two sugar-powdered donuts!" remarked our hero with a big smile.

Chastity then turned her head to face the tennis courts, and reacted bug-eyed as if she'd seen a ghost!

"Why did that man on the tennis court bring his *bowling bag* with him?"

The naked gentleman in his forties was about to serve a tennis ball, while holding his tennis racket in one hand. His back was completely turned to Double-D and Jingle, and his legs were spread apart with his knees bent. He was totally *mooning* the two of them, with his bare rump and bent knees, as he was about to serve.

"What bowling bag?" Jingle wondered.

"That one!" pointed Double-D, indicating the large bag hanging between the server's legs.

"That's not a bowling bag honey," Jingle grinned. "Those are his jumbo cow bells!"

"Holy Hooters!" sputtered our hero, with even bigger eyes!

The player's hanging balls were the size of a bull elephant's!

CHAPTER SIX

Chastity shook her head, focusing back on her investigation. She recalled that during her battle with the Super Nudist kidnappers, the villains and villainesses all looked physically perfect! They were just like supermodels hidden beneath their dark goggles . . . with the strong, handsome, masculine men possessing square jaws and muscular tanned bodies . . . and the fit, topless, big breasted women all drop-dead gorgeous with beautiful faces and luscious lips!

The few Adamite Acres members who did fit those descriptions, didn't seem to 'ring a bell' in Chastity's mind. They weren't the 'right match.'

"Jingle Bells, do any of your members ever go on nude skydiving trips?"

"Skydiving?! Are you kiddin'?!" she shockingly declared. "You couldn't get me to do that for all the tea in China! Neither would most of our members! Besides, we wouldn't want to deal with the liability insurance for a dangerous activity like that!"

"I see," nodded Double-D.

"We're a laid back place for friendly people from all walks of life. Everyone's here to erase stress and leave their cares behind! At Adamite Acres, members can enjoy fresh air, sunshine and fun, relaxing exercise. Our atmosphere of peace and tranquility is conducive to the making of new and lasting friendships too! Members can do whatever they want, without having to worry about what to wear. Yes, nude recreation allows everyone to accept who they are, and to feel comfortable about their own bodies."

A look of seriousness then flashed over Jingle's face.

"We do, of course, maintain certain membership rules, as I mentioned earlier. We're strictly a 'platonic establishment' here, and *do not* tolerate open, public, *sexual activities* of any kind, or other inappropriate behavior! Adamite Acres is _not_ the place for perverts, swingers, exhibitionists, wife-swappers, peeping Toms, sex maniacs, wild orgies, and so on! We're an authentic, safe, traditional, friendly, 'clean' nudist resort . . . genuine, honest and certified . . . not like that *other* place."

"Well, I'm certainly glad to hear that," smiled Double-D.

"We did catch a pickpocket once . . . he hated it here! *Ha, ha!*"

"I'm sure!"

Our hero got curious.

"Jingle Bells, what's that *other* place you're talking about? There's another nudist resort in Driftwood Valley?"

"Yes, the Jaybird Growth Institute, run by that maniac . . . Monty Jaybird."

"Monty Jaybird?"

"That's him . . . Monty isn't a real nudist or naturist at all, he and his followers are just a bunch of sexually motivated degenerates who use the terms 'nudist' or 'naturist' to hide the true carnal nature of their shenanigans! He's nude and rude!"

" . . . and he runs a place called the Jaybird Growth Institute?"

"That's right. Oh, don't get me going on Monty . . . I could bitch all day long about that creep! He was kicked out of L.O.O.N.S. you know!"

"L.O.O.N.S.?"

"The Leisure Organization of Nudists Statewide. It's a group of affiliated nudist and naturist clubs."

"What's the difference between nudist and naturist?"

"No difference really," replied Jingle. "Anyway, Monty tried to cheat his way into becoming President of L.O.O.N.S. by rigging the election! The board totally disagreed with his 'free love,' 'hippy,' 'touchy-feely,' 'get sprung' attitude towards nudism! They tossed his fake ballots out, then his uncovered keister too!"

"Is that so?"

"Yep . . . not only that, the sleazeball was further outraged when L.O.O.N.S. started publishing their own nudist newspaper, which directly competed with Monty's own *Bare Behind Bugle*."

"What's L.O.O.N.S. newspaper called?"

"The Undressed Observer."

Suddenly, a fat man holding an inflated beach ball over his front private parts waddled by.

"Hi, Jingle Bells!" he wavied. The man then did a double-take, seeing the Double-D Avenger. "Hey, aren't you . . .?"

" . . . The Double-D Avenger?" said Double-D, beating him to it. "Yes, I am."

"Wow!"

"I'm just giving our V.I.P. guest a tour," said Jingle.

"I see," he nodded. "Interested in becoming a member?"

"Maybe," she politely replied.

"We'd love to have you," he smiled. "Wish I could stop and chat, but I'm off to the pool. I'm judging the diving contest. Nice meeting you!"

He quickly shook her hand, and then sped off wiggling his big bare butt behind him.

"Nice meeting you."

"Chubby," Jingled called out. "Remember, no cannon balls from the high diving board!"

He turned his head and hollered back. "I know! No cannon balls."

"Why can't members do cannon balls into the pool?" asked Chastity.

"We don't want unexpected enemas!"

"Oh," gulped our hero.

"That was our long time member, Chubby Baton," explained Jingle. "He runs our popular pancake breakfasts. You mentioned donuts a moment ago . . . well Chubby can carry a cup of hot coffee in each hand, *and* a dozen donuts at the same time!"

It was Chastity's turn to do a double-take, when she realized the *only way* Chubby could hold a dozen donuts while both of his hands were occupied with coffee!

"Well, Jingle Bells, I want to thank you so much for your time. It was a lovely tour, but I'm going to have to 'bounce off' now." Our hero made up a kind and polite way to exit. "Please give me one of your brochures and I'll think about becoming a member."

"No problem, Double-D. I've got them back at the office, along with our membership kits which include our pricing and application forms. Of course for a V.I.P. such as yourself, we'd offer a generous discount."

"Why thank you. That's very thoughtful."

Meanwhile, miles away on the roof of the Driftwood Valley City Hall building, missing Mayor Artie Phishel, and councilmembers Max Phuckter, Harry Bottoms, and Helga Hoodwink . . . along with young male intern, Rod Long . . . weren't missing any longer! In fact, there they all were . . . alive and well, and naked as jaybirds! The whole gang had been freed by their mysterious kidnappers! They were now *sunbathing in the nude*, relaxing on comfortable lounge chairs they'd set up on the building's *rooftop!*

"Pass the sunscreen, will you councilman Bottoms?" asked the Mayor.

"Here you go mayor," replied Bottoms, handing him the plastic bottle. *"Ah, this is the life!"*

"Thanks . . . it sure is," agreed the Mayor taking the sunscreen. "You couldn't ask for better weather!"

"It feels so good to take off all my clothes and be free!" remarked Phuckter.

"You said it," agreed Bottoms. "I love the feeling of the warm sun against my naked skin!"

"Me too," said Hoodwink. "The sun is my nudist beauty treatment! I'm a 'nature girl' at heart and I can't get enough of it. This is what my body needs . . . what it longs for!"

"I love baking my body in the sun like a baked potato!" declared Rod.

"Yes, folks, as councilman Bottoms so rightly put it . . . *this is the life!*" smiled the Mayor.

"I want to live outdoors, fully naked . . . naked as a jaybird . . . forever!" added Hoodwink.

"I couldn't agree with you more! In fact, I'm gonna throw away all of my clothes and run around naked *permanently,* just like Adam and Eve used to do!" grinned Bottoms.

"Too bad Eve had to go and eat that damn apple though!" remarked Hoodwink. "A pity she was a *fruitarian!*"

"Can I have some of that sunscreen," asked Rod. "I don't want to get a bad case of 'ball burn.'"

"Here you go, son," said the Mayor, as he tossed the bottle over to the young man. "We wouldn't want that. Nothin' worse than a sunburned scrotum!"

Suddenly, the metal door to the building's roof swung wide open, and a half dozen city clerks, assistants and staff filed out. Their jaws all dropped and their eyes bugged out, the instant they saw the nude mayor and naked councilmembers! The city manager, an older man named Charlie, also popped his head out from the doorway, having heard all the commotion downstairs.

"*Mayor!*" cried one shocked clerk.

"Coucilman Phuckter . . . Councilman Bottoms," stuttered an assistant. "You're . . . *barefoot* all over!"

"Coucilwoman Hoodwink . . . you're . . . you're . . . nude too!" muttered another clerk.

"Yes, and isn't it wonderful darling?" cheered Hoodwink.

"What are you all doing, sunbathing in the nude?! Have you all gone crazy?!" asked Charlie from the doorway.

"Show a little more respect to your Mayor, Charlie," warned the Mayor.

"You're the ones who are crazy," barked back Phuckter. "How on Earth can you walk around in those hot, itchy, sweaty, stinky clothes?! The thought of it is revolting! *Yuck!*"

"Yes! *Yuck!*" snapped Bottoms.

"Mankind's expressiveness has suffered terribly by being confined and falsified by clothing," lectured the Mayor. "Clothes are an artificial barrier to the true-self."

"Nudists have a special fellowship with nature, which you fools can't see . . . yet!" warned Rod.

"But you all can't go around stark naked for Heaven's sake!" pleaded a clerk.

"What if the press finds out? All of Driftwood Valley will be in an uproar! It'll be the political scandal of the century!" cried a panicked staff member.

The Mayor was growing angry! He stood up, fully naked, pointing his accusing finger at the group of gawkers!

"You had all better run along now, the councilmembers and I have vitally important city business to discuss . . . private legal matters! Now scram or I'll summon the Sheriff! Beat it!" spat the Mayor.

"Yes, sir," mumbled back a frightened clerk.

"Yes, Mayor," nodded Charlie.

"Get movin'! You're slower than nudists trying to climb a barbwire fence!"

"We're going, sir. We're going," sheepishly replied a staff member.

"Sorry to have bothered you all," apologized an assistant.

One by one, the scared city employees all filed back through the roof doorway and disappeared. None of them wanted to get arrested or lose their cushy jobs. The last one to leave shook his head in disbelief, as he shut the door behind him. *Boom!*

"That's better," chuckled the Mayor.

"Nicely done Mayor," laughed Hoodwink.

"She's right, sir!" smiled Bottoms. "Bravo!"

"Bravo! Bravo!" applauded Phuckter and Rod.

"When do we pass our new law?" anxiously asked Hoodwink.

"As soon my brother Soupy returns!" the Mayor replied. "We'll file the bill, introduce it in our meeting, discuss it, and then vote on it."

"It will get our unanimous vote!" said Phuckter.

". . . and then you'll sign the bill, right Mayor?" asked Bottoms.

"You bet your nude ass I'm signing it!" reassured the Mayor. "The bill will become local law and then entered into the city's administrative code."

"How wonderful darling!" sighed Hoodwink. "Just think . . . *public nudity* will soon be *completely legal* throughout all of Driftwood Valley!"

Meanwhile, high atop snowy Mount Nipplepotamus, Mayor Artie Phishel's lazy brother Soupy Phishel, was enjoying a sunny day of snow skiing. The extraordinary aspect of Driftwood Valley's unique geography was you could snow ski on Mount Nipplepotamus in the morning, and later that same afternoon, surf some big waves on the sunny beach miles below. The valley was full of amazing diverse typography.

Soupy resembled the Mayor, only he was younger and thinner. He was dressed in a thermal ski outfit and helmet, and had just gotten off of the top of the ski lift. Something nice then caught his eye . . . a cute snow bunny! Soupy instantly waddled over in the snow to the sexy young lady, using his skis and poles for balance. The foxy woman wore formfitting snow clothes, and was waiting her turn to ski down one of the slope's more advanced runs.

"Hey! How are you today?" he asked.

"Fine," she politely replied.

"I'm Mr. Right, and I heard you're lookin' for me," he chuckled.

She wasn't chuckling and rolled her eyes.

"No, I'm city councilman Soupy Phishel. You've probably heard of me," he boasted. "My brother's the <u>mayor</u>!"

"*Oh!*" she happily smiled, as if recognizing him. A second later, a deadpan look flashed over her pretty face. " . . . never heard of you."

"Oh, well," he mumbled, thinking of his next pick-up line. "Nice outfit. Can I talk you out of it?"

"Why, so I can freeze my titties off?" she snapped back.

"You're freezing your titties off? Let me check to see if they're still there."

"If you do, I'll shove this ski pole up your ass!" she snorted, while lifting her pole up in a menacing manner.

"Calm down baby, relax, no need to get feisty. What do you do? Are you an archeologist? Because I've got a big bone for you to examine!" he chuckled.

"Get lost, or better yet, ski down the advance run and break a leg or hug a tree or something!"

"*Ha, ha,* you're cute when you're angry. Hey, why don't you and me go to the ski lodge's ball tonight?"

"What ball?"

"The snow ball."

She rolled her eyes again, and then noticed her run was clear. It was her turn to ski, so off she went, skiing down the hill as fast as she could to get away from the jerk.

Whooosshh!

"Wait, come back . . ." he sighed. "Oh well, there's other fish in the sea, or snow bunnies on the ski slope."

Soupy lowered his helmet's goggles, and then he skied down a different hill . . . the more advance run.

Wa-whoosh!

He was a surprisingly good skier, and zoomed down the mountain like a pro. There weren't too many other skiers on the slopes that afternoon, so Soupy felt like he had the entire place to himself.

Nearby, sinister eyes were spying on him . . . tracking him . . . as he glided down the hill. The eyes behind the tiny pair of binoculars were Coconut's pretty peepers! The Super Nudist lowered the binoculars in her gloved hands, and then she looked down.

"Here he comes! I saw him! Run number eight!" she declared, while slipping her helmet's black goggles back down to disguise her face.

The birthday suit kidnappers had formed another one of their *Super Nudist Pyramids,* right next to some snow covered pine trees! They were somewhat hidden by the tree's branches. The men . . . Banana, Pecan, Walnut, Peanut and Macadamia . . . were lined up side by side, with their arms over each other's shoulders, forming the pyramid's strong base. They stood still in a perfectly straight line. Next, three of the women . . . Lemon, Guava, and Papaya . . . were on top of the men's shoulders! They had their arms over each other's shoulders, forming the pyramid's second level. Finally, the last two female Super Nudists . . . Coconut and Kiwi . . . were standing on top of the ladies shoulders forming the third and final level of the human tower! The two had an arm over each other's shoulders for support, just like the others below them had done. Coconut and Kiwi were about sixteen feet up in the air!

This incredible three-storied human pyramid demonstrated once again, the Super Nudists superb skills at stabilizing themselves and retaining their balance! They were just like Chinese acrobats! It was an amazing feat! The men had their snow skis on, but the ladies had taken off their skies, before jumping up to form the second and third levels of the pyramid.

"Right! Let's go!" declared Banana. *"Super Nudists Pyramid, disassemble!"*

Coconut and Kiwi, on the top level, lifted their arms off each other's shoulders and super jumped back down into the snow. *Zoop! Zoop!* The other topless and bottomless ladies on the second level then followed, doing exactly the same thing. *Zoop! Zoop! Zoop!* Once all five women were safely down, the men slipped their arms off each other's shoulders.

The ladies snapped their boots into their snow skis and grabbed their poles. The chilly air seemed to make their rubbery boobies and pointed nipples a little 'stiffer' and 'pointier!' However, the cold weather and snow didn't seem to bother the Super Nudists in the slightest. The men, with their skis already on, kneeled down to grab their ski poles.

"Super Streakers, go!" commanded Banana.

CHAPTER SEVEN

Off the Super Nudists skied . . . in their signature light-green and yellow goggled helmets with fruit or nut symbols painted on them, and their minimal uniforms of matching colored gloves, boots, utility belts, waving capes and fig leaf jockstraps and Jillstraps.

Waaaa-Whoooossshh!

Like hungry wolves after their prey, they flew down the snowy mountain after Councilman Phishel in perfect formation . . . proving they were just as excellent on snow skis as they were on water skis. One by one they sailed over snow banks, doing complete flips in the air! *Zoom!* Each airborne Super Nudist then landed safely back onto the snow to continue the chase.

The few other skiers on the slopes noticed flashing bare breasts and butts, as the Super Nudists whizzed by! However, the villains and villainesses darted away so quickly, people could hardly make them out.

A snow covered log cabin suddenly appeared in the Super Nudists path! Instead of going around the small structure, the streaking skiers glided up another snow bank and onto the cabin's roof itself! Using the roof like a ski ramp, the Super Nudists rocketed over it, one by one, soaring into the air again! *Whoosh! Whoosh! Whoosh! Whoosh! Whoosh!* Each nudist did a complete spin in the air, and then landed on bent knees in perfect synchronization!

A bewildered park ranger opened the cabin door, wondering what was happening on his roof! As he looked up, the last two female Super Nudists, Lemon and Papaya, flew right over his head! *Whoosh! Whoosh!* They soared over him like greased lightning, but he was still able to get an eyeful of their naked crotches!

"What the hell?!" he joyously declared. *"Nice beavers!"*

The Super Nudists closed in on Phishel, who was totally oblivious to what was behind him. The corrupt politician was just happily skiing along, nearing the end of his run.

Banana was leading the pack, and female Super Nudist Coconut was right behind him. He turned to her.

"Coconut! Your bolas!" ordered Banana.

"Right!" she replied.

Coconut pulled her coconut bolas from her utility belt . . . her throwing weapon made of round weights, resembling coconuts, connected to each other by a long cord. The villainess whipped them around, and then threw them! *Woo-Woo-Woo-Woo-Zoom!*

Her bolas flew through the air, spinning around and around by their cord, like an out of control helicopter propeller! A second later, they struck Phishel from behind . . . *Woo-Woo-Woo Zap* . . . and wrapped around his arms and chest! He crashed into the snow, tumbling at tremendous speed!

"Waaaaahhh!"

He lost his poles and skis, and couldn't stop!

"Aaaahhhh!"

The councilman tumbled and slid down, down, down, totally out of control! Snow flew everywhere! *Vooosh! Boom! Crunch! Crunch!* He was like a runaway snowball, tied up by the bolas, and caused a minor avalanche! When his run reached another step slope, down he dropped! Down, down, down! *Va-Boom! Ka-Crunch! Boom!* Phishel's out of control body plummeted, picking up more and more speed . . . and he drifted onto the second run!

Unfortunately, the sexy lady skier he tried hitting on earlier was in his way!

"Aaaahhh!" he cried.

A second later, his body collided with hers like a runaway bowling ball, knocking her down the slope! *Ka-Pow!* Yes, he 'hit on her' again, *literally!* Her poles flew and she lost one of her skis! She was pissed!

"Ah! You son-of-a . . .!" she screamed, while skidding and flailing down the snowy hill.

The collision didn't stop him, it only ricocheted Phishel back onto his original run! His coasting body finally came to a stop near a large pine tree, as the course leveled off.

Phishel was dazed and his aching body was blanketed in snow.

"Errrgghhh . . . aaahhh. . . . oohhh."

Banana reached him first, then so did the other nine Super Nudists. They slid to a stop, kicking up bits of ice. *Vooosshh!*

"Got him!" smiled Banana. "Great work, Coconut!"

"Thanks," she replied, as she bent down to unwind her bolas from the councilman.

When she was done, Banana grabbed Phishel's arms and Walnut took hold of his legs.

"Ergh . . . ," mumbled Phishel. "What's . . . . what's going on? Who are you guys?"

Banana turned to Guava.

"Guava?" he nodded.

The female Super Nudist understood Banana's subtle message. She shot the councilman in the face with her knock-out gas! *Sssssss!* He was out like a light a second later.

Banana then commanded, *"Super Streakers, go!"*

Off they skied, taking their latest political captive with them! *Voooosssshh! Voooossshh! Voooossshhh!* The Super Nudists disappeared into a snow-covered pine forest.

Minutes later, near the bottom of Mount Nipplepotamus, the villains and villainesses slid to stop in front of a waiting light-green and yellow-colored vehicle. It was a classic 1960's VW Bus, a 'Samba,' with its engine running. There were twenty-three windows wrapped around the sausage-shaped 'hippy bus,' with bi-parting side doors, a sunroof, and a sloping split windshield in front. The Super Nudists whipped off their skis, and piled into the vehicle's open side along with the anesthetized councilman Phishel.

The driver of the bus was the same person who piloted the speedboat earlier. He was a man in his forties with a 'regal air' about him, wearing a light-green and yellow colored helmet, except his had an ornamental identification symbol of a gold *fig leaf* painted on the front . . . just above his black goggles. He slid the stick shift into drive, stepped on the gas pedal, and off the bus went!

Chastity, as the Double-D Avenger, followed the excellent clue given to her by Jingle Bells at Adamite Acres. She booby-bounced over to the Jaybird Growth Institute, curious to see if the Super Nudists were hiding out there . . . and if they were holding Mayor Artie Phishel and councilman Max Phuckter as hostages! It was around four o'clock that afternoon when she arrived.

The Jaybird Growth Institute was nestled in warm and breezy Toupee Canyon, a unique and scenic section of Driftwood Valley. The canyon was out in the middle of nowhere, with a winding two-lane highway leading right through it. There weren't any chain restaurants, big box stores, malls, or gas stations . . . just residential cabins and ranch homes scattered here and there, surrounded by mountains covered with sagebrush, rocks, and pine, oak, and eucalyptus trees. The canyon also had several rivers, streams and waterfalls, along with cliffs of exposed bedrock, and overlooks featuring panoramic views of the mountains.

The southern tip of Lake Tittykookoo, the biggest lake in Driftwood Valley, actually extended into the canyon itself. Lakeside beaches, boating docks and private coves took up the northern edge of Toupee Canyon. Visitors enjoyed swimming, fishing, boating and water-skiing there. The canyon's state park and many wilderness trails were also popular for walking, hiking, mountain biking, horseback riding, birdwatching, and rock climbing.

Toupee Canyon was also famous for being Driftwood Valley's original *hippy* and *outlaw biker* hotspot! The small Bohemian town did have a post office, a fire department, and a few 'mom and pop' shops and restaurants, run mostly by aging hippies, artists and musicians reeking of 'whacky tabaky,' a.k.a. 'weed.' In total contrast to this, the valley's other residents were more conservative, traditional, 'old school' families and couples living in middle-class neighborhoods. These little communities were lined with mid-century homes and very narrow streets.

Double-D wandered up to the redwood fence surrounding the Jaybird Growth Institute, and instantly noticed a big sign near the open driveway entrance. Unlike Adamite Acres fancy, high-end sign, the Jaybird Growth Institute's banner was just a painted canvas, framed and held up by wooden posts. It read *Jaybird Growth Institute,* with the phone number just below it. The words *'Clothing Optional Resort'* and *'Education and Workshops in Human Potential'* were also nicely painted below the phone number. A little warning disclaimer, painted in red, stated *'Ages 18 and Over!'*

Chastity didn't see a sliding front gate . . . the entrance was just a wide open driveway. She moved to one corner of the driveway and could make out a one-story redwood building in the background, the edge of a huge swimming pool, and some lawn chairs with large open umbrellas. The green lawn looked mowed, and beautiful shady trees dotted the lovely property. She could hear people having fun in the background.

"I better play this a little differently," she told herself. "I shouldn't go in immediately as the Double-D Avenger. I'll walk around the outside of the property first and peek over the fence."

She did just that, sneaking around the expansive resort, avoiding the main entrance's open driveway. Every few yards, she would periodically hop up and peek over the redwood fence for brief seconds. Chastity's eyes widened through her bra-mask, when she saw attractive naked people playing tennis and volleyball! She also spotted a nude man relaxing on a beach towel, strumming a guitar.

When she caught a better glimpse of the large swimming pool, she noticed a group of smiling, laughing, young nudists all in their twenties, horsing around near the shallow end! The attractive girls were seated on top of the guys' shoulders, mock wrestling with each other and splashing pool water! Each happy young man held onto his girl's legs, and playfully bounced and bumped into the other guys holding their own ladies. Occasionally, one of the girls would lose her balance, or a guy would lose his grip, and down they went into the sparkly water.

"Whoah! Ahhh!"

"Ha, ha, ha, ha, ha!"

Ka-Splash!

As Double-D circled the property, she took another hop at the fence. A sexy woman in her forties was seen using an outdoor shower, washing her hair in the sun. Her wet boobs were big, shiny and soapy! Nearby, other nudists seated crossed-legged on towels, were having a picnic on the lawn. They were eating apples, oranges, and bananas.

Chastity then blinked her eyes in amazement, as she beheld a miniature golf course in the background. A giant, ten-foot tall fiberglass *golf ball* was standing in front of the course, like a big statue. A handsome, older gentleman bent over to retrieve his golf ball, totally mooning her!

"Huh! No sign of Mayor Phishel, councilman Phuckter, or the Super Nudists," she grumbled to herself. Our hero was unaware that the kidnapped Mayor, the councilman, and the others had been secretly returned to their offices earlier that day.

Chastity, as Double-D, then heard some angry grumbling right behind her! She spun around, and noticed a group of residential ranch-style homes, located *right next door* to the nudist colony! These long, wood and glass ranch houses were all single story, having low-pitched rooflines. An angry woman was outside her house, standing out in the middle of the road, taking photographs of parked cars using her cell phone! She was the source of the grumbling!

Double-D thought she'd ask the woman a few questions . . . to maybe pick up a few more leads . . . so off she went to greet her.

The thin lady was in her late fifties, with short blond hair, big blue eyes, a pointed nose, and a frowning mouth. Red lipstick and blue eye shadow highlighted her white powdered face. She was conservatively dressed in dark pants and a purple turtleneck top. She held her cell phone in one hand, while nervously rattling her house keys in the other.

The frustrated expression on the woman's face suddenly changed to a look of surprise, the moment she recognized the Double-D Avenger!

"*The Double-D Avenger!*" she cried. "Did the police send you over?"

"Ah, no, they didn't," replied Double-D. She paused to carefully think of how to respond. "I, ah, just happened to be in the neighborhood and thought I'd look around a bit, that's all."

"Well, I wish the cops had sent you. Just look at all those nudists' cars!" she pointed.

Dozens of cars were parked, lining the street on both sides, from one end to the other.

"What about them?"

"They're taking up the whole damn road as usual! I've been taking photos and counting each and every one of them, especially on weekends, for evidence. It's a thankless task!"

"Evidence?"

"Yes . . . more 'ammunition' for my case."

"What case?"

"Good heavens Double-D, where have you been? Haven't you heard of my legal case against Monty Jaybird and his Jaybird Growth Institute?"

"I don't even know your name," confessed Double-D.

"Oh, I'm sorry, how rude of me. I'm Adrianna Azzhat."

They quickly shook hands.

"Nice to meet you Adrianna."

"Nice meeting you, Double-D." Azzhat took a deep breath before speaking again. "I've had a twenty-year zoning battle with the

Driftwood Valley Board of Supervisors, resulting in the longest and most expensive zoning case in the valley's history!"

"Bless my over-the-shoulder-boulder-holder! Is that so?"

"Monty has been illegally running his nudist colony, a *resort*, on residentially zoned land! You're not supposed to do that! His motley throngs . . . all buck naked perverts . . . cause endless traffic and noise on Bare Road at all hours of the day and night! There's not enough parking spaces in the nudist resort itself, so it spills out all over our neighborhood!"

She paused to catch her breath again, and continued. "You should hear the moans, groans, and animal cries of ecstasy! We neighbors have no peace and quiet! We're living next-door to *a recreational sexual playground!*"

"*Recreational sexual playground?*"

"That's right . . . a recreational sexual playground! Got a moment? I can show you my legal files. They're in my kitchen."

"Okay Adrianna. Please lead the way," said Double-D with great interest.

Azzhat led our hero into the house, through her open garage, and moments later they were in her kitchen. It was a kitchen untouched since the 1970's . . . a time capsule . . . with bright orange wallpaper, wood cabinets, orange-colored vinyl linoleum squares on the floor, and a hanging wood lamp above the kitchen table.

"Would you like a cup of coffee?" asked Azzhat.

"No thanks."

"Very well."

The angry woman snatched one of the many legal files spread out on her table. She opened it, pulled out a piece of paper, and began reading it aloud.

"Here we go! Listen to this; *A nudist camp involves people congregating in activities while without clothing or any covering of the* *pubic areas or any portion of the <u>crease of the buttocks</u>, exposing such parts in the presence of others!"*

"The *crease of the buttocks,* huh?" questioned Double-D.

"Yes, *the crease of the buttocks!* As I said, Monty's illegally running a nudist resort in our neighborhood! We're sitting on residentially zoned land! None of us neighbors can stand the traffic, the blaring music, the wild cries, noise and outrageous nighttime activities!"

She slammed the paper down on the table.

"Not only that, the whole neighborhood is a fire hazard with all the eucalyptus trees, especially during our hot, dry, summer months! Those nudniks host naked barbeques all the time! I think that S.O.B. 'bought off' the local fire department and the newspaper too! Did you know he's running a psychotherapy office without a license?"

"No, I didn't," replied Chastity as Double-D. She was completely fascinated.

"Naked psychotherapy isn't recognized by professional medical associations!"

"Adrianna, what's the current status of this zoning battle of yours?"

"Monty outspent me, and this resulted in the local law against social nudity being temporarily overturned on the property. He got a 'conditional use permit' to continue his immoral goings on, but I'm fighting that too."

"What did the old law state?"

"No three people . . . unrelated people that is . . . could be seen together if all were naked."

"I see."

"I was even on TV discussing it! The local news hosted a debate between me and Monty, but they had Monty sit in a nice, comfortable, professional looking chair . . . while I was told to sit on a stool. I looked like a <u>stool</u> pigeon, literally! I'm telling you, the media unfairly paints me as an anti-nudity moralist."

Chastity, as Double-D, sympathized with Azzhat, yet at the same time, she was beginning to think the media might right in this one instance.

"You can see them from my backyard too . . . I mean, you can *see everything!*" added Azzhat.

"You can?"

"Come, I'll show you."

Azzhat opened her kitchen's sliding glass door, and the two of them walked out.

"I fired my old attorney . . . I suspected Monty 'bought him off' too!"

The backyard had a small, kidney shaped swimming pool and patio, and a high concrete wall. Chastity was surprised, because she couldn't see the back of the nudist colony.

"I thought you said you could see the nudists back here?"

"You can!" she flatly replied. "If you climb *onto my roof,* you can see them all naked as Jaybird himself!"

Azzhat grabbed a ladder and climbed up onto her ranch house's flat, single story roof. Double-D quickly followed her up.

" . . . but doesn't the law say your wall, and Monty's fence, are reasonable attempts to hide the nudity from you?" asked Double-D as she climbed.

"Not according to my new attorney!"

CHAPTER EIGHT

Once they were on Adrianna Azzhat's roof, Chastity had a bird's-eye view of the back of the Jaybird Growth Institute, including its miniature golf course. Dozens of attractive nudists were enjoying rounds of mini golf.

"*Yuck!* It's so evil and obscene! Shameful and immodest! Untidy too! I'm thoroughly convinced something immoral is going on over there!" spat Azzhat. " . . . and another thing, Monty's septic system is inadequate to support commercial land use and may be a health hazard to the whole community! I hear toilets flushing hundreds of times a day and at night! These flushes generate tremendous noise, creating an adverse impact on the neighboring residents! *Va-Voosh! Va-Voosh! Va-Voosh!* It never ends!"

"Bless my boobies!" declared Double-D.

"I can only look for so long . . . all those unclad keisters make me sick to my stomach! Why would anyone in their right mind want to frolic around naked like that! Let's climb back down."

"Certainly."

Double-D took one last glance from the rooftop, to see if she could spot the Super Nudists or the Mayor. There wasn't a sign of them, so she followed Azzhat back down the ladder.

"As I said, the street we share with Monty, Bare Road, was not constructed to accommodate the high traffic volume . . . traffic caused by Monty's nudists on our surrounding residential community! The traffic is a hundred times greater than it would normally be, if the property were used for single family residential purposes! Given the high fire hazard in the area, the lack of adequate emergency access to Monty's place is a huge danger! That nudist joint is a real public safety hazard!"

"I see," nodded Double-D.

"Years ago, the *old* Sheriff . . . not our current one . . . conducted 'indecent exposure' raids at Monty's place."

"He did?"

"Yes, but then Monty's attorney filed a lawsuit stating the raids were 'abuse of police power,' so the Sheriff had to stop."

"Oh."

"The Sheriff told me so long as Monty and his nudists maintained their privacy behind their property's fence, and they avoided exposing themselves deliberately to the neighbors, they were not guilty of lewdness and were within their legal rights."

Azzhat sadly shook her head. "It's tragic . . . twenty years ago, Monty Jaybird came into our quiet, decent, law-abiding community and shocked every neighbor's sense of decency! He and his followers are total degenerates! "

She then grabbed Double-D by the arm. "But I'll tell you this, Double-D . . . I'll never give up the fight! I've done everything in my power to see the Jaybird Growth Institute close its doors, and I'll continue to do so! My baby was nine months old when I first filed my case, and now he's in college! I divorced his dad years back."

"May I ask why?"

" . . . he became a nudist too! I caught him sneaking over the wall one night!"

Chastity bit her tongue, so she wouldn't burst out laughing.

"I'll just keep spending my weekends counting and photographing cars! As I told you, it's a thankless task."

They took an exit on the side of the house, and found themselves back out front by the garage again.

A car full of nudists . . . dressed, but soon to be nude . . . suddenly passed by, looking for a place to park! Azzhat reacted bug-eyed and rattled her house keys at them!

"*Go away!*" she yelled.

The passing car, with its windows rolled up, was too far away to hear her.

"I wish I was a unicorn, so I could stab all those obnoxious nudies with my head!"

Azzhat then glanced at her watch, and went bug-eyed again.

"Oh, look at the time! I gotta get ready! I'm hosting my church's monthly meeting here at my house tonight! It starts at seven o'clock. I'm co-chair of the 'Love Thy Neighbor' committee, and our pastor the rest of the ladies will be here! I must get the refreshments out of my refrigerator."

"I see . . . well, have a nice church meeting Adrianna!" Double-D cheerfully replied. "Thank you so much for filling me in on everything. I greatly appreciate it. I'll talk to the Sheriff next time I see him. Hopefully something can be done to solve your neighborhood traffic and noise troubles! *Ta-Ta!"*

"Thanks Double-D! *Ta-Ta!"* waved Azzhat.

Double-D didn't Booby-Bounce right away . . . she decided to stick around a little longer. As soon as Azzhat disappeared back into her garage and shut the automatic door, our hero continued her trek around the outer perimeter of the nudist resort property.

The sun began to set for the night, as our hero nearly completed her circle around the extensive Jaybird Growth Institute. There were still no signs of the Super Nudists or Mayor Phishel, as she periodically peeked over the fence. Chastity was somewhat disappointed, because she was certain the villains and villainesses were hiding inside.

Suddenly, an eighteen-year-old teenager *somersaulted over* the redwood fence, hollering like crazy!

"Waaaaaa-aaaaahhh!"

He was totally dressed, not naked, as he flew over then hit the grass! *Boom!* Double-D watched as he tumbled head over heels into some sagebrush. *Crash!* A second later, a small round object was also tossed

over the fence, and it nearly clobbered the young man in the forehead.
Boom!

Double-D dashed over to help him up.

"Hey, what the heck do you think you're doing?" she exclaimed.
"Are you okay?!"

"I'm fine, I guess. Nothin' broken, I don't think," he frantically
replied. "Who are you?"

"The Double-D Avenger, busty costumed crime-fighter."

The pimply-faced teen smiled. "The Double-D Avenger?! I've
heard of you!"

"What were you doing in there?"

He looked down, totally embarrassed. "I didn't mean any harm,
really. I just peeked over the fence and saw some beautiful ladies playing
tennis, so I . . . "

". . . hopped over to get a better look?" said Double-D, completing
his sentence.

"Yeah, I'm sorry! I know I shouldn't have done it."

"What did you do, use a trampoline to bounce back over the
fence?"

"No, *she* threw me over."

"Who threw you over?"

"One of the angry naked ladies playing tennis."

"A single nude woman was strong enough to throw you *that high*
and *that fast* over the fence?!" she sputtered.

"Yeah, and you should have seen her *run* too! She must have gone
fifty miles an hour when she spotted me! I've never seen a person, man
or woman, run so fast in my life."

Chastity, as Double-D, reacted bug-eyed! She couldn't believe
what she was hearing.

The teen then examined the small, black clump of metal, plastic
and glass that landed in the dirt.

"Look what she did to my phone!"

Chastity took the round clump and analyzed it.

"It's a cell phone all right . . . or I should say . . . *was* a cell phone," she calculated. "Were you taking pictures of them?"

The teen bowed his head again in disgrace. " . . . yes."

"Shame on you!" scolded Double-D. She took another look at the crushed phone. "Only a person with super-human strength could crush a phone like this."

"That's right!"

"What did she look like?"

"Bare, beautiful, and bodacious! She was the sexiest lady I've ever seen! They all were! They were perfect! Like *'Goddesses!'* That's why I couldn't control myself! I just had to take a closer look."

Chastity nodded her head, recalling how the female Super Nudists looked in their helmets and skimpy costumes. They were all drop-dead gorgeous beneath their goggles . . . flawless.

"What your name?"

"Tom," he told her, taking his crumpled phone back.

"Well, listen Tom, you get out of here and don't come back. Nobody likes a *peeping Tom,* Tom! I mean . . . well, you know what I mean Tom! Don't ever trespass on private property again . . . you're lucky you weren't seriously injured or worse!"

"Yes, ma'am," he said, as he limped away. *"Later."*

"Ta-Ta!"

Chastity thought carefully, whispering to herself. "They *are* in there . . . that young man and his phone prove it. I think I'll have to investigate the inside of the Jaybird Growth Institute first thing tomorrow morning . . . but not as the Double-D Avenger . . . as *Mona Lot!"*

Our hero then took a running leap and bounced up into the nighttime sky!

"Booby-Bounce!"

Boi-oing-oing-oing!

It was past seven o'clock and Adrianna Azzhat was nervously pacing back and forth in her living room. The dining room table with snacks, coffee and tea was all nicely set for her 'Love Thy Neighbor' church meeting. Dozens of folding chairs were set up too, but no one had arrived yet. She frantically looked at her watch. Something seemed wrong.

"Where on Earth could they all be?" she wondered. "It's not like the pastor to be late! He's usually early! Where is every one?!"

The mysterious green and yellow VW Bus, the 'Samba,' was parked on the lawn, directly *in front of* the nudist resort's big sign! This was because of an overflow of parked nudist cars filling the driveway! The bus had nowhere else to park! The Jaybird Growth Institute's entrance banner . . . the painted canvas, framed and held up by wooden posts . . . was completely hidden from view! From the street and driveway, people could not read the sign *Jaybird Growth Institute,* nor see the phone number listed below it. The words *'Clothing Optional Resort'* and *'Education and Workshops in Human Potential'* were obstructed too, and so was the disclaimer stating *'Ages 18 and Over!'* All anyone could see was the long, empty VW bus, and the wooden posts of the hidden sign behind it.

A tiny compact car . . . a classic 1950's imported convertible . . . drove up to the entrance driveway with its headlights on. It stopped, and the fat man behind the wheel looked very confused. He was holding a piece of paper in one hand, while gripping his steering wheel with the other. The gentleman looked around, searching for any sign of an address marker or a mail box. There wasn't any. Out of desperation, he finally parked right there, near the middle of the street.

He opened his driver's side door, and struggled to get out of the tiny vehicle, since he was so huge! The forty-something year old man was morbidly obese, at least four hundred pounds, and he stood six-feet tall. He had a friendly, comical, clean-cut face, but since he was lost, his expression was one of great confusion. The tubby man had to literally *crawl* out of his tiny car onto the pavement, and then use the hood of his parked vehicle to get back up again. He was wearing a dark, conservative suit and tie, with black leather shoes.

Sweating like a pig, he adjusted his coat and tie, and then reached back into his car to retrieve a notebook with religious papers on the passenger seat. His name was *Pastor Weensy!*

Six other cars then drove up right next to him. One of the vehicles rolled its window down, and a conservatively dressed lady called out.

"Pastor Weensy!"

He turned around.

"Hello, Cordelia!"

"Is this Adrianna's house? I've never been to it."

"Neither have I," he confessed. "I think so, looks like others are already here. They've taken up the whole driveway."

"Where should I park?"

"Find a place up the street."

"Very well," replied the woman.

The car zoomed away and was followed by five others. Pastor Weensy waddled up to them and pointed to Cordelia's moving car.

"Good evening Pastor Weensy? Is this the place?" asked another conservatively dressed lady from her car window.

"I think so, just follow Cordelia," he said, pointing up the street.

As the second car drove off, Weensy became a traffic director, motioning the other church members to park up the road.

Moments later, he and the six conservative 'church ladies' gathered together and strolled right into the place! The ladies, all part of the 'Love Thy Neighbor' committee, actually strolled . . . the pastor waddled.

"Adrianna has a big piece of property," commented one woman.

"Glad we found it, we were lost! Her directions were less than legible," said another.

"Tell me about it," remarked another lady.

Wild 1960's 'Go-Go' music was heard in the background, and the pastor noticed!

"Sounds like Adrianna's got some lively music playing," he commented.

The pastor and his stuffy 'church ladies' turned a corner, getting a full view of the Jaybird Growth Institute's main lawn and outdoor dance floor. The whole place was illuminated with colorful lights, and the lively nudists were having a *'Go-Go' dance contest!* A dozen beautiful nude ladies were dancing up a storm on both the dance floor and on a large stage! The stark naked beauties were swinging back and forth, waving their arms up and down, and snapping their fingers in time to the fast music!

The hot and foxy women rolled their heads, and wiggled their pelvises back and forth. As they bounced to the music, their large rubbery breasts bounced too, swaying up and down, and back and forth, and around and around! Bare jugs, tatas, honkers and globes jiggled, shook, and wiggled! Some of the 'Go-Go' vamps spun around, clapping their hands . . . and they weren't the only ones clapping! The naked men seated on lawn towels totally loved every second of this contest, and were madly applauding . . . on top of their cheering and whistling! There were so many bare boobies quivering and quaking, it was hard for the guys to keep track of them all!

"*Yeah!*" shouted one dancer.

"*Whoah!*" cried another 'Go-Go' girl.

"*Sock it to me, baby!*" yelled another.

"*Go, baby! Go!*" cheered one of the nudist men.

Some of the wild dancers began doing high leg kicks, flashing their nookies, poontangs, fuzz boxes, and furburgers to the audience! The men went crazy!

"*Woo-hoo!*"

"*Yes!*"

"*Ow!*"

"Work it!"

Pastor Weensy and the 'church ladies' were in *total shock!* They froze in place . . . as if in *suspended animation* . . . wide-eyed with jaws dropped. They could not believe what they were seeing!

The pastor, especially, couldn't take his bug eyes off the 'Go-Go' sirens wobbling globes, hood ornaments, and kalamazoos!

As the music's tempo increased, the dancers picked up their pace! The seductresses twitched like crazy, whirling around and clapping their hands, while their booties and lady bubbles trembled! They did lots of fancy footwork and smiled, showing off their pearly white teeth!

The loud, swinging Go-Go music was fantastic, and the Jaybird nudists were having a ball!

Pastor Weensy finally snapped out of his trance, and was able to spit out a few sentences.

"Ladies . . . I don't think . . . we're at . . . the right . . . place!" he sputtered.

"This is . . . outrageous! Blasphemous!" muttered one woman.

"It's Sodom and Gomorrah!" agreed another 'church lady.'

Others got up the nerve to chime in.

"Shocking!"

"Monstrous!"

"Shameful!"

"Sinful!"

"How dare Adrianna give us directions to this . . . this *outdoor den of iniquity!"*

"Come ladies, let us flee from these disrobed devils . . . this cesspool of wicked, immoral nudity!" instructed the pastor.

The 'church ladies' quickly scurried away, with Weensy waddling behind them. The Jaybird nudists and 'Go Go' dancers were having so much fun, they never even knew the strangers had been there!

CHAPTER NINE

Back outside the property, the 'Love Thy Neighbor' committee members raced to their parked cars.

"We'll discuss this tomorrow ladies! I'm phoning Adrianna tonight!" declared the distraught pastor.

"Yes, pastor," one of them frantically yelled back.

"Good night, pastor," shouted another distressed lady.

"Good night," he nervously answered back.

All alone, the morbidly obese gentleman waddled over to his small compact car. He opened the door, and had trouble squeezing his big fat body back into his driver's seat. Struggling, he whipped off his coat and threw it onto the passenger seat. He then managed to get one foot into the car, and pushed down on his other foot, to climb in. The tiny vehicle squeaked and rocked as he did this.

He collapsed inside the car, but was now stuck, lying on his right side. He carefully lifted up his left leg, to use his left shoe to close the car door. It wouldn't close! Therefore, he had to get back up and wiggle out of the diminutive vehicle. Now he was getting angry, and sweating like a pig again!

He bumbled around and climbed in again on all fours. Once inside, he needed to shut the door, but his left leg was now stuck hanging out the door's open window. He fumbled opening the door again and fell out onto the pavement! *Ka-Plop!* Determined to get in one way or the other, the pastor took a few steps back, and then *charged like a rhino* into his vehicle. *Zoom!* The overweight man flew right into his compact car! *Ba-Boom!* Now he was really stuck! His tubby body was like a chubby frankfurter stuck between two mini hot dog buns!

Meanwhile, back in Adrianna Azzhat's living room, it was nearly seven-thirty! Azzhat was livid, nervously pacing back and forth in her living room, in front of her dining room table filled with refreshments.

She frantically looked at her watch for the fiftieth time! Something was definitely wrong.

She glanced at the table, and looked at the church flier she had printed and handed out to the group. Her eyes suddenly bulged out!

"Oh, no! No! No! No!" she howled. "That's the *wrong address!* That damn copy place mixed my lawsuit paperwork with the church letter! *Aaaaaaahhhh!!!!"*

Azzhat dropped her flier and ran out the door faster than any Super Nudist!

Back at Pastor Weensy's parked car, the pastor's body was still stuck in his compact vehicle. He had no choice but to open the passenger door and climb out again. After floundering around, he managed to do it. The second he was out, he quickly waddled around the car and tried to squeeze back into the driver's side. Sweat poured down his face, but miraculously, he finally managed to do it. Success! He was in! He slammed the car door in anger, sweating and panting for breath . . . then felt around for his car keys!

"Oh, no! Where the hell are my keys?!"

He looked around, and noticed them on the pavement! He had accidentally dropped them when he fell out of the car the first time. Weensy wanted to cry!

"Pastor Weensy!" hollered Azzhat, as she ran up to the car. "Pastor Weensy, I'm so, so sorry! There was a terrible mix-up at the copy place! My legal papers were accidentally shuffled in with my church paperwork. The meeting fliers have the wrong address printed on them!"

"You can say that again!" he angrily spat. "Would you mind grabbing my keys, they're on the ground."

"What? Oh, certainly!"

She knelt down, snatched his car keys, and handed them to him.

"Thank you," he spat.

"Where are the others? My living room is all set for our 'Love Thy Neighbor' committee meeting. I've arranged some lovely refreshments for everyone . . . let me show you the way. I'm just next door."

"The ladies left, and I'm leaving too! To hell with your refreshments! We need time to recover . . . to relax and calm down from this outrageous, nasty, dirty, appalling, and obscene surprise! I thought I was going to have a heart attack in there! We've had enough shocking and nauseating vulgarity for one evening! Good-bye!"

"You mean, you and the ladies went inside and saw my . . . *neighbors?*" she asked with bug-eyes.

"Indeed we did, and we got a wicked and offensive eyeful!"

Her mind raced, trying to think of how to respond. "Well, pastor, you're always telling us to remember to *love our neighbor,*" she said with a forced smile.

"Yes, but not to love loathsome, abominable, *nudnik neighbors!*"

With that, he started his car's engine, and sped away!

Zaa-Zooomm!

Azzhat turned to face the Jaybird Growth Institute.

"*Oooooo! I hate you, Monty Jaybird!*" she screamed, shaking her fists. "*I hate . . . hate . . . hate . . . hate . . . hate you!*"

Of course, her loud temper tantrum was completely drowned out by the blaring Go-Go music playing inside.

Back at Chastity Knott's house across town, our exhausted hero was getting ready for bed. She lived in a beautiful, two-story, Spanish style house with stucco walls. It was in a nice upper-middle class neighborhood, and the house sat on a hillside with a magnificent view of Driftwood Valley. Ornamental rot-iron gates covered the arched entranceway to her front door. The open driveway was large enough for three cars, and a lovely old olive tree grew next to it. The town's lights twinkled down below in the nighttime background, like millions of little stars.

Inside Chastity's bedroom, the cutie nudie was out of her shower and fully dry. Her large TV was playing in the background. Before hitting the sack, she threw on a skimpy bathrobe and opened her large wardrobe closet full of beautiful clothes.

Our hero then grabbed her cell phone and dialed the Jaybird Growth Institute. Someone immediately answered on the other end.

"Oh, hello? Is this the Jaybird Growth Institute?" Chastity asked, while grabbing the TV's remote to turn down the volume.

She listened for a second and smiled. "It is? Great! I'm glad you're open this late. Ah, my name's Mona Lot, and I've heard marvelous things about your clothing-optional resort and educational facility. I was wondering if it would be possible for me to make an appointment to visit your place tomorrow. I know its short notice, but I'm very interested in becoming a new member."

She listened.

"I'm a single female, twenty-five years old, and I live in Driftwood Valley." Chastity was originally in her fifties, but the magical Crockozilla Fruit acted like a 'fountain of youth' or 'youth elixir,' transforming her into a twenty-five year old woman again!

Chastity paused to listen to the person on the other end.

"Oh yes, I consider myself a naturist . . . I parade around naked all the time in my house. In fact, I always have to put on a *hat* just to look out a window."

There was another pause.

"The Leisure Organization of Nudists Statewide?" she curiously repeated. "Oh, yes, I remember . . . ah, no, I'm not a member of L.O.O.N.S. . . . but I *have* previously visited Adamite Acres, and had a nice time there. I've heard you facilities are much, much nicer."

Chastity listened carefully and then a huge smile appeared on her face.

"I can attend a 'one day vacation and introduction' conducted by a staff member *tomorrow morning* at *eleven am?* That's awesome, thank you, yes, please pencil me in," she happily exclaimed, as if she'd won a prize.

She listened once more.

"Right . . . there will be some 'get acquainted time,' a tour of the grounds, a light snack, and all the membership information will be explained . . . got it. A thirty-dollar visitor's fee for women . . . that's fine. Well, it all sounds wonderful! Thanks so much! I really look forward to seeing you tomorrow. *Ta-Ta!*"

She ended the call.

"Fantastic! That's done!" she told herself, as she put the phone down. "Eleven tomorrow morning . . . that'll give me time to pay a visit to Dr. Della-Kwak. Maybe she's got some medical answers regarding this nudist brainwashing business."

Chastity then focused her attention back to her wardrobe closet. On one particular shelf was a hat box with a short, dark wig inside. This was the brunette wig she'd use tomorrow in her disguise as *'Mona Lot.'* It was her 'Mona Lot' wig! The dark hairpiece helped disguise both her Double-D Avenger and Chastity Knott identities.

She took the hatbox, grabbed a black, low-cut blouse from its hanger, and pulled out a tight pair of jeans to go with it. Beyond the hanging rows of jeans were some of Chastity's past Double-D Avenger disguises, including an English Beefeater's costume!

She opened the hatbox, pulled out the pretty, stylized brunette wig, and began brushing it.

"Mona, your hair's a mess!" she joked to herself.

Once her Mona Lot disguise was all laid out, she grabbed the TV remote and turned the volume up again. Suddenly, a televised newsflash appeared, and two newscasters, a man and a woman, made an amazing announcement.

"This is a Driftwood TV 5 news alert. Driftwood Valley city councilmembers Max Phuckter, Harry Bottoms, Helga Hoodwink, and Soupy Phishel, voted today to legally permit public nudity throughout all of Driftwood Valley," stated the male reporter.

Chastity was stunned!

"Holy Hooters!"

The female reporter continued.

"Mayor Artie Phishel signed the bill into law just moments ago, and spoke to the press. A warning to our audience, this segment does contains nudity."

"Mayor Phishel?! He isn't kidnapped anymore? Phuckter's back too?!" she spat, looking as if she'd seen a ghost.

The news report cut to earlier footage of the Mayor proudly celebrating the new law at the city hall's press conference.

"This is a proud moment in our history, because today my friends, public nudity is finally legal throughout all of Driftwood Valley!" cheered Mayor Phishel.

"I don't believe it!" stuttered Chastity, as she sat on the edge of her bed.

"Yes, every citizen is now guaranteed the unfettered freedom of complete nudity, thanks to the progressive new bill the council passed and I just signed. It's a magnificent achievement for free speech and our first amendment! Yes, ignorance, prudishness and hypocrisy are now things of the past. Driftwood Valley will now prove to the rest of the country, that public nudity isn't lewd, and that men's and women's bodies are clean and wholesome, not something to be ashamed of, or to feel guilty about. They are the temples in which we live."

As the camera pulled back from the podium, Chastity could see the mayor and the rest of the city councilmembers were all completely naked!

"They're all . . . !"

"Councilwoman Hoodwink had this to say," narrated the male reporter in a voice-over.

Footage of Hoodwink then was run, as the mayor stepped aside from the podium to let her speak.

"Nudism is a road to self-respect, self-confidence, and it leads to a better understanding of life," Hoodwink explained, wobbling her big rubbery boobies as she turned to face different cameras. "It's a healthful lifestyle for Driftwood Valley, because nudists bask in the sunshine and bathe in the fresh, open air. One can achieve great mental satisfaction, physical fitness and a feeling of freedom and oneness with all other fellow nudists who share this open communion with nature."

"They're using the same 'flowery talk' the Sheriff was yapping about this morning," declared a puzzled Chastity.

A reporter at the press conference than asked a question.

"What about negative backlash from the public? Are you worried?"

"Not in the slightest," smiled the Mayor, stepping back to the podium's microphone. "The law doesn't *require* the citizens of Driftwood Valley to go 'au naturel,' it merely gives them the *legal option* to do so if their little 'nudist hearts' desire. The councilmembers and I are convinced that everyone will eventually come on board and toss away their clothing! Once people try it, they'll like it . . . in fact, they'll *relish* parading around in their birthday suits, just as we do!"

Another reported shouted out a question.

"Mayor, we've had reports that you were kidnapped earlier, and so was councilman Phuckter. Can you shed some light on this?"

"Kidnapped? Oh, how silly!" chuckled the Mayor. "I was extremely tired after having dinner at Chastity Knott's English Pub the other night, and didn't want to risk driving home alone . . . so being a responsible citizen, I phoned some friends, and they *streaked over* to get me."

"I'm not so sure if that plug helped or hurt me!" Chastity joked.

"As for me," cut in councilman Phuckter, "the battery in my golf cart went dead, so some friends of mine also *streaked over* to give me a hand."

"Wait a second . . . they're both denying their kidnappings?!" she spat, staring at the TV.

Our hero's mind raced like crazy, trying to piece together this bizarre jigsaw puzzle.

The news report then cut back to the studio.

"The new public nudity law goes into effect immediately. We'll have other late-breaking news after these messages," ended the male reporter.

The news program then cut to a live TV commercial of Driftwood Valley's infamous used car salesman, Cactus Wilmington. Wilmington, owner of Cactus Wilmington's Used Car Supermarket, was a tall, slim man in a white cowboy hat. He had a friendly smile, and around his neck he wore a jade bolo tie. The cowboy car salesman was in his fifties, he was clean-cut, and had salt-and-pepper hair.

Cactus began his TV pitch, as the car lot's sales flags blew in the nighttime wind. Fast hillbilly banjo music played in the background during the live commercial.

"Howdy again folks, Cactus Wilmington of Wilmington's Used Car Supermarket. If you're shoppin' around for a used car, come on down, I know I got the car you're lookin' for," he said directly to camera. ". . . and I can save ya a gang of money too! Here's where your friends are, here's where the bargains are. Ya outta drop by and see me first, give me first chance at the deal."

As Cactus began strolling past his lineup of used cars, the camera pulled back and the TV audience could now see that he was *completely nude* from the neck down.

"Take a look at this here dandy. Ignore the sticker price, ask for the discount price," he instructed.

Chastity's jaw dropped and her eye's popped out!

"It's *a dandy* all right! I'm afraid to ask what the discount price for *it* is!" she exclaimed, not looking at the car, but staring at the cowboy's exposed, hanging ramrod. "Cactus Wilmington's 'gone nudist' too?!"

Chastity had enough for one night, and switched off her TV. She got up, removed her bathrobe, and tossed it on a chair. She then moved to her pillows, lifted her soft, fluffy bed cover, and hopped in naked. She always made it a point to sleep in the nude . . . it was so comfy-cozy for her. Before shutting her eyes, she grabbed an old teddy bear resting on one of her pillows.

"Nighty-night, Russ," she affectionately whispered to the stuffed animal. She named her toy bear in honor of a man she'd once known many years ago. The gentleman, who'd been in the entertainment industry, used to have an out-of-control breast fetish.

I have a big day tomorrow, she thought to herself. *Those Super Nudists are the criminal masterminds behind all this, and they're hiding out at the Jaybird Growth Institute. They've clearly brainwashed everyone, and I may be the only one who can stop 'em! I'll fill Billy in on this first thing in the morning. No use bothering him now, he and Connie will be closing the pub soon.*

With that, Chastity let out a big yawn, and then closed her eyes, falling fast asleep. The busty beauty was out like a light.

The next morning at Driftwood Valley Hospital, Chastity, as the Double-D Avenger, paid her visit to Doctor Della-Kwak's office. Della-Kwak, the fifty-something blond, scatterbrained quack, was Chastity Knott's physician, but the wacky doctor never made the connection between Chastity and the Double-D Avenger. She thought the pub owner and the superhero were two separate people. It was Doctor Della-Kwak who originally suggested Chastity visit South America to find the magical Crockozilla Fruit, to help cure her of a past terminal illness. The phenomenal plant's miraculous healing properties not only cured Chastity, but also gave her super-human strength, powers, and a new youthful appearance!

Della-Kwak was surprised to see our busty costumed crime-fighter in her patient reception room. She'd helped Double-D out with cases in the past, as was about to do so again.

"Double-D!"

"Hello, Doctor! Good morning! How are you?"

"I'm fine, and you?"

"In the pink and protuberant, as usual!" she proudly boasted. "Doctor, I need to ask you a few questions for a new criminal case I'm working on. Can you spare a few moments?"

"I've got a patient coming in for his yearly physical, but for you Double-D, I'll gladly give you all the time you need. Step into my office."

"Thanks!"

The two of them quickly disappeared into Della-Kwak's private office. Inside, medical diplomas were hanging on the white walls, and a nude, muscular, male statue . . . a Greek-like sculpture . . . was proudly displayed on the desk. The wacky doctor periodically enjoyed pinching the statue's bubbly bare butt.

"Brainwashing!" declared Double-D, as she took a seat.

"Brainwashing?" asked the doctor, while sitting in the chair behind her desk.

"Yes. Know anything about it?"

"Well, brainwashing is good for you! No one wants a dirty mind!" she chuckled.

"Doctor, I'm serious!"

"Oh, sorry . . . ah, brainwashing . . . brainwashing is the idea that the human mind can be manipulated, or controlled, or altered by using certain psychological techniques. The brainwashed subject's no longer able to think independently or critically. New, unwanted ideas or instructions are introduced into the subject's mind, totally changing his or her values, beliefs, behavior, and so on."

"How's it done?"

"Electroshock, high doses of drugs, hypnotic suggestion . . . these are just a few of the methods. I also heard of a man who was so bald, he got brainwashed every time he took a shower!"

Double-D rolled her eyes, as Della-Kwak continued.

"Prisoners of war were brainwashed in the past, and cult religions brainwash their followers by deceptive and indirect techniques of persuasion and control," she added. "Double-D, is some new villain in Driftwood Valley brainwashing victims?"

"I'm convinced of it," our hero firmly stated. "How can it be reversed?"

"Reverse brainwashing? I really don't know. The whole subject is still 'up in the air.' Some in the medical field say there's not enough scientific proof that brainwashing actually works to take a firm position one way or the other. Brainwashing may be effective, or it may not, depending on many factors."

"I see," said Double-D.

"It's like a medicine made from ducks to cure all illnesses."

"A medicine made from ducks that'll cure all illnesses?"

"Yes. That's 'quackery'!"

Double-D rolled her eyes again.

"Time often heals all psychological wounds. If subjects are weaned off of any brainwashing drugs, or are no longer exposed to psychological brainwashing techniques, or hypnosis, their minds should eventually return to normal. They say intensive psychotherapy can successfully deprogram or reverse the effects of brainwashing too."

"Well, I've heard all I need to hear," said our hero, rising from her chair. She then reached out to shake hands. "Thank you, Doctor! As always, you've been of great help to me!"

"No problem. Please keep me posted Double-D. If you need any more advice, call me anytime."

"Will do!"

As they shook hands, a busty nurse knocked on the door.

"Come in," said the doctor.

"Excuse me, Doctor," the nurse apologized. "Your patient Buster Coochi is here for his physical."

"I'll be right there. Thanks."

"I'll let you go. Thanks again Doctor!" waved Double-D.

"Bye-bye!"

The two of them exited out of the office, Double-D to the reception room, and the doctor to an examination room.

Della-Kwak knocked on the door, and then entered. She instantly stopped in her tracks, shocked to see her patient, Mr. Buster Coochi, standing in the exam room waiting for her . . . stark naked and sporting a humongous, upraised, speedo torpedo!

"Mr. Coochi!" stuttered the Doctor. "Did the nurse ask you to undress?"

"No," smiled Coochi. "I've gone nudist! I'm happy to see you!"

"I can *see* you are," replied Della-Kwak, staring down at his aroused crotch with bug-eyes and raised eyebrows!

Outside the hospital's main entrance, Chastity, as the Double-D Avenger, raced out to the street.

"Booby-Bounce!" she cried.

Off she flew, rocketing up and away from the hospital! *Boi-oing-oing-oing-oing-oing!* A small group of patients, doctors and nurses on the entrance sidewalk looked up in awe, as Double-D hurtled off into the wild blue yonder!

CHAPTER TEN

It was nearly eleven that morning, when Chastity drove her classic 1970's Corvette Stingray thru the Jaybird Growth Institute's main entrance. Chastity was wearing her short, brunette wig in her disguise as 'Mona Lot,' and she easily found a parking spot for her gorgeous metallic blue sports car, which sparkled in the sunlight. She checked her purse, which had her entrance fee, and then she hopped out. Chastity, as Mona, looked 'hotter than a Mexican's lunch,' in her skin tight jeans and black, low-cut blouse . . . which exposed her gargantuan melons!

Our undercover hero wiggled her hot little bootie towards the administration office, a one-story redwood building in the background. A huge swimming pool appeared on her left side, along with some lawn chairs and large open umbrellas. On her right side was the enormous, outdoor dance floor and stage. Chastity, as Mona, once again noticed the lovely green lawn and beautiful shady trees, which dotted the magnificent property. She also spotted some attractive young nudists in their twenties, three women and two men, joking around in the hot jacuzzi.

As she approached the administration office's front door, it instantly opened, and a ravishing naked woman with long red hair greeted her.

"Mona Lot?"

"Yes!"

"Nice to meet you, I'm Candy Delight, New Membership and Hospitality Director," she explained, reaching out her hand to shake.

Mona shook her hand, and both ladies overinflated beach balls jiggled! Delight's honkers were nearly as big as Chastity's/Mona's!

"Glad to meet you," smiled Mona. "You're the person I spoke to on the phone last night?"

"Yes. Thanks for showing up on time for your one day vacation and introduction."

"I always make it a point to be punctual. I'm just glad you were able to squeeze me in on such short notice."

"No worries. Come in and have a seat."

"Okay!"

Delight ushered her into the office, and once inside, they quickly took their seats at one of the desks. Mona then pulled thirty dollars from her purse.

"Here's my admission fee," said Mona, while handing over the cash.

"Thank you," replied Delight, taking it.

Delight whipped out a few sheets of paper and handed them to Mona, along with a pen.

"These are a few papers I'll need you to fill out and sign," she explained. "Our application form, the waiver, and some other paperwork."

"Sure thing," replied Mona, as she began signing away.

"I'll also need your Driver's License."

"Here it is," she said, taking it out of her purse.

Chastity had a super realistic 'fake ID' made for her Mona Lot disguise. Delight took the license and scanned it, believing it was one-hundred percent legit.

"While you're finishing the forms, I'll fill you in on our place."

"Wonderful."

Chastity, as Mona, began to recognize Candy Delight from somewhere. Somehow, Delight's jawline, nude breasts and near perfect body all 'rang a bell.' Chastity's mind began to race.

Was she one of the Super Nudists I fought with earlier?!

Our hero then refocused her attention on the paperwork, so Delight wouldn't become suspicious.

"The Jaybird Growth Institute is a non-profit, public-benefit organization dedicated to education and the dissemination of information regarding the healthfulness and naturalness of the nude human body."

"I see," replied Mona, looking up from her forms.

"Our institute advises and encourages individuals and organizations that contribute to the acceptance and appreciation of human social nudity through the publication of books and videos, and through the establishment of nude recreation and clothing-optional resorts and facilities."

"Very impressive," Mona added. She then handed over all her signed papers. "There you go."

"Thank you, Mona," said Delight. The busty director quickly filed the forms away.

The front door suddenly swung wide open, and in waltzed a handsome nude gentleman in his forties! He stood around six feet tall, was clean cut with short dark hair, and had a perfect, athletic body . . . a physique like that of a classic 1950's *natural* body builder. His muscular shoulders, biceps, chest, six-pack abs, and legs were not too big and not too small . . . and he possessed a 'regal air' about him. His eyes sparkled on his friendly, smiling face, and the man's enthusiastic, positive energy, seemed to powerfully radiate out from his entire body! He was full of pep, zeal and vitality!

"Oh, Monty!" declared Delight. "Meet Mona Lot, our newest visitor. She's interested in becoming a member."

He turned to face Mona and smiled, showing off his sparkling white teeth.

"Terrific meeting you, Mona!" he happily cheered in his strong, educated, British accent. "I'm Monty Jaybird, Executive Director of the Jaybird Growth Institute."

Jaybird spoke and moved swiftly, like a happy army drill Sargent, or a hyper-active salesman. He grabbed Mona's hand, but instead of shaking it, he *kissed* it!

Mmm-wahh!

"Oh, Mr. Jaybird," stuttered a surprised, blushing Chastity/Mona. "It's an honor to meet you!"

"Please, call me Monty."

"Okay, Monty."

For a quick second, our undercover hero looked down and glanced at Jaybird's titanic salami and meatballs! She was stunned at how 'herculean' they were, and quickly raised her eyes again . . . since she didn't want to seem perverse!

"I was just telling her about the institute," explained Delight.

"I see," nodded Jaybird. "Well Mona, we'd love to have a beautiful young lady like you as a new member."

Jaybird moved to an oversized map of the institute, which was hanging on the wall. It was a detailed, illustrated chart showing all of the property's buildings and amenities.

"The Jaybird Growth Institute serves as a home for residents of Driftwood Valley and visitors world-wide who wish to experience clothing-optional living. We're primarily supported by individual annual membership dues, plus a maintenance donation paid by members and their guests when they use the grounds."

He grabbed a long pointer and used it to direct her attention to various spots on the map.

"The institute sits on over twenty acres of land, which we own. Our expansive, sunny lawn, spotted with shade, provides space for sunning, resting, reading and quiet conversation," he lectured. "Our sauna, hydrotherapy pool, mediation area, and silent garden offer space for rejuvenating the body and mind."

He pointed to other spots.

"The tennis courts, swimming pools, and miniature golf course, provide an active visitor with space for exercise and fun. Notice we have two pools. Our seminar rooms hold large groups for classes, and our one-of-a-kind library offers literature of interest to nudists and naturists."

Mona happily admired his flawless and tanned muscular buns every time he turned his back to her.

"How impressive," she applauded.

"Thank you," smiled Jaybird, as he continued. "This is where our barbecue and picnic areas are located. We also have a gourmet restaurant, serving the finest, 'farm-to-table' healthy and organic meals, as well as fresh fruit smoothies, juices and shakes."

"Sounds delicious," said Mona. "What's that sand?" she asked, pointing to a spot on the map.

"That's our very own beach with volleyball court on the edge of Lake Tittykookoo! We're one of the only nudist resorts in the country to have its own 'private cove' for skinny-dipping and boating! We have a speedboat for nude water-skiing too."

"Nude water-skiing? Can outside strangers on the lake see us naked?" she wondered.

"No Mona, the edge our property surrounds our private cove, and we never swim, paddle or water ski past our property boundaries. We warn outsiders and lookie-loos to keep their distance from our small portion of the lake too."

"I see."

"Yes, the Jaybird Growth Institute's clothing-optional policy permits total relaxation in a safe, accepting environment."

The office's back door opened, and in walked a handsome young man in his mid-twenties. He was like a younger version of Monty Jaybird, totally nude and perfectly tanned, with a muscular physique. The main difference was this young guy had short blond hair and blue eyes.

"Ah, Oscar, meet Mona Lot," said Jaybird.

"Hi Mona! Nice to meet you!" he grinned. For a split second, Mona reminded him of someone . . . but he couldn't be sure.

"This is Oscar Dong," added Jaybird.

"Nice to meet you too . . . Oscar!" smiled Mona.

Chastity, as Mona, *did* recognize Dong . . . his supermodel body, nose, lips and jawline clearly 'rang a bell.' Her mind raced.

He has to be the Super Nudist in that banana helmet who wore the big fig leaf!

She took a quick glance down, and her eyes bugged out! He was bigger than Jaybird in the 'jackhammer department!'

Yep! That explains the big fig leaf . . . she thought to herself. A moment later, she had second thoughts.

Wait a second Chastity, don't jump to any sudden conclusions! Maybe he just looks like the 'Banana guy' . . . I can't be one-hundred percent certain. I'll need to investigate further.

"Oscar, why don't you give Mona a tour? I've got to gas up the bulldozer," said Jaybird.

"Yes sir," Dong gladly replied.

Jaybird turned to Mona.

"We're widening our parking lot," he explained. "Mona, get those clothes off and enjoy your vacation at the Jaybird Growth Institute."

"Undress here?" she nervously stuttered.

"Oh no, of course not . . . in the ladies changing cottage," clarified Jaybird.

"Ah," she nodded in relief.

Jaybird began to exit, but then he turned once again to face her.

"I almost forgot . . . Mona, before I go, I must explain our Jaybird Growth Institute's Credo to you," he stated.

Grabbing the pointer again, he directed her attention to a four point list hanging on an opposite wall. Mona rose from her chair and walked over to Jaybird and the printed list.

"Number one . . . there is an essential wholesomeness in the human body and all of its functions."

Jaybird then pointed to the next statement.

"Number two . . . exposure to sun, water, air, and to nature is a helpful and basic factor in building and maintaining healthy attitudes of mind and in the development of a strong body."

Mona nodded her head in agreement with each sentence of the credo.

"Number three . . . man and his sexuality are part and parcel of our living, and no separation or division is possible without denying what man is and what he was created for."

Jaybird finally pointed to the credo's last part.

" . . . and finally, number four . . . the depiction of man in his entirety and completeness in photographs and text requires no apology or defense, and only with such an attitude of mind can we find true modesty . . . for modesty comes from within."

"That's a very nice credo Monty," complimented Mona.

"Thank you."

Chastity, as Mona, was starting to get a bit confused, because this man . . . Monty Jaybird . . . seemed to be saying nothing but wonderful, positive things! It was a beautiful credo and she agreed with many of the statements. He didn't seem like a villain.

She then thought she'd use the opportunity to ask about the feud with Adrianna Azzhat. Perhaps she could dig up some information that could be useful.

"Oh, one other quick question," said Mona.

"Yes?"

"Monty, I heard some rumors about a twenty-year zoning battle with the Driftwood Valley Board of Supervisors and one of your neighbors?"

Jaybird smiled.

"Adrianna Azzhat!"

"Yes . . . Adrianna Azzhat."

"It's been the longest and most expensive zoning case in Driftwood Valley's history! *Ha, ha, ha, ha, ha!*" he laughed. "But I won in the end, getting my 'conditional use permit' to continue operating the institute. Adrianna's done a magnificent job of creating much ado about nothing . . . and spending a pretty penny for it. Social nudity is a civil liberty. As you heard, we're bulldozing our parking lot to expand it. This will lessen the traffic on Bare Road."

"Oh, that's good to know," said Mona.

"Adrianna Azzhat won't be problem for much longer," chimed in Candy Delight with a sinister smile.

"That's right," chuckled Dong.

"Oh?" questioned Mona.

Jaybird stared at Delight and Dong with sharp eyes and subtly shook his head 'no,' as if telling them to 'shut up.' He then continued chatting with Mona like nothing was wrong.

"To Adrianna, I'm sin personified, I'm the pits! *Ha, ha, ha!*" he chuckled. "Geology isn't the issue, traffic isn't the issue, commercialism isn't the issue, noise isn't the issue, and a possible fire hazard isn't the issue. The woman's just a paranoid, psychotic, moralist nut . . . period! She's got nothing better to do with her time!"

"I see," nodded Mona.

"I've been hounded by that crazy 'do-gooder' . . . who's been seeking to prove that nudism provides a friendly environment for licentiousness! If Adrianna had her way, every art gallery and museum on Earth would run out of fig leaves to tape over countless nude paintings and naked statues."

"Oh."

"You wanna know something else Mona?"

"What?"

"Once upon a time, over fifty years ago, Adrianna, was little, bare-assed nudist herself!"

Everyone laughed at Jaybird's silly joke.

"Ha, ha, ha, ha, ha, ha, ha, ha, ha!"

"Ha, ha, ha, ha, ha, ha, ha, ha, ha!"

"Ha, ha, ha, ha, ha, ha, ha, ha, ha!"

"Well, enjoy your lighthearted day of joyous, naked pleasure!"

"Thank you," smiled Mona.

"Here at the Jaybird Growth Institute, you'll have the unfettered freedom of complete nudity!" declared Jaybird, as he dramatically waved his arms to make the point.

Oscar Dong and Mona exited the administration building, and the handsome young man led the way to the men's and women's changing cottages.

"The ladies changing room is just up ahead and you can use one of the secure lockers to store your purse and clothes. The locker key is attached to an elastic wrist band you wear."

"I see," said Mona.

"Once you've changed, grab one of the towels and take it with you, along with your key."

"A towel for the pool and hot tub?"

"Yes, and also to sit on. We always use towels whenever we sit on chairs and benches."

"Got it," she nodded.

After strolling down a winding stone path, Dong stopped and directed her to the lovely changing room.

"Here you are," he stated, holding his right arm out towards the cottage.

The ladies cottage looked like a pretty little 'storybook house' painted all in pink.

"Thanks. I'll only be a moment," she nervously replied.

"By the way," he added, "there are complimentary flip-flops you can use to walk around in, if you're uncomfortable walking barefoot. The ones displayed have all been sanitized."

"Thanks, I'll use a pair."

Mona raced up the concrete steps, opened the cottage door, and disappeared inside.

The small room looked like a cute, neat living room with a pink couch and pink chairs, and a line of pink lockers on one wall. A beautiful fruit basket was displayed on a pink table, and a ceiling fan with bright lights lit up the entire pink room.

Chastity, as Mona, didn't pay too much attention to the cute room she was in . . . she was too nervous! Her mind began to race as she thought to herself . . . *Chastity, what the hell have you gotten yourself into this time? I don't know if I can go through with this! How can I parade around totally naked in front of that handsome guy and the other people here? I'm so embarrassed.*

She shook her head, and continued thinking . . . *Chastity, you can do this. You have a mission to accomplish! You've got to find evidence of those Super Nudists, and bring them to justice. You've got to figure out how they're brainwashing people! Sometimes superheroes need to make personal sacrifices . . . and this is one of those times.*

"Okay," she told herself. "Here I go . . . off it all goes!"

CHAPTER ELEVEN

Our hero slowly undressed in the ladies changing room, taking off her top, shoes and pants. It was almost as if Chastity was performing a sexy striptease act from a classic burlesque show! She then undid her bra and out popped her super enormous dairy pillows! *Ba-Boing! Boing! Boing!* They majestically sprung out and bounced around like titanic rubbery balloons, wiggling and jiggling, as they were 'freed!'

Her gravity-defying, up thrust and perky, areolas, nipples, and oversized globes, were utterly superb! She was outrageously abundant . . . the physical embodiment of woman!

When Chastity, as Mona, took off her panties, her pretty little 'Bermuda Triangle' was magnificently revealed for the whole world to see. It was a perfect little 'vertical smile,' with neatly trimmed blond pubic hair.

Our hero looked down and suddenly became alarmed!

"Uh-oh! My hair 'down there' doesn't match the hair 'up here' . . . my brunette wig!" she sputtered to herself. "Oh, no . . . I didn't think of this! *My drapes don't match my carpet!* Will this blow my cover? Chastity think . . . many ladies dye the hair on their heads, so that's what I'll say if asked about the difference in color. There shouldn't be anything to worry about."

With that, she gathered up her clothes, panties, oversized brassiere, socks, purse and shoes, and tucked them away neatly inside of one of the empty lockers. The locker was number sixty-nine. Once that was done, she removed the locker door's key, and slipped the elastic key band over her right wrist.

She then looked over towards a wall and saw a whole line of different sized ladies flip flops and sandals. Mona carefully glanced at the different sizes and found a perfect pair for her pretty feet. Once she slipped into them, she snatched one of the white, warm, folded towels from a rack. The clean, fresh towel had just come out of the laundry, and Mona modestly held it over her 'Alter of Venus.'

She then had another thought.

Wait a second . . . could the female Super Nudists costumes be hidden in here? They all wore black goggles and light-green and yellow colored helmets with a fruit or nut symbol painted on them. They also wore light-green and yellow colored gloves, boots, utility belts, capes and those strange metallic green fig leaves.

Our hero quickly opened all the unlocked lockers, searching for any signs of the female Super Nudists costumes, helmets, capes, boots, or fig leaves. There was nothing . . . nada . . . zip.

She thought some more.

Nothing! Unless, the costumes are in some of the locked ones . . . but how could they squeeze the boots and utility belts in there too? The lockers are a bit small. No, they're obviously hiding their Super Nudist costumes someplace else.

Chastity then remembered another important thing.

"Sunscreen!" she reminded herself. "I've got to put some on!"

She used the key on her elastic band to reopen her locker, and grabbed a soft bottle of sunscreen from her purse. In a flash, she squeezed it all over her naked body, and slowly and seductively rubbed the shiny lotion on her face, neck, shoulders, huge jiggly puffs, stomach, thighs, legs, and impeccable derriere. She left a little bit on her shoulders, so Oscar Dong could rub it on the parts of her back she couldn't reach.

Chastity, as Mona, looked truly spectacular, with her fully nude body shimmering and glimmering like shiny wet rubber! She looked incredibly erotic covered in the wet sunscreen, and was so red hot, men seeing her would be tempted to call the fire department!

Outside the ladies changing cottage, Dong was starting to grow impatient, wondering what was taking Mona so long. He had ducked into the men's changing cottage and grabbed a white towel, which he was now holding. His eyes widened as soon as Mona opened the changing room door and slowly crept out. She was clearly embarrassed, covering her pubic area with her own towel, as she shuffled towards him. Trotting down the concrete stairs, Mona's shiny wet Montezumas bounced up and down with each step! *Ba-Boing! Ba-Boing! Ba-Boing!*

Dong's breath was taken away, and his heart began racing a mile a minute! His blood pressure was skyrocketing! He couldn't believe how beautiful, stunning, and drop-dead gorgeous Mona was . . . not to mention how perfect and magnificent her jumbo-sized, sweater-stretching airbags were! The sexy young woman was literally glistening and sparkling in the sunlight, thanks to her still wet sunscreen. He'd never seen such extravagant breastworks in his life, and wondered if Mona was too much for one man to love and adore!

The young man was so excited, aroused, and attracted by Mona's twinkling beauty and sex appeal, he popped the biggest 'boner' in America! He was falling madly in love . . . and in lust . . . with her! It was 'love at first *nude* sight!'

Chastity, as Mona, couldn't help but notice his sudden 'Big Boy,' and ironically, she too was falling in love . . . and in lust . . . with Oscar Dong! Warm, tingling feelings spread all over her body, and she felt a little intoxicated looking into his charming blue eyes!

"Ah-hem," uttered Dong, clearing his throat. "Mona, I think you look lovely! Honest!"

"I believe you," she blushed, looking down at his rock-hard horizontal exclamation point.

"Pardon me for my 'flag at full mast,'" he joked. "Sometimes these tent poles suddenly pop up out of nowhere around here."

"I understand," she smiled. "There's some extra sunscreen on my shoulders. Would you mind rubbing it on the parts of my back I missed?"

"Not at all!" said happy Dong.

The handsome guy held his towel between his thighs, and then he enthusiastically rubbed the lotion all over her shoulder blades and down the center of her back. Now Mona's complete body looked like shiny wet rubber! When Dong was done, he took the liberty of wiping the excess lotion off his hands by using Mona's springy and bouncy butt cheeks. *Zip! Zoop!*

"*Oh,*" she remarked, pretending to be surprised. In reality, she loved it! "Thank you, Oscar."

"My pleasure!" he declared with a big smile. "Let's continue with the tour."

"Sounds good."

As he began to show her around the vast property, Dong ran math equations in his head, in order to 'calm down' Mr. Happy. They casually strolled around the place, holding their white towels.

Chastity, as Mona, slowly started getting used to walking around fully nude in front of others, and as time went on, she became more and more comfortable in her own skin.

"Funny," confessed Mona, "I'm starting to forget all about being naked. What a strange sensation . . . and realization!"

"This is your first time?" he asked.

"My first time? *Oh, ah,* I meant, my first time *here,*" she fibbed, realizing she almost blew her cover.

"Gotcha. Lots of first-timers feel that way," he reassured her.

Mona loved the sun's warmth and the canyon's slight breeze tickling her naked body, as she waltzed around free a jaybird! She was really starting to enjoy being an undercover nudist!

Attractive Jaybird nudists, both men and women, were seen relaxing on towels and lawn chairs, and enjoying pleasant conversations amongst themselves.

"The Jaybird Growth Institute is a garden spot in Toupee Canyon, where couples and singles can enjoy outdoor recreation *naturally,*" Dong explained. "We designed our parklike facilities and policies to provide a peaceful green refuge from the hyperactive noise of urban living."

"I see," nodded Mona.

"As Monty mentioned, the first sentence in the Jaybird Credo states our belief that, 'There's an essential wholesomeness in the human body and all its functions.' Our policy of clothing-optional is part of our dedication to providing a life-enhancing environment where freedom-of-choice is truly meaningful."

"I understand."

"Great, Mona. Yes, we're in a bit of the back country out here, close to the big city . . . it's comfortable and relaxing . . . and we have a positive attitude towards laughing, loving and living in a nudist environment."

"Sounds heavenly," smiled Mona.

"You know, clothing can be dangerous to your health! Toxic chemicals in clothes have been linked to cancer and skin irritation."

"Is that so?"

"Yes . . . and damp, wet bikinis often give women skin irritations and bacterial infections."

"*Eww!* I'm glad I'm not wearing one now!" she exclaimed.

"So am I," he grinned. "You know, a moderate amount of sunlight on skin is very healthy! The sun's beneficial UV rays help the body make vitamin D, which prevents many illnesses and builds strong bones. You need sunlight to set your body's internal clock for better sleep, weight loss, and emotional well-being."

"*Hmm* . . . that's interesting Oscar."

Our hero then saw folks seated at tables near a redwood building, enjoying some meals.

"Is that the restaurant?" she asked.

"Yes! Delicious sandwich wraps, acai bowls, salads, burgers, pizzas and homemade soups are served."

"I see the restaurant's smoothie bar is packed," she added, noticing nudists enjoying their delicious beverages.

"It always is! We can grab a shake, some cold-pressed juice, or a smoothie later, if you like."

"I'd love to!"

A volleyball game was taking place, with many of the fit young nudists jumping up and down, keeping the ball in play. Many players were laughing, having the time of their lives!

Mona noted some of them had 'white buns,' while the rest of their bodies were perfectly tanned.

"Funny some of the players have white behinds," she joked.

"Cotton tails!"

"Cotton tails?" she repeated.

"Yes, that's what we call them," he chuckled.

Near one of the large, sparkling pools, nudists were sunbathing and swimming, while a guy in his thirties performed a spectacular dive from a high diving board. *Zoooom! Ker-Splash!*

"Nice dive," she remarked.

Mona then did a double-take spotting a sixty year old man wearing an artist's beret, an ascot scarf, and nothing else! He was helping a young Asian woman sculpt a clay figure on a table . . . a sculpture that resembled a giant, upright and erect weenie!

"Who's that gentleman? I think I've seen him someplace before," she said.

"That's the famous Bart Kookie, creator of the stop-animation TV series *Dungbee*," explained Dong.

"Oh, that old show about a little brown ball of dung that came to life?" she asked.

"That's right. Mr. Kookie had a midlife crisis and left his wife and kids to become a hippy nudist. He attended one of our 'date nights,' and meet his new nude girlfriend . . . who's forty years his junior."

"Ain't that something!" remarked Mona, while rolling her eyes. "Are they making what I think they're making?" she mumbled.

Dong called out to Kookie.

"Hey Bart, what are you guys sculpting?"

"I'm helping Ghigh-na create *a snake*," Kookie hollered back in reply.

Mona giggled and so did Dong.

Kookie then did a double take seeing Mona's lovely zoomers.

"Giving a tour to a new member?" he asked with sudden intrigue.

"Yes, meet Mona Lot . . . our 'soon-to-be' new member," Dong explained.

"Hi Mona," said friendly Ghigh-na.

"Nice to meet you Mona!" added Kookie. "Welcome to the Jaybird Institute, you're going to love it here."

"Thank you! Nice meeting you too . . . Ghigh-na . . . Mr. Kookie!" she happily replied.

"See you guys later," said Dong.

"Bye!" waved Ghigh-na.

"Au revoir," chimed in Kookie.

Mona and Dong continued on, and they soon approached the institute's beach on the edge of Lake Tittykookoo. Nearby, a young woman wearing a frilly bathing cap was seen scrubbing the back of her boyfriend under an outdoor shower. On the lake itself, a few nudists were frolicking in the water, and a couple women were rowing around in a kayak.

Two women and one man unexpectedly raced past Mona and Dong. They were all holding hands and joyously laughing, as they dashed into the water and splashed around.

Another couple, two skin divers wearing diving masks, snorkels, and flippers, had difficulty kissing near the water's edge. Their masks and snorkels kept getting in the way!

"Here's our own private cove that Monty was telling you about."

"This is the tip of Lake Tittykookoo?"

"Yes."

Iron monkey bars, parallel bars, swings, tight ropes, and athletic rings were all set up on the sand. A fit, muscular guy was seen acrobatically swinging from one metal chain ring to another, like a monkey swinging from vine to vine. He was wearing a backwards baseball cap and nothing else. Mona was impressed by his flying athletic abilities on the rings. *Za-Zip! Za-Zip! Za-Zip!*

"He's good on those!" she declared.

"I'm not too bad on them myself," Dong winked to her.

On the opposite side of the beach, other naturists were practicing archery with bows and sharp arrows. *Zoom* . . . went the arrows straight into their colorful wooden targets. *Zing!* One woman in sunglasses was so good, her arrows hit the bullseye target every time!

"Wow!" cried Mona. "William Tell, eat your heart out!"

Dong chuckled.

"Are you good at archery?" she asked.

"No, I'm pretty bad, actually . . . but I *aim* to improve!" he laughed. "Get it?"

"Yes, I get it!" she giggled.

Mona's attention turned to a rocky cliff on the right side of the beach. Small rocks and pebbles were falling down to the sand! As our hero looked up, she was surprised to see six athletic nudists rock climbing, using a rope, climbing boots and gloves.

"Oh . . . they're pretty high up!" she exclaimed. "That looks a little dangerous."

"They know what they're doing," Dong told her. "Our rock climbing cliff is known a 'Buff Bluff.'"

"Buff Bluff?!"

As she took a better look, our hero got more than an eyeful of pickles and beavers!

"I see . . . in more ways than one!" she joked.

Just then, a cute couple in tennis shoes strolled past them, holding hands. They were clearly in love, and held their towels in their free hands.

"Hello!" they greeted, while smiling.

"Hello!" replied Mona.

"Showing a new member around?" asked the cheerful young man.

The guy's dark pubic hair was so overgrown his pickle and nuts were practically buried beneath it all!

"Yes, meet Mona Lot, our 'soon-to-be' new member!" explained Dong.

"Nice to meet you!" he smiled.

"Hello Mona," said the pretty young woman. "Welcome!"

The young lady was thin and attractive, with a gold necklace around her neck and an attractive yellow flower in her hair.

"Thanks . . . nice meeting you both," nodded Mona.

The couple continued on their way, and Mona turned to Dong.

"You've got some very friendly people around here! They're so warm and welcoming."

"You can say that again. Most of our members are really nice."

"That's awesome."

The tour continued and as Mona and Dong circled the property, they approached the busy tennis courts. A group of serious women were totally focused on their tennis match. Mona noticed some of the ladies big Tom-Toms were bouncing around *more than* the speeding tennis ball! One player wore a straw hat, and her tennis partner had short red hair with matching red earrings and lipstick. On the opposite side of the court, a woman had her hair tied up in a bun and her boobies were slightly sagging. Her tennis partner was a short Hispanic lady with the muscular physique of a female body builder!

Our hero had a brainstorm! *Could one of those ladies have been the player who tossed peeping Tom, Tom, over the fence? Was one of them a Super Nudist?*

Dong interrupted her train of thought.

"Do you play tennis?" he asked.

"Huh? Do I play? Oh, yes," smiled Mona.

"You do? We should play sometime."

"I'd love to Oscar."

Dong and Mona then moved on to the miniature golf course!

As they strolled along, conflicting thoughts raced through Chastity's/Mona's mind . . . .

Jingle Bells at Adamite Acres told me this place was full of perverts, swingers, exhibitionists, wife-swappers, sex maniacs, wild orgies, and so on . . . but so far, I haven't seen a single trace of that inappropriate behavior anywhere! None of it! Adrianna Azzhat repeated the same thing . . . but where are all those open, public, sexual activities I was supposed to see? This wonderful place looks and feels exactly like the 'clean' nudist resort Adamite Acres was! In fact, it offers so many more activities and fun things to do, it blows Adamite Acres away!

She shook her head and continued thinking . . .

I wonder why Jingle Bells and Adrianna would have lied to me? Or did they?

CHAPTER TWELVE

Oscar Dong interrupted Chastity/Mona's train of thought.

"Not too many nudist resorts have their very own miniature golf course, but we do, and there it is!" he proudly stated.

"Amazing," stuttered Mona.

A giant, ten-foot tall fiberglass *golf ball* was standing in front of the course, like a big statue. Nudists playing the outdoor golf game had to try and hit colorful golf balls on tricky felt pathways leading to eighteen different holes. The object of the game was for players to hit their balls using as few swings as possible with their golf clubs. The putting greens the golf balls rolled over were in different zig-zag paths, which made the game challenging. These felt trails also had different obstacles set up to block the way of the balls into the holes, making the game even harder. Some of these obstacles were little windmills, castles and other funny, toy-like fantasy buildings placed on the course.

"Playing naked miniature golf is like putting around a magical fairyland," said Dong. " . . . and at night, the whole place is colorfully lit up by outdoor lighting!"

"It is?"

"Yep. Even the golf course's man-made pond, the flowing waterfall, the water fountains, and winding rivers are all illuminated at nighttime."

"How charming!"

The course had beautiful grounds too, filled with evergreen bushes, freshly cut grass, and gorgeous, blooming flowers of all shapes and colors.

Mona's eyes popped out when a hairy man bent over on the course to pick up his golf ball! *Boom!* She got another hairy eyeful!

"Boy, he's got so much body hair, I thought Bigfoot was mooning me for a second!" Mona chuckled.

"*Ha, ha, ha, ha, ha!* You're right!" laughed Dong. "Maybe we could play a round of miniature golf later tonight."

"I'd like that."

Not far from the miniature golf course were several trampolines. Young naked ladies were bouncing up and down on them, and their sizable pumpkins simultaneously lolloped and leapt at the same time! *Ba-Boing! Ba-Boing! Ba-Boing! Ba-Boing!* Dong found the bouncing trampoline women . . . and their bouncing boobies . . . delightfully erotic! One chick had her hair in a ponytail, and it flew up and down in time with her ta-tas! Another bouncing beauty had a tattoo of a flying bird on her thigh, which looked like it was flying away with each bounce!

"You like to bounce on trampolines?" asked Dong.

"Yes! I'm been known to *bounce around* a lot," she confessed, with her superhero tongue planted firmly in her cheek. " . . . and there's a lot of me that bounces!"

"I can see that!"

They both laughed, and Mona's big jiggly puffs jiggled.

"Mona, I gotta tell you . . . I love to watch you laugh!"

"You do?"

"Yeah, cause *so much of you* has a good time!"

They cracked up even more!

Mona was then shocked to see a nude woman riding up on a horse!

"I know Monty mentioned it, but I'm surprised you have naked horseback riding!" she commented. "That woman reminds me of Lady Godiva!"

"You're right," grinned Dong. "I once heard that Lady Godiva had a terrible gambling problem."

"Oh?"

"Yeah, she put everything she had on a horse."

"Very funny," sneered Mona.

Near an orange tree, a couple of naturists were picking some fruit. The man was lanky with a goatee beard, and the lady was a gorgeous black woman in sunglasses.

"You've never tasted better oranges . . . they're like pure sugar!" Dong told her.

"That's an orange tree? Oh, wow!" said Mona.

Winding around the vast property, Dong and Mona passed the sauna room.

"There's our sauna. Inside, you sit on wood paneled benches and soak up the hot dry air, sweating out all of your body's impurities."

"I see," she nodded.

A couple nude men were seated on a bench outside the sauna room, playing a game of chess. They were locked in total concentration, staring down at their chess board. One man was completely bald, and the other was burly with a beard.

The nudist library was next on the tour, and Dong and Mona took a quick look inside.

"This is our library. I'll give you a fast peek, but remember to only whisper when we're inside."

"Got it."

In the library, several naturists were seated on towels at tables, reading various nudist books and magazines. A sexy, buxom, lady librarian was seated at the front desk, reading a naturist magazine too. She was Asian and wore vintage 1950's cat eye reading glasses with stylized frames. When she noticed Dong and Mona walk into the room, she put a finger up to her lips, indicating for them to remain quiet. Dong and Mona smiled and nodded, getting her message.

The library's single story room was packed with bookshelves. Mona examined some of the magazine titles, which included . . . *Buck Naked Today, Disrobed Adventures, Undressed Idea, Peeled Digest, Birthday Suit Trend,* and *Streakers Weekly.*

A young guy with an athletic build, a mop of curly hair on his head, and *a small weenie* approached the librarian.

"Excuse me," he whispered. "Do you have that book for men with small wee-wees?"

The librarian glanced at her computer screen.

"I don't know if it's in yet," she whispered back.

"Yeah, that's the one," he said.

Mona and Dong overheard the hilarious exchange, and fought like hell not to burst out laughing! Our bug-eyed hero put the white towel she was holding over her mouth, and Dong turned his head away. After a few moments, they composed themselves and Dong waved goodbye to the librarian with nice cans. The bountiful woman in her fancy cat eye glasses politely waved back, as Dong motioned Mona outside.

Once they were out in the fresh air and bright sunshine again, Dong turned to her.

"Thank goodness I was able to keep from laughing," giggled Mona.

"I know! Me too," agreed Dong. "If you'd like to spend some more time in there, we can do it later."

"I'd like to. Some of those magazines looked interesting."

Circling back towards the main entrance, the couple passed some nudists playing ping-pong, and an outdoor yoga class was also in progress. The nudist men and women struck a 'spread eagle' yoga pose which was sexy and erotic in nature! Mona's eyes widened! Nothing was left to the imagination!

"That's a *unique* yoga position!" she commented.

"It's called the *Air Out Third Leg and Camel Toe Position.*"

Mona shook her head, and then to her surprise, she beheld a big circular running track, like the type you'd see around a college football field. A couple of healthy, robust nudists were jogging and running around the track.

"You've got a running track too?"

"Yes, we do."

A little light bulb turned on inside Chastity's / Mona's mind. She wondered . . . *do the Super Nudists use this track to practice their streaking?*

"Do you ever use that track?" she asked.

"Oh yeah, I *streak* around it all the time," he replied.

Our hero raised an eyebrow when Dong said the word 'streak.' Mona then heard some relaxing music coming from the second pool area.

"Music?" she asked.

As she turned, she saw nudist musicians . . . a flute player, a harpist, and a guitarist . . . performing a soft, melodic tune. The hippy guitarist was a guy with such long hair, he looked like a woman from the back!

"That's lovely . . . so relaxing," she stated.

"Yes, they're talented."

The music was so soothing and calming, a cute couple had fallen asleep on a big towel while listening to it. They snored away in each other's arms.

As Dong and Mona neared the administration office, our hero saw another bungalow by the main pool.

"What's in there?"

"Oh, that's our hypno . . . I mean, hydrotherapy pool," he explained.

"Hydrotherapy pool?"

"Yes, unfortunately, it's closed for maintenance at the moment."

"I see."

She then thought for a moment . . . *Did he just say 'hynpo?'*

Mona's attention was abruptly drawn to a group of happy nudists near the hydrotherapy bungalow . . . naturists who were *body painting* each other! A young man using a paint brush was painting a middle-aged woman with wildly colorful paint! The woman's breasts were painted as two 'eyes,' her belly button was the 'nose,' and her pubic section was painted as the 'mouth.' The entire front of her body was painted like a comical cartoon *face!*

She also had some paint on her beautiful behind! The woman, who loved being painted, looked bizarre and hilarious . . . like something out of the psychedelic 1960's!

Three other older gentlemen were doing the same thing, body painting a trio of younger nude women with different colored paints. Each lady had a crazy, colorful, *'nude face'* painted on her midsection.

"What are they doing?!" asked surprised Mona.

"Body painting."

"Body painting?!"

"Yes, the paint's safe and non-toxic," explained Dong. "City Councilwoman Helga Hoodwink seems to really be enjoying it!"

Mona's eyes bugged out!

"That's Coucilwoman Hoodwink?"

"Yes, and the artist painting her is her intern Rod Long. They're new members, along with Mayor Artie Phishel and councilmen Max Phuckter and Harry Bottoms."

Chastity, as Mona, couldn't believe what she was hearing!

"Those other men, body painting those three young ladies, are *the Mayor* and councilmen *Phuckter* and *Bottoms?!*"

"Yes."

She took a closer look, and realized it *was* the Mayor! He was chuckling and dramatically waving his paint brush all over the woman's breasts to create her 'eyes.'

"It *is* him," stuttered Mona. " . . . but aren't they all supposed to be down at city hall, doing their jobs . . . running the town's business? Why are they 'goofing off' here at the Jaybird Institute?!"

"I heard Monty say something about the Mayor and his staff taking the day off for the *'three R's of nudism.'*"

"The three R's of nudism?" wondered Mona.

"Yes . . . *Rest, Relaxation,* and *Recreation.*"

Mona glanced back at the body painting group, and observed the Mayor chatting away with his hot artistic subject.

"You look sensational, honey!" declared Phishel to his 'living canvas.'

"Thank you Mayor," replied the bodacious young lady with short dark hair.

"Did you hear about the soldier who had his body painted?" Phishel asked.

"No, I didn't hear about the soldier who had his body painted."

"He's now a *decorated* veteran," he joked.

The two of them laughed away.

The others were having just as much fun, giggling and joking around, as they body painted their own subjects.

"Rod darling, paint my fanny again with that brush! I love it when you tickle it!" Hoodwink told him.

"Yes Helga," nodded Rod.

He dabbed his paintbrush in pink paint from the palette he was holding, and a second later, he was tickling Hoodwink's sexy bootie with it! She loved every second of it, and squirmed, twitched, and shivered with every thrilling brush stroke. Her big boobies rocked and jiggled at the same time too!

"Oh Rod, yes! Yes!"

Councilmen Max Phuckter teased his busty female model, by tickling her large milk shakes with his paint brush.

"Coucilman Phuckter . . . behave yourself!" teased the protuberant, body painted lady.

"Sugar-tits, you remind me of a big-boobed gal I once dated . . . we had fun times together!" grinned Phuckter.

"You did?" she asked.

"Yeah, those were some fond *mammaries!*"

The young woman being painted by Councilman Bottoms had short red hair and her face and body had freckles. She asked him a question, while looking down at the 'nose' painted on her belly button.

"Why is my nose in the middle of my stomach?"

"Because that's the *scenter!*" chuckled Bottoms.

"You're a real comedian, aren't you?" she remarked, while rolling her eyes at his play on words.

Mayor Artie Phishel's lazy brother, Soupy Phishel, then wandered out from behind the hydrotherapy pool's bungalow. His *entire body* had been *painted,* with the front of it resembling a wild hippy's face! His male nipples were painted as two stoned 'eyeballs,' and his long, hanging manhood was colored as the face's absurd 'nose!' A toothsome nude lady quickly followed him, holding a paint brush in one hand and a palette in her other. Both the artist, and her live, psychedelic artwork, couldn't stop giggling.

"Hee-hee-hee-hee-hee!"

"Hee-hee-hee-hee-hee!"

"Oh, there's the mayor's brother," noticed Dong.

"She painted *him!*" exclaimed Mona. She looked down and did a double take. "My, what a *big nose* he has!"

Dong chuckled.

"Your *nose* is twelve inches long!" remarked the female artist to her male subject.

"It can't be twelve inches long, otherwise it would be a *foot!*" replied the younger Phishel.

The two of them roared.

Chastity, as Mona, was stunned Mayor Phishel and the rest of the councilmembers were just yards away from her!

"Holy Hooters!" spat Mona.

"Would you like to meet the Mayor?" asked Dong.

Our hero *panicked,* because the Mayor *knew* Chastity Knott! If he could see through her Mona Lot disguise, her cover would be blown! She had to keep away from him at all costs!

Oh God! If he recognizes me in this wig, I'm finished! I've gotta hide my face! she frantically thought, while turning her head away.

"Ah, maybe some other time," Mona nervously said in reply. "Oscar, you've convinced me . . . I'd love to join the Jaybird Institute! Let's go back to the office right this minute and I'll pay my yearly membership fee. I brought extra money with me in my purse. The annual membership is five-hundred dollars, right?"

"That's right," he smiled. "Okay, we'll head back. We're not far."

"Wonderful," she said. "Let's go."

CHAPTER THIRTEEN

Chastity wanted to get as far away from the Mayor as humanly possible, in case he was to look over at her! She also realized she needed to spend more time at the nudist resort, in order to have absolute proof the Super Nudists were there. The Mayor and councilmembers clearly set off 'red flags' in her mind, convincing her she was at the right place!

As they strolled on with their towels, Dong had an idea.

"Listen, lets grab a bit to eat at the restaurant, and then we can participate in this afternoon's 'Body-Self Image Workshop.' You'll love it! Afterwards, we can go swimming."

"What about my membership?"

"I'll process it before you leave . . . no worries."

"Okay," she agreed. "Are we going to swim in one of the pools, or the lake?"

"It's your choice."

"Maybe the pool," she suggested.

"Sounds like a plan," he smiled. "The water's warmer."

Mona and Oscar Dong loved their meals at the Jaybird Growth Institute's healthy, farm-to-table restaurant. Of course they were seated on their towels, which they draped over the restaurant chairs. The café itself was a mid-century modern redwood building, with indoor and outdoor seating. The smoothie bar had a side window, so nudists who just wanted a drink could get one without having to go into the restaurant itself.

Mona had the famous chicken salad wrap on whole wheat. It was made with organic chicken breast, celery, red onion, mayo, mustard, lettuce, tomato, and spices. When it arrived, Mona turned to the waitress.

"I'm sorry, I forgot to ask . . . is there any lemon juice in this chicken salad?" she asked.

"No, there isn't," replied the pretty, naked waitress.

"Oh good, thank you."

The waitress spun around and raced off to the kitchen to place another table's order. As she did so, the couple noticed she had a very lovely behind. Dong smiled, and then turned his attention back to Mona.

"Why can't you have lemon juice," he wondered.

"It's just an old childhood allergy of mine," she fibbed.

Mona took a big bite of her wrap and loved the delicious taste of it!

Lemon juice is the only substance that can weaken Chastity Knott's super powers as the Double-D Avenger! She has a terrible allergic reaction to it, since lemon juice curdles milk and it also curdles our busty hero's blood . . . blood filled with the Crockozilla Fruit's magical vitamins, minerals, nutrients, and miraculous powers.

When Chastity, as Mona, casually 'wrote it off' lemons as an old childhood allergy, Dong never thought anything more of it.

He had the tuna wrap on wheat, made with wild-caught albacore tuna salad, mayo, red onion, celery, carrot, parsley, mustard, lemon juice, alfalfa sprouts, lettuce, tomato and organic spices. Dong relished every bit of his sandwich too!

"How do you like your chicken salad wrap?" he asked.

"Love it! Best I ever had!" she told him. "How's your tuna wrap?"

"The greatest, as always!"

"Hey, I was wondering, is the chef back in the kitchen naked too?" she asked.

"Yes, but he's *extremely careful* how closely he *stands* next to the hot stove."

Mona giggled, covering her mouth with her hand, so Dong wouldn't see any of the food she was chewing.

The couple washed their wraps down with the restaurant's magnificent drinks. Mona had the famous cold-pressed carrot juice, which not only contained organic carrot juice, but also had celery, apple, parsley, beet and ginger! She never tasted better juice . . . it was so naturally sweet, refreshing and healthy!

"*Mmm* . . . this carrot drink is heavenly! So yummy!"

"Glad you like it," he said.

Dong went for the popular berry smoothie, which had organic blueberries, bananas, almond butter, coconut oil, chocolate plant protein, and almond milk. It was so delicious, he chugged it all down in seconds.

"I can tell you hated your berry smoothie," she joked.

"Yeah, it only took me five seconds to finish it!" he smiled. "We serve the best smoothies in all of Driftwood Valley!"

After lunch, Mona and Dong casually headed over to the redwood building where the Jaybird Growth Institute's seminars and workshops took place. It was almost one-thirty that afternoon . . . time for the 'Body-Self Image Group Workshop.'

Our nude couple walked into the building, which was not far from the nudist library. Inside, Monty Jaybird was seated cross-legged on his towel, and several other naked men and women were doing the same thing. There were four women, and four men. The group formed a semi-circle on the hard wooden floor.

"How was the tour?" Jaybird asked, as Dong and Mona strolled in.

"Marvelous!" smiled Mona.

"Glad to hear it," he replied. "Oscar, Mona, take a seat, and we'll get started."

"Yes, sir," nodded Dong.

As Mona and Dong settled in on their towels, Jaybird began the workshop.

"Welcome to the Jaybird Institute's Body-Self Image Group Workshop," he announced. "The purpose of this class is to encourage 'body acceptance,' not 'body shame,' and to help you become more aware of what your nude body is and what it says."

Jaybird stood up and began to pace around in front of the group, like a college professor giving an important lecture.

"Students . . . it's important to look at yourself, to get in touch with yourself, to talk about yourself, and to really examine your feelings about who you are and what your body says. You see, when people have negative body images of themselves, this adversely affects all aspects of human functioning. Yes, if society were to accept the realities of the body's structure and its functions, humanity could become quite different."

Jaybird moved over to a group of artists' easels already set up, with papers and drawing pencils. Each easel stood over five feet tall.

"Everyone take your places in front of an easel and draw me a picture of yourself . . . draw what you think you 'look like.' There are enough easels for all ten of you."

Mona turned to Dong and giggled, and he smiled back. The couple quickly took their places in front of two easels, and began drawing their pictures. Dong was a talented artist and he drew a pretty accurate illustration of his supermodel body and handsome looks. Mona's illustration was hilarious, resembling a cartoon figure with gigantic, oversized watermelons!

Jaybird observed the various work, and nodded his head in approval.

"Students, this is all very good," he applauded.

He then stopped at Mona's easel, and glanced at her cartoon figure's voluptuous hood ornaments!

"Mona, how do you feel when you look at your drawing's extremely large breasts?"

"I feel fine . . . I love'em . . . and so do many men," she bashfully explained.

"They do?" asked Jaybird.

"Yes, guys have told me I look like 'Miss America' . . . and a good part of *Canada too!*"

"Wonderful," nodded Jaybird. "That's the type of positive body acceptance I like to hear."

Jaybird noticed some of the men in the room getting aroused while leering at Mona. Even Oscar Dong was starting to get a 'woodie.'

"Ah, if anyone gets an erection, that's permissible."

He then moved to Dong's professional looking illustration . . . which made the handsome young man look like a muscular comic book superhero!

"What about you, Oscar?"

"I'm proud of my body and everything works . . . including my vagee-gee miner."

"I'm sure it does," said one of the enthusiastic nude ladies.

Chastity, as Mona, felt a slight twinge of jealousy hearing the young woman's comment.

"Good, good," he nodded to Dong.

Jaybird then moved to an overweight man in his fifties. The gentleman, 'Mr. Gassaway,' drew a cartoon-like picture of himself with a pot belly.

"What about you, Mr. Gassaway?"

"Well, I need to lose my beer belly," muttered the uptight Gassaway.

"We have diet and exercise programs here to help you do that," explained Jaybird. "However, it's important that you accept and love your body, once you get it to where you want it to be."

"I see," he nervously replied.

Jaybird moved on to the next easel. The cute, sexy young lady standing in front of it drew a picture of herself with a stunning, red hot fanny! In reality, the woman's rear end truly was exquisite! She had a perfect, jaw-dropping, marvelous booty!

"You've emphasized your charming and delightful derriere, my dear."

"Yes, Monty, I think it's my best _ass-set_!" she smiled.

"I agree a hundred percent!" chimed in the uptight Gassaway.

Jaybird turned to the other nudists.

"You see students, here's another example of positive body acceptance," he praised.

Jaybird reviewed the remaining nudists' work, and most of them were happy with their drawings.

"Now, it's time for the mirror," he announced.

Jaybird waltzed over to a full length wall mirror, and turned to face the group.

"You've all reviewed drawings of yourselves . . . now let's analyze the real thing. Mona, please come over and stand in front of this mirror."

"Okay," she replied, a bit nervous.

Once she was there, Jaybird continued with his instructions.

"Face the mirror, and tell me what you see."

"I hate to sound immodest, but I see a pretty twenty-five year old woman with big boobs."

The others in the group, especially the men, smiled.

"That's very good," agreed Jaybird. "What are your feelings?"

"I'm happy"

"Good, good. Touch the top of your head," he instructed.

Chastity, as Mona, was worried now . . . because she didn't want her brunette wig to slide off! Her mind raced . . . . *I better be very careful how I touch my wig! If I goof, my cover might be blown, especially if the Mayor's still hanging around the property!*

She patted the top of her hair . . . her wig . . . ever so softly.

"Splendid. Now, move your hands down your body . . . feel your hefty Lady Bubbles," instructed Jaybird.

Mona did as she was told, and was starting to 'turn on' all the guys in the room again. She slowly, and seductively, rubbed her big rubbery balloons . . . including her rosy nipples! Even Monty was beginning to pop a raging, throbbing hard on! When our hero saw his 'stiff riser,' her eyes bugged out!

Chastity, as Mona, was seriously trying to participate in the group workshop. She didn't fully realize her 'mau-mau massaging' was playing out like a scene from some adult movie!

"Now touch your nose, then your teeth," continued Jaybird.

Our hero did everything as instructed.

"Can she touch her Lady Bubbles again?" asked Gassaway.

"No, she cannot," snapped Jaybird. "Ah Mona, touch your stomach, your legs, and then your sensational buns."

Mona obeyed her teacher, and when she got to touching and rubbing her tight butt cheeks, the guys went crazy yet again. At one point, our hero rubbed and pulled both ass cheeks apart, unintentionally giving her audience a quick flash of her pink starfish and tight little beaver.

It was Dong's turn to react bug-eyed!

"Splendid, now stick out your tongue."

Mona did it, and blew a 'raspberry' to her reflection in the mirror.

Pppooooooppppp!

"That's enough of that Mona, thank you," he grumbled. "Now look closely in the mirror. Would you like to spend time with that person? Are you in good company?"

"Yes, she looks friendly."

"How would you rate your body?"

"I'd give it a twelve," shouted Dong.

"I'll second that," chimed in another male nudist.

"I'm asking Mona," clarified Jaybird.

"I guess a ten out of ten," Mona softly said. "I chalk it up to good genes."

"Do you accept your real body in its entirety, or is there any shame about a particular part?"

"Not particularly . . . I love my body."

"Is there any part of your body you forgot? Be honest. You've got nothing to hide."

"You ain't kiddin'!" remarked Mona, looking down at her nude body. "No, I think we covered it all . . . I mean, reviewed my *uncovered* body."

"Wonderful," exclaimed Jaybird.

He then faced the group. "Students, this therapeutic feedback can help dispel negative attitudes as well as reinforce positive ones. These disrobed workshops are preventative psychiatry."

Jaybird turned back to Mona. "Please have a seat, and let's have Mr. Gassaway come up."

Mona nodded and took her seat back on her towel.

"Great job Mona!" smiled Dong, congratulating her. "I loved it, honest!"

"Thanks Oscar," she smiled back.

The nervous Gassaway shuffled in front of the mirror, and his body seemed incredibly tense. The man's pot belly looked even bigger in front of the mirror.

"Mr. Gassaway, you seem a little tense today," noticed Jaybird. "Tell me, what do you see in the mirror?"

"I, ah, I don't know," he nervously replied.

Jaybird turned to the group.

"Students, I sense Mr. Gassaway has a little bit of body shame, not complete body acceptance. Do any of you notice anything else?"

A good-looking guy raised his hand.

"Yes?" asked Jaybird.

"His whole body seems muscularly tense," suggested the young nudist.

"Anyone else?" asked Jaybird.

"He seems to be holding a lot of tension in his buttocks," remarked a glamourous nude woman in full makeup.

"His buttocks?" commented Jaybird.

"Yes, his buttocks," she confirmed. "It looks very tight . . . like he's squeezing it, because he's nervous."

Jaybird took a quick glance at Gassaway's tight caboose.

"You're right," nodded Jaybird, as he glanced down at Gassaway's keister. "Mr. Gassaway, you do seem to be holding a lot of tension in your buttocks. Let it out!"

"Okay!" Gassway replied.

A gigantic explosion of *excess gas* suddenly filled the entire room, coupled with a horribly loud, booming noise!

Baaaa-rrroooooooppppppffffhhhh-Fooooop-Fooooopp! Poop!

"*Oh my God!*" cried the glamourous woman!

"*Oh man!*" shouted another nudist.

Mona and Dong turned to each other with bug eyes again, and quickly held their noses.

"Mr. Gassway! That wasn't excessive tension . . . that was *excess gas!*" scolded Jaybird, waving his hand in the air. "Class dismissed! Open the windows on your way out!"

Mona and Dong snatched their towels and raced out of the room as fast as they could, along with the other fleeing nudists!

"I've heard of 'touchy-feely' sensitivity groups, but that was ridiculous," said Mona.

"I agree," chuckled Dong. "Let's get some fresh air!"

CHAPTER FOURTEEN

Mona and Dong spent the rest of the afternoon enjoying each other's company. They went swimming in the main pool and had a ball splashing around and having fun. Our hero bounced around in the wavy water, and her big U-Boats bobbled around too.

In order to prevent her wig from falling off in the pool, Mona dashed back to the ladies changing cottage to get her waterproof silicone *swim cap*. She had cleverly tucked it away in her purse. Once it was on, Mona's brunette wig was safe and secure under the watertight cap. Retro style pink, yellow, and orange flowers decorated the cartoon-like bathing cap!

Oscar Dong was totally into Mona Lot! He delighted in her naked company . . . and burned for her . . . lusted over her!

Whenever Mona ducked underwater, she flashed her shiny bare bottom, mooning Dong and the other swimmers . . . before disappearing under the sparkly chlorinated water!

Dong showed off his diving skills, doing a perfect dive from the high diving board. Mona was totally impressed seeing his excellent dive! She then thought she'd show him what she could do! She got out of the pool, and quickly walked over to the high diving board. She scrambled up the ladder, and slowly walked out onto the long, springy board. She looked down at the deep end below her, and then did a quick bounce on the board. *Boi-oing!*

She flew up a few feet, and then down she went! *Splash!* However, she probably shouldn't have done it, because the sudden impact of her super boobs on the surface of the pool caused nearly *a third of the water* to fly out! *Ka-Crash! Voooshh!*

Dong was amazed, and Mona giggled while holding her boobies. The other nudists in the pool and on the patio were shocked. Some sitting on lounge chairs got soaked by Mona's *'Booby Tidal Wave!'*

"Oh my goodness," she declared. *"Whoopsie . . . I'm so embarrassed!"*

Dong just shook his head.

"Who overfilled this pool?" she asked, making excuses for her super-booby blunder.

The couple dried off using fresh towels, and Mona removed her flowery bathing cap. Her wig beneath it was perfect . . . it was dry and good as before! Meanwhile, the water flooding the pool's patio quickly disappeared down the irrigation drains, and a lifeguard refilled the pool. He easily did this by turned a valve near the hidden pool equipment, and a jet of fresh water streamed back into the pool from the deep end.

Our couple then decided to play a round of miniature golf. Mona and Dong had more fun using their iron putters to hit colorful golf balls into the different course holes. The miniature golf course was filled to capacity with other nudists, and everyone was having a ball playing on the different holes!

Mona and Dong would scramble up to the little fantasy structures and houses, and 'horse around.' They 'made-believe' they could go inside the fun, tiny castles, windmills, and other mini buildings . . . decorations such as a little haunted house, a candy house, a Chinese pagoda, an Alaskan Igloo, an Arabian palace, a lighthouse near the big pond, and a mini replica of England's Big Ben clock tower.

There was plenty of laughter, and the naked crowd had a great time putting around the course.

As they played their last hole . . . hole eighteen . . . Mona *nearly* brushed up against some odd, three-leaved vegetation.

"*Watch out!*" cried Dong.

The handsome young man dropped his putting iron and grabbed Mona! He pulled her away from the dangerous plants.

Our hero was shocked, as Dong held her tightly against his strong chest, six-pack abs, and semi-hard firehose.

"*What?*" she shouted in surprise.

"*Poison Oak!*"

"Poison Oak?!"

"Yes! Always remember, *'leaves of three, let it be,*'" he lectured. "We've removed nearly all of it from the property, but sometimes poison oak still pops up in certain spots. If you'd brushed against it, you'd be itching like crazy for days!"

"Oh, thank you Oscar. You saved me from those dangerous plants!"

"Like I said, never forget . . . 'leaves of three, let it be.'"

"Right! I'll remember," she sweetly replied.

Their eyes locked as he continued to hold her in his strong arms. Overwhelmed with emotion, he gave her a light kiss on the lips.

Mmmm-waaaahhh!

Chastity was caught off guard, but she too was overcome with emotion . . . and she romantically kissed him back! They were in love . . . and in lust!

After a few seconds, the good-looking young man stopped his kissing and moved back.

"I, ah, hope that little kiss wasn't too soon," he softly said. "I'm taken away by your beauty Mona. I've never met a more attractive lady in my life! I'm crazy about you . . . you seem like my ideal woman!"

"Thank you, Oscar," she blushingly replied. "I like you too . . . and I have a deep feeling you might be the yin to my yang!"

She paused for a moment, blinking her bashful eyes.

"I'm overwhelmed by everything I've experienced today . . . and by meeting such wonderful, handsome guy like you."

"Thanks," he told her, while taking her hand. "Monty only asked me to give you the quick tour, but I wanted to accompany you the whole time you were here!"

"I'm glad you did," she sheepishly replied.

She then let out a little yawn. *Aaahh . . .*

"Tired?" he asked.

"Yes, it's been a long day. I got up early this morning," she confessed.

"What time is it?"

"Around six," he said.

"I think I better head on home now."

"No worries. I'll take care of your membership back at the administration office. You've got to come back tomorrow! We're having our big Saturday night talent show!"

"Talent Show?"

"Yeah, members perform all sorts of entertaining acts on our outdoor stage near the front entrance. There's a five-thousand dollar prize for the winner."

"Five-thousand dollars? Sounds interesting."

Chastity, as Mona, thought to herself.

Not only do I want to see Oscar again, but I still need to find hard evidence of the Super Nudists . . . so far, I've only had little clues they're present on the property. Entering that talent contest might give me an opportunity to do a little more detective work.

"You should enter the contest," he declared.

She thought about it for a moment, and then smiled.

"Okay Oscar, I think I will," she cheerfully replied.

"Awesome! I'll sign you up as a contestant, after I complete your membership paperwork. First, I'll take you back to the ladies changing cottage."

"Great!"

"I hope you enjoyed your one day vacation and introduction."

"Oh Oscar, I loved it," she told him.

Dong lovingly held her hand, as the two of them strolled back to the ladies changing cottage.

Off in the distance, Mona and Dong noticed clouds of dust rising in the air, along with the loud noise of a yellow bulldozer. Brown smoke belched from the black smokestack near the driver's enclosed cab. As they got closer, they saw naked Monty Jaybird operating the big bulldozer, using the machine's wide front shovel to push dirt and small rocks away from a slope.

"Looks like Monty's cleared enough space for another dozen cars in the parking lot," observed Dong.

"I see . . . hopefully that'll reduce the neighborhood traffic troubles," she commented.

"It will."

"Man, that's one humongous bulldozer!" she added. "Looks like an army tank with those metal treads!"

"Yeah . . . it's got one-hundred and sixty-eight horsepower and weighs over forty-three thousand pounds!"

"Bless my over-the-shoulder boulder holder!" she joked.

The two of them chuckled and continued on their way.

Back inside the ladies changing room, Mona instantly put her clothes back on . . . her skin tight jeans and black, low-cut blouse . . . which showed off her gargantuan melons! As she glanced around the small space, she once again noticed its cute, neat living room with the pink couch and pink chairs, and the line of pink lockers on one wall. She admired the beautiful fruit basket displayed on the pink table, and the ceiling fan with bright lights that lit up the whole pink room.

A million thoughts and emotions raced through her head, as she mentally talked to herself.

Even though I'm on an undercover mission as the Double-D Avenger, I genuinely meant what I said to Oscar. I did enjoy my visit, and am surprised that nudism is no big deal. I was very comfortable parading around in my own skin. I'm also falling in love with handsome, kind, Oscar! I sort of hope he isn't a Super Nudist . . . how could such a nice guy be a super criminal? It's hard to believe!

She then stared at the lovely fruit basket.

Hey, that gives me an idea . . . an idea for my act tomorrow night!

Her eyes widened and a big grin appeared on her face.

In a flash, Mona and Oscar were back in the administration office. Candy Delight, the New Membership and Hospitality Director, was not in the room . . . the couple were alone. Mona signed her membership contract, she paid the fee, and was handed her plastic membership card which Dong had printed out for her. He also signed her up for tomorrow night's talent show. Once that was all done, he escorted her back out to the parking lot, where her classic 1970's Corvette Stingray was parked.

"That's a beautiful classic! I love the old Stingrays!" he smiled. "That metallic blue is an awesome color Mona!"

"Thank you!" she gently replied. "Well, thanks again for the fantastic day Oscar. I loved it. I'll see you tomorrow morning. Maybe I can get in some waterskiing before the talent show!'

"Sounds great . . . I'll join you! See you tomorrow!"

He embraced her, and they gently kissed again.

After a few sweet moments, the couple's lips separated, and Mona turned to climb into her sports car.

"Good night," she whispered.

"Good night," he smiled back.

She opened the car door and hopped into the driver's seat. This was never an easy task, because her super-stacked abbondanzas always took up too much space between her driver's seat and the steering wheel. All of a sudden, she felt a sneeze coming on.

"Aahh . . . aaahh . . . aah-chooo!"

She sneezed and *blew the car horn* at the same time . . . thanks to her outrageously abundant double-ds! *Honk!*

"Whoopsie!" giggled Chastity. "This car's such a tight fit, my big boobs always honk the horn whenever I cough or sneeze!" she chuckled, winking to Dong.

"Ha, ha, ha," he laughed. "Well, there *is* pollen in the air, out here in Toupee Canyon!"

"That's for sure," she agreed.

Our hero started the motor, and seconds later her Stingray zoomed out of the Jaybird Growth Institute's main entrance. *Za-Zooommm!* Dong waved goodbye to his new love, until she was out of sight.

Monty Jaybird suddenly appeared behind him . . . and he was not happy.

"Why were you with Mona all day long? I only told you to give her the quick tour?" scolded Jaybird in his British accent.

"Sorry Monty, I . . . " stuttered Dong.

"I know, you're in love with her . . . just like you're in love with all the other busty ladies around here! Well, never mind about that now . . . I've got three more important assignments for you and the team. I'm closing the place early tonight."

"What time?"

"Seven o'clock . . . the excuse is we need to prepare for tomorrow night's talent show. Now go join the others immediately."

"Yes, sir," he nodded.

"I'll be there shortly to fill you in on the plan."

Later, around eight o'clock that night, something sinister was about to happen at the Driftwood Valley Wax Museum. The front of the museum resembled a magnificent mid-century modern palace, with long, tall, white walls and pillars, and automatic sliding-glass doors at the entrance and exit. A huge, flashing neon sign was erected in front of the building, which read *Driftwood Valley Wax Museum* in sparkly lights.

Inside, the museum's eighty-five year old caretaker, whose nickname was 'Romeo,' was making his last rounds of the night before closing. The old man was a tall, slim fellow with a smiling face and a friendly personality. His grey hair was receding, and he wore large glasses with round plastic frames. A salt-and-pepper colored moustache appeared below his long nose. Romeo's wardrobe consisted of a loud, red Hawaiian shirt, baggy red pants, and a red jacket with embroidered stars all over it.

Holding his feather duster, he entered his favorite section of the museum, the Chamber of Horrors. The chamber's spooky group of life-sized displays featured a tall wax figure of Frankenstein's Monster standing in a detailed mad scientist's laboratory. Across from the Frankenstein set was a flight of stone stairs with a wax figure of Dracula holding a female victim in his arms. In the next room, an Egyptian mummy was lying on a slab, with his arms crossed. The wax mummy was displayed in a set resembling the interior of a pyramid's royal tomb. The chamber's entrance had a frightening figure of a werewolf, standing with his arms up in an attacking pose. The wax wolf-man was displayed in front of an old castle window.

Atmospheric lighting illuminated the scary wax displays, while sounds of howling wind, thunder, and creepy shrieks, moans and groans, were heard from hidden speakers throughout the chamber.

Romeo often chatted with his wax figures, believing they were real.

"Well, Frankie, it's nearly closing time" he told the Frankenstein Monster, while waving his feather duster around. "I'll go shut off the spooky sound effects."

The slightly senile old man shuffled towards a control panel behind a black curtain, but then he stopped dead in his tracks! Some *new* wax figures had been set up near the Phantom of the Opera display! The figures were of *the Super Nudists!*

Each athletic nudist stood perfectly still, not moving a muscle. The five men and five women were wearing their black goggles and signature light-green and yellow colored helmets with fruit or nut symbols painted on the front forehead areas. Lemon, Banana, Walnut, Papaya, Peanut, Coconut, Kiwi, Macadamia, Guava, and Pecan were pretending to pose as wax dummies, in their minimal uniforms of light-green and yellow colored gloves, boots, utility belts, capes and metallic green *fig leaf* jockstraps and Jillstraps.

"Who on Earth put those new figures there?!" wondered Romeo. "They don't belong in the Chamber of Horrors, they need to be displayed in the Superhero section!"

Romeo did a double take at the females' bare breasts.

"Someone forgot to put *brassieres* on those lady dummies too!" he exclaimed. Romeo then took a closer look at Guava's humongous breasts. *"Criminy!* What a pair . . . she's super-stacked! I bet if I look up the word "boobs" in the dictionary, her picture's there!"

Banana suddenly cried out, *"Super Nudists, go!"*

"Huh?!" shrieked Romeo in total surprise.

The birthday suit bandits *came to life* and surrounded him! He hollered in fear!

"Waaaahhhh!"

The octogenarian tried fighting them off with his feather duster, but busty Guava gave him a quick shot of her knockout guava gas! *Sssssss!* Within seconds, Romeo was out like a light . . . stiff as his wax monsters on display.

Super Nudist leader Banana somewhat resembled Oscar Dong, but was he really him? It was hard to tell under his black goggles and helmet. His near perfect, nude body looked similar, but so did all the other male Super Nudists muscular physiques. The men all resembled fit, super models . . . with flawless bodies like those of the classic Greek gods.

CHAPTER FIFTEEN

Not far from the museum, Doctor Della-Kwak . . . the fifty-something year old blond, scatterbrained quack . . . was relaxing at home after a long day at work. She lived in a gorgeous, mid-century modern, cliff-top home. The single story house resembled a compact steel and glass box. It was called a 'cliff-hanger' because the home was held up by huge support beams buried deep into the side of a steep hill. The strong columns resembled the home's 'legs,' allowing half the house to 'hang over' the cliff . . . and out into midair.

Della-Kwak had just plopped into bed, and was admiring her magnificent nighttime view of Driftwood Valley down below. Millions of city lights twinkled on and off in the distance. The view from her bedroom was like the perspective you'd get from an airplane. The mid-century boudoir, with minimal mod furniture, was wide open with walls made entirely of glass! Her spectacular panorama was even better than the view Chastity Knott had at her house!

Della-Kwak still had some privacy though, because neighbors could not see through the solid, white-painted brick wall sections where her bed and bathroom were located.

The sexy Milf was feeling horny that night . . . especially after the 'nude surprise' her patient, Buster Coochi, had given her earlier that day! She just couldn't get his hot, sexy image out of her mind . . . the image of Buster standing there in the exam room, stark naked and sporting a humongous, upraised, speedo torpedo!

Feeling incredibly frisky, Della-Kwak leaned over and slowly opened the top drawer of her bed's end table. She then pulled out a *huge silver vibrator*, along with a tube of lube. She quickly rubbed the lubrication jelly all over the rocket-shaped vibrator, and then whipped off her bed covers! The next things to be whipped off were her lacy bra and panties!

Fully nude, Della-Kwak was quite attractive for her age! She had a lovely face . . . thanks to a recent facelift . . . and her voluptuous body was ravishing. Her boobs were nearly as big, fresh, and rubbery as the Double-D Avenger's! She was a sexy, middle-aged, hottie in heat!

Lying on her back, she supported her head and shoulders by using several soft pillows. The hot and bothered doctor then spread her legs wide open, showing off her magnificent, golden-haired coochie! She held the buzzing rocket in her right hand, and gently placed the slippery vibrating tip of it directly on her love bud!

Buzz-buzz-buzz!

The woman instantly went crazy, lifting up her left leg with her left hand! Her feet and toes wiggled around, as she lustfully rode a pulsating wave a pure ecstasy! Glimpses of pretty red nail polish flickered, as her painted toes wiggled.

"*Oh, yeah!*" she cried, totally turned on. "This battery-powered dildo is much better than my old one! That old one was a *dil-don't!*"

She passionately took in some deep breaths and exhaled them out! The battery-powered joystick did not move any lower! She held it carefully over her clamhat, slightly rubbing it over the magic button.

Buzz-buzz-buzz!

"*Aaaaahh! Wwwooooo! So good!*" she delightfully squealed, while tingling her bean.

"*Oh, yeah!*" she repeated, in a series of breathy pants.

"*Ah, ah, ah, ah, ah!*"

Della-Kwak then passed the noisy oscillator to her left hand, and grabbed both of her legs with her right, holding them way up in the air. The lustful woman continued her peanut polishing with the wondrous trembler! When she held it on the hood of her fun buzzer, and her eyes rolled into the back of her head! Her lips parted . . . the ones on her *face* that is . . . and her fast huffing and puffing continued!

"*Ah, ah, ah, ah, ah!*"

Buzz-buzz-buzz!

"*Oh!* This vibrating boner is so doggone good, I'd love to *suck it* . . . but I don't want to chip a tooth!" she lustfully gasped.

"*Aaahh! Ooooh!*"

She then forced the head of the greased silver rocket *deeper* into her pink guitar! Suddenly, her toes pointed straight up to the ceiling! *Zing!*

"*So good! Mmmmmmm!*" she passionately moaned. "I think the only reason women get married is because vibrators can't mow the lawn or take out the trash!"

Buzz-buzz-buzz!

She let go of her legs and they hovered over the bed, with her knees still bent.

Della-Kwak felt the orgasmic waves deep within her honey pot growing stronger and stronger . . . and her eager wet beaver started to fly up and down off the bed, in perfect sync with each fast wave! Her big white boobs, with light brown areolas and nipples, quivered and shivered! The doctor's rock hard nipples pointed straight up to the ceiling, like two pudgy rockets ready to blast off to the moon!

"This thing's a better lover than any man I've had!" bellowed the feverish physician.

Buzz-buzz-buzz!

Her eyes *really* widened all of a sudden!

"*Ah, here I go!*" she cried out, about to climax.

The overexcited Milf rode and humped her pulsating, trembling rocket like it was a miniature bucking bronco in some Wild West rodeo! Her crotch area was convulsing faster and faster, as her thighs and legs wiggled and jiggled! She was literally bouncing off the bed, as her 'tinkerbelling' was about to reach its grand and glorious end!

Suddenly, Della-Kwak went completely *spastic* and *crossed her eyes*! She kicked her legs and lifted her torso up and down! The oversexed Milf 'went to the moon,' figuratively speaking, on her vibrating rocket! *Zoooom!!*

"Aaaaaaaahhhhh! Yes! Yes! Yes! Aaaaaaahhhhh!" she feverishly screamed, reaching her 'orgasmic zenith.'

Once it was over, she took a few deep breaths to relax and calm down, while switching off her noisy love machine. Slowly, she got up out of bed, wiped a little sweat from her forehead, and shuffled off to the bathroom with a big, happy smile on her face. Her glistening panty hamster was happy too! As she slid the bathroom door open and turned on the lights, she stopped *dead in her tracks!*

Surprise! The *Super Nudists* were in there, *waiting for her!* Lemon, Banana, Walnut, Papaya, Peanut, Coconut, Kiwi, Macadamia, Guava, and Pecan *ambushed her!* There was plenty of space for all ten of them, because the mid-century mod bathroom, complete with oversized bathtub, enclosed shower, toilet area, and multiple mirrored sinks, was enormous!

Della-Kwak screamed in fear, seeing the nude intruders in their goggles, helmets and minimal uniforms of light-green and yellow colored gloves, boots, utility belts, capes and metallic green *fig leaf* jockstraps and Jillstraps!

"Waaaaaahhhh!" cried the naked doctor.

Guava gave her a quick shot of her knockout guava gas! *Sssssss!* Within seconds, the doctor was out like a light.

"Sounds like she had a really good time!" male Super Nudist Macadamia joked.

"Too bad we couldn't see it," remarked male Super Nudist Pecan.

Banana turned to male Super Nudist Walnut.

"Walnut, you carry the Doctor," he ordered.

"Right," nodded Walnut.

"Maybe *I* should buy one of those things for myself . . . they sound like fun," grinned female Super Nudist Coconut.

"Me too!" chimed in female Super Nudist Kiwi.

"Super Nudists, retreat!" cut in Banana.

Like a team of indestructible Chinese acrobats, the Super Nudists dashed out of the bathroom and into the wide open bedroom. Walnut threw the unconscious Della-Kwak over his shoulder with ease. Male Super Nudist Peanut forced open one of the large windows, and then he and the rest of the team *jumped out!*

One by one, the helmeted Super Nudists dove off the edge of the cliffhanger home, falling down, down, down into the step canyon! *Zoom! Zoom! Zoom! Zoom! Zoom! Zoom! Zoom! Zoom! Zoom! Zoom!* They were skydiving again, only this time *without parachutes!* Their light-green and yellow capes violently waved behind them!

Remarkably, as each unclad kidnapper neared the bottom of the steep canyon, they started to run like crazy in midair! They looked like funny characters from some 1940's slapstick cartoon! When their racing boots finally hit the dirt slope, they continued streaking down the cliff on foot . . . at close to fifty miles per hour! The super villains and villainesses were literally *running down the side of the steep hill*, completely unharmed! Ten dust clouds trailed behind them!

Doctor Della-Kwak, who was out like a light, was unharmed! Walnut had her safely in his arms and over his shoulder, as he super streaked down the side of the cliff!

Once the Super Nudists reached the bottom of the hill, they all levelled out. A second later, the group disappeared into the night, bolting down a dark residential side street.

Around ten o'clock that same night, right next-door to the Jaybird Growth Institute, Adrianna Azzhat was lying in her bed. It was past her bedtime, and unlike Doctor Della-Kwak, Azzhat was fully dressed in her clown-like polka dot pajamas . . . which included a long sleeve mid-length top and pants. She tossed and turned, trying to get to sleep.

Suddenly, she heard wild 1960's 'Go-Go' music playing outside! Her eyes popped wide open! The sound was deafening!

"Oh no, not again!" she roared. *"Not again! It never ends! That damn music's so loud it sounds like they're in my backyard!"*

She wondered for a second.

"They better not be in my backyard! I'll arrest every one of those disrobed devils!" she howled.

Springing out of bed, she instantly slipped on her matching polka dot house slippers! Her bedroom was a perfect time capsule from the 1970's, with orange shag carpeting, orange drapes, wood paneled walls, hanging green plants, and an orange 'cottage cheese' ceiling with 'sparkles' in it.

Azzhat dashed out of her bedroom, and zipped down the hallway to her kitchen! She threw open her kitchen's sliding glass door, and raced outside. The backyard's lights were on, illuminating the small, kidney-shaped swimming pool and patio.

The furious woman glared at the high concrete wall separating her property from the Jaybird Growth Institute. To her surprise, the nudists had not trespassed on her property, but the booming 'Go-Go' music was blasting her eardrums.

"Turn off that damn music, or I'll call the cops!" shouted Azzhat to the wall.

Mad as hell, she grabbed her ladder and climbed up onto her ranch house's flat, single story roof. Once there, Azzhat had a bird's-eye view of the back of the nudist resort, including its miniature golf course.

"You guys think it's funny to put a loud speaker right up against my wall?!" she screamed. "Well, we'll see how funny it is when the Sheriff comes over and arrests all your naked asses! I already reported that *hole* you made in my wall, separating my property from your nudist colony! The police are *looking into it!"*

She scurried over to the roof's edge, to get a better look over the wall. She couldn't see a thing . . . no nudist pranksters, and no loud speaker. The nudist resort was deserted.

"So, you little bare-assed hooligans are hiding are you?"

"No, we're right here!" replied Banana.

"What!?" exclaimed Azzhat.

She turned around and the Super Nudists stepped forward from out of the shadows . . . like ninja ghosts! *Boo!*

There they all were . . . right there on the roof with her . . . Lemon, Banana, Walnut, Papaya, Peanut, Coconut, Kiwi, Macadamia, Guava, and Pecan, in their black goggles and minimal Super Nudists costumes! Moonlight reflected off their shiny helmets!

"Waaaaaahhh!" screamed Azzhat, as she turned to run.

The frantic, idiotic woman was so scared she didn't look where she was going! She literally ran straight off the roof of her house . . . and plunged into the swimming pool below! *Ka-Splash!*

The Super Nudists chuckled, as they jumped down to the patio. *Zip! Zip! Zip! Zip! Zip! Zip! Zip! Zip! Zip! Zip!*

Dazed and frightened to death, Azzhat frantically bobbed around in the deep end of the water. Her drenched polka dot pajamas were weighing her down a bit.

"Aaaaaahhh!" Azzhat gurgled, as chlorinated water filled her mouth. *"Someone . . . call . . . the . . . Sheriff!"* she cried, spitting the water back out.

Banana turned to male Super Nudist Walnut.

"Walnut, fish her out."

"Right," nodded Walnut.

"Guava," said Banana.

"Yes?"

"When she's out, give her the gas."

"I'm way ahead of you," Guava smiled.

Banana then turned to female Super Nudist Lemon.

"Lemon, hop over the wall and turn off the music. Take our boombox back to the outdoor stage."

"Will do."

As the delirious Azzhat was pulled from the pool, Guava's knock-out gas blasted her wet face. *Sssssssss!!!*

"Ah!"

"Nighty-night Adrianna," Guava chuckled. "We're finally rid of you! You've been a thorn in Monty's side for far too long!"

Banana and the rest of the Super Nudists joined in the laughter.

Back at Chastity Knott's English Pub, Chastity was clearing a table in the outside patio section. It was nearly eleven o'clock that same night, and the pub's patio was beautifully lit with strings of hanging Italian lights. Our hero had such a strong work ethic, she didn't want to leave all of the pub's chores to her cousin Billy and busty waitress Connie Cans. Most of the pub's customers were inside . . . not many were out on the patio.

Billy, taking a short break, dashed over to Chastity, so they could have a quick, private talk.

"Thanks for helping out this late, but you've had a long day. Go home," he urged her. "Connie and I can close tonight."

"Well, okay, if you say so," she reluctantly replied.

Billy looked her straight in the eye.

"Chastity, I'm worried about your going back to that Jaybird Institute tomorrow," he whispered. "Those Super Nudists could kill you . . . they've got the same strength and speed as Double-D . . . and it's ten against one!"

"I know Billy, but I was able to 'blow them away' . . . literally . . . during our first fight," she confidently explained. " . . . and I won't fall for their knock-out gas trick a second time!"

"But . . . "

"Please stop worrying. The Double-D Avenger can handle them. Remember, I've got indestructible tits," she said, while placing a reassuring hand on his shoulder. "I know I'm close to finding them . . . and bringing them to justice. All the clues are right out in front of me; the mayor and the councilmembers, their sudden legalization of public nudity, the crushed phone and super tennis players, and a couple people I met who bear resemblances to some of the Super Nudists. I can't be certain, but I saw facial similarities."

" . . . and you're convinced they've been kidnapping and somehow brainwashing key individuals in Driftwood Valley . . . turning them into radical nudists?"

"Absolutely," she replied. "It's like *one* . . . "

Chastity cupped her right boob with both hands and slightly shook it. *Shakey-shakey!*

". . . and *one* . . . "

She then cupped her *left* boob with both hands and slightly shook it. *Shakey-shakey!*

" . . . adding up to *two!*"

Chastity finally grabbed *both* her right and left boobs and slightly shook them together as she said the word 'two!' *Shakey-shakey! Shakey-shakey!*

Having made her clever verbal and visual point, our hero stopped jiggling her big melons. She thought carefully before continuing.

I've deliberately decided not to tell Billy about my feelings for Oscar Dong. It's too early for that, and besides, if Oscar's connected to the Super Nudists, or he's one of them . . . God forbid . . . I'll have to break off any relationship before it even begins.

She resumed with Billy.

"They've got to have a hideout hidden somewhere on the Jaybird property, and I know I'll find it. I've got to legally catch them in the act of their next crime and figure out how they've been brainwashing their victims. The Mayor and the councilmembers have clearly lost their minds."

"I hope you can, you're Driftwood Valley's only hope, especially since they turned the Sheriff and Deputy into devout nudists," he replied. "We'll get no real help from them."

"You're right about that," she agreed, as her mind raced. "I've got to find out how those villains got their super powers too!"

"Man, I still can't believe you went undercover, fully nude, at that nudist colony! *Ha, ha, ha,*" he chuckled. "My cousin . . . *a nudist!*"

"Billy, as strange as it sounds, it was no big deal really. After a few minutes, I got used to walking around naked, and never really thought more about it. Everyone else was in their birthday suits. I must confess, there *was* a sense of freedom doing it, and I think it was good for my whole body to get some sunshine, fresh air and exercise."

"Yeah . . . makes sense I guess," he grinned.

Suddenly, a gorgeous woman in her thirties, Anita Heirbags, walked out onto the patio *completely nude!* She was quite cantilevered in the bare breast department! Chastity and Billy turned to see her, and their eyes bugged out! They recognized her as one of their regular customers!

Heirbags stepped outside to make a call, holding the cell phone in her hand.

"Anita!" stuttered Chastity. "What . . . what are you doing here . . . barefoot all over?!"

Billy couldn't say a word . . . he just stood there in total shock . . . staring at the red-hot, sexy lady! He thought he was seeing a foxy nude centerfold from some men's magazine, *magically come to life!*

"Chastity, I've gone nudist! It's legal now," smiled Heirbags. "I used to race to the mall for the latest fashions, but now I don't care about clothes anymore."

"Really?" sputtered Chastity.

"That's right," replied Heirbags. "I was also getting sick and tired of guys always trying to look down my blouse whenever I sat at the bar!"

Chastity turned to Billy, as Billy turned to Chastity! They couldn't believe what they just heard and nearly burst out laughing!

CHAPTER SIXTEEN

Early the next day, the weather was perfect! It was a gorgeous Saturday morning with blue skies and warm sunshine. Summer was in full swing, and things were jumping at the Jaybird Growth Institute. Lots of adult nudists were scattered throughout the property, enjoying the resort's many recreational activities. Attendance was greater than usual, because everyone was excited to see, or participate in, that night's talent show! Each contestant was hoping to be the lucky winner of the five-thousand dollar prize!

On Lake Tittykookoo, a powerful speedboat raced past the Jaybird Institute's private beach, towing a very busty, nude, female water-skier! The classic speedboat was a light-green and yellow-colored fiberglass beauty from the 1960's . . . aerodynamic and sleek. It was the same boat the Super Nudists had used when they kidnapped city councilman Harry Bottoms!

Behind the speedboat was Chastity in her 'Mona Lot' disguise, standing on a pair of waterskies! *She* was the big boobed water-skier, with her brunette wig hidden under her retro-style pink, yellow, and orange flowered bathing cap! Chastity/Mona was a great skier, and she loved the thrilling feeling of zipping over the cool water . . . naked as a jaybird! Her entire body was sprinkled by water flying up from her skis and from the rear of the speedboat towing her. Of course, she looked sensational . . . all wet and shiny . . . like a stunning nude goddess magically streaking across the sun sparkled lake! Our hero was all smiles . . . giggling and laughing, while waving to the speedboat's driver up ahead of her . . . Oscar Dong!

Smiling Oscar turned around to wave back, while keeping his other hand steady on the boat's steering wheel. He was mesmerized by her au naturel lusciousness, as his short blond hair blew in the wind. The front of the speedboat was lifted up in the air a bit, as it zoomed forward, leaving a white foamy wake in the water.

Mona rocketed over the lake like a pro, while holding onto her tow line. She carefully kept her knees slightly bent, and her arms straight. Of course, her colossal hooters and tight naked bootie were exposed for the whole world to see, as a trail of wavy, white foam jetted out behind her. Her hefty breast cannons pointed straight ahead, like two enormous guns on a fast-moving Navy battleship!

Suddenly, a floating, bobbing ski ramp appeared up ahead! Dong turned again and gave Mona a thumb's up signal. She nodded back, giving him the same sign. Having his 'green light,' Dong gunned the boat, and Mona approached the ramp at lightning velocity! The speedboat, with its roaring motor, pulled to the right, rushing just past the ramp . . . and Mona skied straight up it! *Za-Zoom!* She was airborne!

Her waterski jump was perfect, as she soared through the air like a big breasted seagull! After a few seconds, she landed back onto the water, making a swift splash! *Ka-Sploosh!* Mona didn't stop . . . she just kept speeding ahead at full throttle!

"Whoo-hoo!" she joyously cried. Our hero then mumbled to herself, "Good thing I kept my super humdingers completely still during that jump, otherwise I would have *overshot* the boat thanks to the centrifugal force of my catapulted tits! *Hee, hee, hee!*"

Dong waved to his new love, while laughing. They were both having a ball!

After their waterskiing fun, the two of them decided to grab a little lunch at the Institute's healthy, farm-to-table restaurant. Mona and Dong woofed down their yummy sandwich wraps and delicious fruit smoothies, and then they were off to play a round of tennis. It was an exciting match, since Dong was an excellent player. Chastity/Mona was a good tennis player too, but she kept getting distracted by her handsome new boyfriend's huge, dangling weenie, that kept swinging all over the court! In fact, it was swinging more than his tennis racket!

Yes, instead of keeping her eyes on the tennis ball, Mona's eyes were focused on Dong's dong!

"Hey, keep your eyes on the ball, not my banana," he jokingly shouted over the net. He then realized he used the word 'banana' and reacted. "Ah, I mean my third leg!" he corrected himself.

Chastity, as Mona, was puzzled.

"Banana?" she mumbled, as her mind raced.

The rest of the afternoon flew by, as the couple enjoyed their lighthearted day of joyous, naked pleasure! Mona and Dong did some archery, a little horseback riding, and then they took a soak in the large outdoor hot tub. Their muscles were a little sore from all of their physical activities, so the tub's strong jets of hot water were soothing and relaxing. Of course, Mona's enormous breasts bobbed around in the water, causing minor waves in the hot tub! Her areolas and nipples looked like the eyes of some gigantic octopus, popping out of the water and staring!

Chastity, as Mona, intended to continue her detective work on the property, but because Oscar Dong was with her the entire time, she never had an opportunity to snoop around.

"Can we try the indoor hydrotherapy pool next?" she curiously asked. There was something about that hydrotherapy bungalow that had piqued her interest yesterday.

"Ah, maybe later," he said with a little unease, as if hiding something.

"It's still being repaired?"

"I don't know . . . I'll ask Monty."

"Okay," she nodded. "Oscar, can I ask you something?"

"Sure."

"Why did you become a nudist?"

"I don't know," he smiled. "I used to skinny dip as a kid. I guess because it's fun! It's thrilling, exciting. I like the freedom from clothes, the physical and mental health benefits, my overall tan, and the fun activities. I've made some great friends . . . and met some beautiful, open-minded women . . . like you Mona."

The handsome young man then looked around to see if anyone was watching. Most of the nudist guests were enjoying other parts of the property, so the two of them were all alone in the hot tub. Dong used this chance to float over to Mona and steal another passionate kiss! Caught off guard, she romantically kissed him back. She was really falling for him! After a few seconds, their hungry lips parted.

"Oh, Oscar . . . someone might see us in here," she breathily whispered, looking into his dreamy blue eyes.

"Nobody's around," he whispered back. "Mona, I love you like a monkey loves a banana!"

He realized he goofed yet again, saying the word 'banana.'

"I mean, like a dog loves a bone!"

"Well, speaking of *bones,* take look at *yours!* It's the size of the Alaskan Pipeline . . . and just as hard!" she giggled. "Better calm Mr. Happy down, before someone sees him!"

"Around you, that's impossible!"

He moved in for a second kiss, and this time their make-out session lasted longer. He held her in his strong arms as they lustfully tongue-wrestled, and his lean, muscular body rubbed up against hers. Our excited hero was wildly aroused, and so were her hot bazooms! They rose out of the water like two surging ocean buoys!

Dong was about to kiss them too, but Mona moved back in the bubbling water.

"Oscar, look at the time," she said, pointing to the outdoor clock hanging on a wall.

It was close to five o'clock.

"I better get ready for tonight's talent show!"

"You're right," he agreed in frustration. "Okay, let's dry off and I'll take you back to the ladies changing cottage."

"Thanks, I just need to go to the car for my costume."

"Costume?" he wondered.

"Oh, it's not much of one really . . . I mean, after all, we're at a nudist resort!" she joked.

He chuckled, as they both stepped out of the hot water.

At that moment, a loud helicopter suddenly appeared in the sky! *Dee-Dee-Dee-Dee-Dee!* Mona and Dong looked up, as it circled the entire institute at a low-altitude. The chopper's rotor generated a strong thrust, which blew lots of wind down at them!

"What's it doing?!" wondered Mona, as the breeze whipped around her wig's hair. "Is there a fire, or something?! Is that the police?!"

"Naw, it's just another *flyby,*" he replied, totally unimpressed. "Usually happens on weekends."

"A flyby?"

"Yeah, that eggbeater's part of the Driftwood Valley Helicopter Tours! The pilot thinks it's funny to give his paying passengers a *peak* at all of us naked down here! Those lookie-loo tourists are probably laughing their heads off right now . . . and getting their jollies!"

"How terrible! They're perverted! We may be *nude,* but they're *rude!"*

"I know, just ignore them. They'll be gone in a minute."

"Hmm!" snorted our indignant hero, as she tried to cover her walloping rack with her hands and arms. *"That should be illegal!"*

The highly anticipated talent show started right on time, at precisely seven o'clock that night! High flood light beams shot down to illuminate the outdoor stage, which wasn't far from the main entrance. This was the same stage were the wild 1960's 'Go-Go' dancing had taken place . . . the unclad scene that shocked and frightened away Pastor Weensy and his stuffy 'church ladies!'

A delightfully warm breeze was in the evening air, and the bare audience sat on lawn towels or folding chairs. Every stark naked spectator in the crowd was mesmerized by the different acts that appeared on stage.

The first nude act was the musical hippy trio known throughout the resort; the flute player, the harpist and the guitarist. They specialized in soft, relaxing, tranquil music, and the male guitarist's hair was so long, he always resembled a woman from the back!

Once their boring number was over, the audience was awakened by a rotund German man playing a fast, lively polka on his accordion! The smiling naked musician quickly worked his right hand's fingers on the accordion's keyboard, while his left hand's fingers hit the chord buttons. All was fine and dandy, until he got his German knockwurst stuck in the accordion's bellows as he was *compressing them* together!

"Aaaahhh-ooooo-waaaahhh!!" he cried. *"Ach du lieber!"*

He scrambled off stage, as the audience howled.

The next act up was a peeled juggler riding a unicycle, followed by a bare-assed ballet dancer, and a nudnik ventriloquist act featuring a dummy/puppet in his birthday suit!

"You know how Pinocchio found out he was made of wood?" asked the undressed dummy.

"No, how?" replied the ventriloquist operating him.

"His hand caught on fire!"

The crowd loved it.

Chastity, as Mona, was standing unclothed in the wings, nervously waiting her turn to go on stage and perform. On the top of her head was a colorful and festive South American *fruit hat!* The exotic headdress was adorned with all kinds of tropical fruit . . . bananas, berries, cherries, mangos, papayas, pineapples, and so on. She had laid out a long gold skirt, a ruffled red blouse, and several necklaces and bangles on a backstage table. On the floor beneath the table she also placed a pair of platform sandals. Our hero's costume and act was inspired by the gorgeous fruit basket she'd noticed while in the women's changing cottage.

She then did a double-take when she saw her long-time friend Romeo, the old wax museum caretaker, shuffling onto the stage! He was naked as the day he was born . . . which was eighty-five years ago! The only thing he had on were his large glasses with the round plastic frames.

Fast rockabilly music started playing over the loudspeakers, and he grabbed a microphone. Romeo then starting singing a 1950's rock and roll number!

"You ain't nothin' but a Jaybird . . . naked all the time! Yeah, you ain't nothin' but a Jaybird . . . naked all the time! Ya never put on clothin', and you're a real good lover of mine!" he warbled.

For a moment, Chastity/Mona worried Romeo might recognize her, but then she realized she didn't have time for that nonsense! Besides, she was pretty well disguised under her fruit hat!

In the cheering and whistling audience, Monty Jaybird was all smiles. Seated next to him on his right was Oscar Dong, and on his left was Monty's girlfriend/assistant Candy Delight, the new membership and hospitality director. Surrounding them were several other good looking people who closely resembled the Super Nudists!

Doctor Della-Kwak, in the raw, sat between two of the handsome, smiling, male models. Of course, she was admiring their big muscles! The doctor was so focused on feeling their pecks and biceps, using both of her hands, she paid no attention to what was happening on stage!

"Make another big muscle for me!" she passionately begged.

"Sure," replied the smiling, sexy stud.

He flexed the pectoral muscles on his chest again, and the doctor nearly fainted in ecstasy!

"Ooooo! Oh my goodness!" she gasped. "All that prime rib and no au jus or horseradish!"

Seated behind Della-Kwak was Mayor Artie Phishel and City Council members Helga Hoodwink, Max Phuckter, Harry Bottoms, the mayor's brother Soupy Phishel, and intern Rod Long. Further back, were the naked Sheriff and his stupid Deputy! The birthday suit gang was all there!

Back on stage, the next act up was a barbershop quartet! Four naked male singers sang their four-part harmony without any instrumental accompaniment, while a pretty young lady, Peggy O'Seal, danced in front of them holding a fancy umbrella. The guys wore Gay Nineties style straw hats, and red and white stripped vests . . . but nothing else! O'Seal, in her early twenties, was cute as a button, with her perky bonbons and tight, little derriere! Her lacy umbrella was actually a dainty pink parasol, which she twirled around in her feminine hands. The men were all smiles as they sang about the sexy lass;

Who's that girl not wearing clothes? That's Peggy O'Seal!
Who's stark naked from head to toe? That's Peggy O'Seal!
If she streaks like a proud little rogue, if she talks with a cute little brogue,
Sweet personality, naked rascality, that's Peggy O'Seal!

The quartet's witty song continued for several more bars, and then it was over. The men and their dancing girl took their bows and exited. The next act came on almost immediately . . . a chorus line of tap dancing women . . . only these gals had enormous, gigantic breasts! All of them! They made the Double-D Avenger's boobies look like microscopic A-cups!

Each lady appeared to be shaking two overinflated, elephantine beach balls, as they madly tap-danced across the stage. They were all completely nude, except for the loud tap shoes on their swift feet. It looked like someone had given each of them a 'hot foot,' because they were trembling and wiggling around so fast, and making such a thunderous racket with their feet! *Rat-tat-tat-tat-tat-tat! Rat-tat-tat-tat-tat-tat!*

The noisy, absurd act was ridiculous and the audience roared! It wasn't over soon enough!

Just when Chastity/Mona thought she had seen it all, Adrianna Azzhat, *completely in the nude,* appeared on stage next . . . pushing a rolling table! A dozen different sized, copper cow bells were on it, all laid out in keyboard order from biggest to smallest! Our hero's eyes nearly popped out!

"Adrianna Azzhat?!" gasped Mona. "They finally got to her too?!"

Some happy, upbeat, pre-recorded music started playing, and crazy Azzhat frantically jiggled the different hand bells in perfect time with the melody! Most of her long ringing notes matched those of the fast jazz tune being played over the loudspeakers. As she raced from one end of the table to the other, Azzhat's sagging melons looked like swinging, low-hanging fruit! *Zoop! Zoop! Zoop!*

The screwy broad had a big smile on her face, and her eyes were like those of someone possessed or unhinged! It was as if some wild whacko had been let out of an insane asylum, and wound up on stage to perform . . . shaking her different bells like a frenzied cartoon character! It was the most hilarious musical act anyone had seen!

Once she was done, Azzhat took her bows, and the audience applauded and cheered! She then pushed the cow bell cart off stage as fast as she could. Backstage, Chastity, as Mona, quickly turned her head as Azzhat strolled past, so she wouldn't be recognized. Odds were Azzhat wouldn't make the connection between Mona Lot and the Double-D Avenger, but still, Chastity didn't want to take any chances.

In the audience, Jaybird, Dong and Delight could not stop laughing.

"Isn't it extraordinary how Adrianna finally came around to loving her neighbors?!" chuckled Jaybird.

"It sure is Monty," remarked Dong with a big smile.

"So nice of her to drop her lawsuit against us too!" chimed in Delight.

On stage, Chastity's/Mona's big moment arrived! Brazilian samba music blasted from the loudspeakers, and out our hero danced in her gigantic fruit hat! She flamboyantly rocked back and forth, stepping forwards and backwards, swaying in time with the fun, bouncy Latin music! Her arms floated all over the place too, along with her shaking body. As she mamboed, she carefully balanced her head, so her eye-catching fruit hat wouldn't fall off!

After a few bars of music, Mona began to sing along with it, while she danced all over the stage. She smiled, showing off her pearly white teeth, and used a Spanish accent when she sang. Every few bars, she would also flash her eyes to the audience, as if someone had pinched her bare behind! *Boo!* Her big boobies seemed to love to samba too, because they kept bobbling around . . . up and down, back and forth, right and left . . . long with her!

"*Chick-chicky-boom! Chick-chick-a-boom! Chick-chicky-boom! Boom-boom-ba- boom!*"

The audience loved her instantly and their applause was deafening!

"*Chick-chicky-boom! Chick-chick-a-boom! Chick-chicky-boom! Boom-boom-ba- boom!*"

Monty turned to Dong with his eyebrows raised.

"I see why you find Mona so appealing!" Jaybird grinned. "She's a very talented young lady!"

"You think so?" smiled Dong.

"Yes, in more ways than one."

Delight overheard their exchange, and a jealous frown appeared on her pretty face.

Back on stage, Mona keep singing and dancing to the sensational samba music!

"*Chick-chicky-boom! Chick-chick-a-boom! Chick-chicky-boom! Boom-boom-ba-boom! Let's all do . . . the Brazilian chicky-chick-a-boom-boom! Chick-chicky-boom! Chick-chick-a-boom! Chick-chicky-boom! Boom-boom-ba-boom!*"

As her singing continued, Mona would quickly reach up and grab a piece of fruit from her hat, to 'show and tell' what she was singing about. The first piece of fruit was a banana.

"*Chick-chicky-boom!   Chick-chick-a-boom!   Chick-chicky-boom! Boom-boom-ba-boom! I made some shoes from my bananas using clippers, the peels looked so lovely as my new slippers! Chick-Chicky-boom!*"

Putting the banana back on top of her head, she then whipped off a coconut. She really was a marvelous singer, as she serenaded the audience in her make-believe Spanish voice.

"*I went to market and bought coconut shampoo . . . Chick-Chicky-boo . . . but later realized I didn't have a coconut to shampoo . . . boo-hoo-hoo!*"

Putting the coconut back on her fruit hat, she then whipped off some cherries.

"*Chick-chicky-boom!   Chick-chick-a-boom!   Chick-chicky-boom! Boom-boom-ba-boom! A man told his boy 'cherry trees smell, son!' Boom-boom-ba-boom! Cause George Washington, the old president, 'cut one!' Boom-boom-ba-boom!*"

Mona made a face and waved the air in front of her nose, as if she got a whiff of something unpleasant! Putting the cherries back on top of her head, she grabbed one of her bananas again, and used it as her next prop.

"*A sunbathing nudist named Miguelito, avoided sunburn by using a hat to cover his 'burrito!'*"

Mona held the banana down towards her crotch, with the banana's curve pointed upwards . . . as if it were a man's tube steak during a full erection!

"*Then a bitchy lady walked by saying 'if you had manners, you'd lift that hat!' Miguelito replied 'it would lift itself you weren't so ugly and fat!' Chick-Chicky-boom!*"

She instantly twisted the banana's curve so it pointed downwards . . . to simulate a man's one-eyed worm becoming flaccid!

The audience laughed, as Mona put the banana back on top of her fruit hat . . . then to everyone's surprise, the samba music's fast tempo abruptly slowed down! It morphed into a slow, jazzy, 'bump and grind' melody . . . like a piece of classical burlesque music! Mona's samba dancing reflected this change, as her movements slowed down too. She slinked around and would periodically snatch one of her wardrobe pieces off stage. In a flash, she'd then step back onto the stage and slowly *put the article of clothing on!*

First she grabbed her long gold skirt, and slowly and seductively put it on in front of the entire audience! The men in the crowd went nuts! *They were totally 'turned on' sexually!* Mona was doing a 'reverse strip tease,' and to guys at a nudist colony . . . used to staring at nude women all day long . . . this seductive 'putting on of clothing' to cover her private parts was actually an incredible 'turn on!'

Jaybird's jaw dropped! Dong's jaw dropped even lower!

"Oh yeah, baby!" cried Dong! *"Love it! Put it on! Put it on!"*

"Woo-hoo!" applauded Jaybird! *"Yes! Put it on! Put it on!"*

Candy Delight was even more jealous now!

Mayor Phishel and councilmen Phuckter and Bottoms were cheering at Mona's 'reverse striptease' too! Intern Rod Long was also in heat, and councilwoman Hoodwink certainly took notice.

"Rod darling, never mind that girl on stage," urged Hoodwink, while trying to block his view of the stage with her head. "Watch me *cover* myself with this towel instead!"

Hoodwink hopped up. She then pulled the towel she was sitting on, up and over her hood ornaments!

Nearby, the Sheriff and the Deputy were suddenly horny as hell too, thanks to Mona's sexy act!

"Yeah, baby!" shouted the excited Sheriff.

"Work it!" howled the randy Deputy.

A curious expression then appeared on the knuckleheaded Deputy's face.

"Hey Sheriff?"

"What?" he snapped back, while keeping his eyes glued to the stage.

"Don't you think that girl in the fruit hat looks a little like Chastity Knott?"

"That's crazy!" spat the Sheriff. "No woman could have tits as big Chastity's!"

"The Double-D Avenger does!"

"That girl in the fruit hat isn't Chastity, and she ain't the Double-D Avenger either! Now shut up! I'm trying to enjoy the strip show!"

"Right, sir! Sorry, sir! Guess you're right," muttered the Deputy. "Chastity isn't a nudist and neither is Double-D . . . at least I don't think they are," he sheepishly mumbled to himself.

Back on stage, Mona tormented her male audience even more by slowly putting on her necklaces and bangles, in perfect time with the bump and grind samba / stripper music! The men continued to whistle and howl, as Mona then slowly and teasingly put on her ruffled red blouse! This was a little tricky, because it was like trying to stuff twenty pounds of potatoes into a five pound sack!

Finally, our hero brought the house down when she grabbed her platform sandals from the wings and returned to slowly slip them on . . . one foot at a time! She wiggled her pretty toes as she did this, and got a standing ovation!

The samba music's tempo sped up again, back to its normal rhythmic beat, and Mona blasted out her last few chicky-boom-booms!

"Chick-chicky-boom! Boom-boom-ba-boom!"

On that note, she kissed her audience goodbye, and wiggled off stage! Mona brought the house down, and everyone in Toupee Canyon must have heard the audience's deafening applause blasting out of the Jaybird Growth Institute!

CHAPTER SEVENTEEN

Back in the crowd, Doctor Della-Kwak was still completely oblivious to what had just happened on stage! The wacky quack never looked once! She was too preoccupied examining the big muscles on her naked boy toys seated next to her!

"You studs remind me of an Arab bodybuilder I once dated," she told them. "He was a Protein Sheikh!"

The boy toys didn't get it.

Nearby, Jaybird turned to Dong.

"She's perfect," commented Jaybird. "She's got such talent."

"True! She's a terrific athlete too!" nodded Dong.

"So you told me," mumbled Jaybird, while carefully thinking to himself.

"She's won the contest?" Dong asked.

"Yes, and not only that," Jaybird grinned.

"What else?" wondered Dong.

"Yeah, what else?" curiously chimed in Delight, while putting her hands defiantly on her hips.

"I want her as part of our 'inner circle!'" he demanded. "She'd be ideal. The perfect candidate . . . looks, brains, athletic ability . . . she's single, lives alone . . . Mona Lot has everything I require!"

"Our inner circle?!" frowned Delight.

"Candy, you keep out of this! Remember who's 'Boss Nudie' around here!" snapped Jaybird.

"When?" inquired Dong.

"Tonight."

Ten minutes later, Jaybird appeared on stage, in the buff and holding a microphone. The crowd wildly applauded as he walked out to greet them.

"Ladies and gentlemen, I hope you all enjoyed this evening's nude entertainment," he enthusiastically stated in his British accent. "Based on all your applause, I trust you did! I'm now happy to announce the winner of our talent show. It was a tough decision with all the amazing acts that performed for us tonight, but the judges and I have finally come to the conclusion that Mona Lot and her Brazilian samba number is our winner! Mona, please come out!"

Mona was shocked she won, and she slowly stepped back onto the stage to more applause, still fully dressed and wearing her tall fruit hat.

"Congratulations my dear," Jaybird told her. "You were awesome tonight, and I'm proud to hand you this five-thousand dollar check!"

Our hero's eyes bugged out as she took it.

"Oh . . . why thank you Monty! Thanks everyone!"

She gave him a quick hug, but Monty couldn't stand the itchy feeling of clothing up against his nude body!

"Honey, I appreciate the hug," he whispered to her, holding his microphone away towards the floor, ". . . but I can't stand the itchy feeling of that ruffled blouse rubbing up against my bare chest! It makes my delicate, uncontaminated, 'devote nudist' skin crawl!"

"Oopsie!" she whispered in reply, totally embarrassed. She stopped hugging and took a few steps back. "Sorry Monty."

He nodded to her, while brushing his chest with his free hand. He then raised the microphone back to his lips and faced the audience again.

"Well, *ah . . . ah . . .* this concludes tonight's show. Folks, due to all the work the staff and I put into this very special event, we'll be closing the institute early this evening. We thank you all, from the bottom of our nudist hearts, for coming today, and you're all welcome back first thing tomorrow morning. We'll be open bright and early for another day of joyous, naked pleasure! Bye-bye! Take care!"

The crowd slowly got up and eventually made their way back to the changing cottages, in order to get dressed and exit the resort from the parking lot. As they were leaving, Dong joined Jaybird and Mona on stage.

"Mona, I'd like you to stay a little longer," Jaybird told her.

"You would?" she wondered.

"Yes, we're closed, so it'll only be you, me and the staff. We now have the entire resort to ourselves."

Dong chimed in.

"You wanted to try the indoor hydrotherapy pool, and Monty says it's repaired now," explained Dong. "The heater's working great, so are the jets and the water's nice and warm."

"That's right," nodded Jaybird.

That hydrotherapy bungalow had piqued Chastity's/Mona's interest the first time saw it, and now she'd have the chance to check it out for herself. This was an offer she couldn't refuse.

"Okay guys . . . that sounds really nice!" smiled Mona. "Just give me a minute to pack up my stuff and I'll pop over."

Ten minutes later, Mona, fully nude and holding a white towel, strolled into the redwood bungalow housing the hydrotherapy pool. It was strange for her to see the entire resort completely devoid of other nudists! The place seemed deserted . . . everyone was gone. The bungalow itself was close to both the administration office and the main pool.

Once inside, she instantly saw the huge indoor Jacuzzi . . . a rectangular pool big enough for at least fifty people! Nude Greek statues of handsome men and beautiful women, life-sized and created in white marble, decorated large room. Surrounding the pool were Greek columns, benches, running fountains and a stunning assortment of indoor tropical plants. The whole space was illuminated by recessed ceiling lights, but strangely, there were *no windows!*

Jaybird, Dong, and Delight were already in the pool, enjoying the bubbling, steaming water.

"Welcome to our asylum for the sane and elite, in the middle of an insane society," Jaybird proudly declared.

"Thank you," replied happy Mona.

"Come on in Mona," Dong told her. "The water's perfect!"

"I'm coming."

She tossed her towel on a bench, then slowly stepped in, holding onto one of the silver hand rails.

"Aaah!" she cooed. "The water's perfect! Oh, I love it! This hydrotherapy pool's lovely!"

"It most certainly is," smiled Jaybird.

"Take a seat behind one of the jets . . . it'll massage your whole back!" suggested Dong.

"Okay!"

She picked a spot next to the trio, and leaned back against one of the powerful underwater jets. Mona was in heaven!

"Oh, I really love this," she happily moaned. "It feels so good!"

"Mona, come over here for a sec . . . I want to show you something up on the ceiling," Jaybird coolly said, while floating near the center of the pool.

"Sure thing Monty," she replied.

She waded over to him in the waist-high water and then looked up.

"What's up there?"

"Watch the lights," he calculated.

Jaybird moved to the pool's edge and grabbed what looked like a TV remote control. He pressed a red button. *Click!*

Suddenly, hundreds of recessed ceiling lights turned on, and began flashing in every color of the rainbow! The entire room transformed into a colorful, psychedelic light show . . . which cast weird, twinkling globs of moving colors all over the place! Weird electronic music was also heard through hidden speakers. The bizarre tune was slow, soft and soothing.

"Oh, wow! Those disco lights are amazing . . . looks like the inside of a lava lamp . . . everywhere!" she chuckled.

Our hero then felt a bit woozy.

"Hey, I'm getting a little . . . a little dizzy . . . I . . ."

Jaybird caught Mona before she sunk into the water. His right arm had her shoulders, and his left lifted her legs. Holding her in his strong arms, he began rocking her like a little baby in the hot water. As he did this, she was still gazing up at the mesmerizing light show playing out across the ceiling. She couldn't stop looking.

"Don't worry Mona, I've got you! You're safe with me," reassured Jaybird in his English accent. His eyes were solely on her . . . he never looked up at the lights on the ceiling. "Just relax . . . look into your subconscious and discard any fears and doubts. Avoid emotional fog through clear, organized thinking."

Dong and Delight also had strange looks on their faces, as if the colorful psychedelic light exhibition was hypnotizing them too, along with Jaybird's soothing voice! Only Monty Jaybird seemed 'immune' to the mysterious lights and music.

As Mona gazed at the bizarre colors, worrying thoughts ran through her drowsy brain.

So this is how . . . how he does it! Those lights up there . . . those strange colors . . . it's some kind of light machine or strobe projector . . . and his words . . . they can hypnotize! That electronic music is also doing something . . . it's weird . . . creepy! I've got to fight this . . . but it's so hard . . . those enchanting lights . . . I can't stop looking . . . they're penetrating my brain . . . I feel like I'm gonna fall asleep . . .

Jaybird continued, rocking her in his arms and speaking softly.

"You are being relaxed into a deep meditative state, where I will reach into your unconscious mind and rewire your mind patterns. Breathe in time with the rhythm of the soft music. Feel your mind floating . . . disassociated from your body."

She panicked!

Oh no, I can't let him do this! I . . . I . . . can't! I feel like I'm falling . . . falling deeper and deeper into his trance! My wig might fall off in this water too . . . and if it does, my cover's blown. I've got to try and keep my head up! Oh, please stay on! Please stay on!

Our hero had a frozen look on her face.

"Your brain frequencies are being lowered, equalizing the left and right hemispheres, so my subliminal suggestions can be firmly planted into your unconscious mind," Jaybird softly said.

The skinny dipping Svengali continued.

"Mona, you will follow my every order from now on. You're going to be a devout Super Nudist, one of my elite, skilled warriors. We need you! You will faithfully support us in our mission of global nudity. Modern civilization is repressive and inhibitive. It admires the artificial and denigrates the natural, but as a Super Nudist, you shall rectify this, along with your fellow teammates."

Jaybird then began to slowly spin her around in the water. Mona remained focused on the flashing ceiling lights, like a pretty zombie, as she spun around and around.

"First our country will go one-hundred percent nudist, then eventually, the rest of the world will too. Every person on the planet will become a staunch nudnik! We've had great success here in Driftwood Valley! One by one, our leaders will all become devout nudists dedicated to public nudity. There will be nudists in every home, every shopping mall . . . and in apartments, condos . . . office buildings . . . supermarkets . . . banks . . . hospitals . . . parks . . . gas stations . . . . everyone in the country will be naked as Monty Jaybird twenty-four hours a day, seven days a week, month after month, year after year! Clothing will be a thing of the past! You, Mona, will help make this happen! Millionaires and factory workers will be 'stripped' of their exterior signs of social and economic status, and will interact on an equal level . . . all across the country . . . and then globally. This is the peaceful, harmonious, untroubled nudist world of the future . . . Monty Jaybird's undressed utopia . . . but first, we must change the minds of the public."

Our hero mentally scolded herself.

Chastity, snap out of it! Keep that head up, so your wig doesn't float off! You've got to think of something to block what Monty's saying . . . you've got to ignore his hypnotic words! He'll turn you into a Super Nudist, with no will of your own! Try to look away from those lights! The Crockozilla Fruit gave you super powers, and it must have boosted and strengthened your brain too! Use that powerful mind of yours!

She struggled to take control of her thoughts again.

I've got it, I'll think of something from the past . . . a trip down 'memory lane' . . . but what? Hmmm! I know, I'll think about how I became the Double-D Avenger, and my different, remarkable adventures! That's it! Think Chastity! Think! Remember! Remember everything . . . and don't look at those psychedelic colors!

She managed to close her eyes, and Monty thought this was simply a normal symptom of his hypnotism.

"You will follow my every order. As a Super Nudist, you'll lead a naturally hygienic life in the open and have a close fellowship with nature through direct contact with the sun, air, light, water, warmth, and cold. I will give you amazing super powers and speed! No one will be able to stop you! You'll have great mental satisfaction, physical fitness, and a feeling of freedom and oneness with your fellow Super Nudists . . . who all share this open communion with nature."

Chastity/Mona's trip down 'memory lane' began . . . she vividly remembered everything that happened in her past, as if it were yesterday. Monty's words slowly disappeared, the more she fought and concentrated.

Stupendous circumstances led to Chastity Knott becoming the Double-D Avenger – busty costumed crime-fighter. It all started when she had to see her doctor for a routine check-up and mammogram. Her then cowboy boyfriend Bubba couldn't believe they made x-ray equipment *that big*. At the doctor's office, Chastity was devastated when she was given a *terminal diagnosis!* She knew smoking ninety cigars a day would lead to trouble for her . . . and her 'twins' . . . and now it had.

Chastity's equally busty female physician, Dr. Della-Kwak, explained that modern medicine had no cure for her titty trouble. The scatterbrained quack then offered an unorthodox suggestion. Della-Kwak, who was also a blond and around the same age as Chastity back then, had heard that the outer peel of the legendary *Crockozilla Fruit* possessed miraculous healing powers. Not giving it a second thought, Chastity flew down to South America to find that magical plant. It was her *only* hope.

She temporarily closed the pub, and wound up parading through the jungles of South America in search of the plant. Unfortunately, her tequila drunken guide, Ronaldo, led her on a wild goose chase through the hot, humid jungle. Chastity was just about to give up, when a statuesque jungle woman stepped out of the bushes to greet them. Her name was Orbs, and she was the gorgeous, dark skinned leader of the famous Ta-Ta Tribe. Orbs wore a skimpy leopard skin bikini, and had the hottest, sexiest ass in all of South America. In fact, Ronaldo was so 'turned on' seeing her, he could barely contain himself. He thought Orbs was so bodacious, desirable, and luscious.

Chastity was surprised Orbs could speak English, so the sexy leader explained her tribe had American cable and Wi-Fi back at the village. Chastity then told Orbs she was in search of the legendary Crockozilla Fruit, confessing she needed its *healing powers,* or else she'd be a *double-d goner.* Orbs understood, and kindly showed her the way to the magical plants. Chastity was forever grateful, and trembled in anticipation.

Orbs, Chastity and Ronaldo trekked through the wilderness, encountering wild animals . . . many who paused what they were doing to check out the large boobs on both human females. As they passed an enchanting waterfall, the trio entered a jungle clearing with several strange looking plants. The plants resembled huge yellow *bananas* on long green stems. Below each banana were two green nuts or *'balls.'* To be honest, each plant resembled a horny male's private parts, *fully aroused and erect.* A strange looking, carved tiki statue stood nearby, guarding over the plants.

Orbs began doing a religious tribal dance, worshipping the Crockozilla Fruit. Chastity and Ronaldo were amazed, and when Orbs gyrated her sexy butt, Ronaldo nearly exploded in his pants. When the short, erotic ceremony was over, Orbs confirmed that the penis-looking plants were indeed the legendary Crockozilla Fruit.

"The outer peel is sucked on and licked," explained Orbs, repeating what Dr. Della-Kwak had previously told Chastity. The Ta-Ta leader then proceeded to demonstrate.

Getting down on her knees, the beautiful black woman gently held a plant's two balls, and then opened her mouth wide enough to *suck on* the nine-inch long banana. She made a lustful *"Mmm"* sound, as she sucked it with her warm, wet, hungry tongue.

Ronaldo's eyes bugged out, as Orbs 'went down' on the banana. *"Aye, caramba!"* he cried, as he tossed his empty tequila bottle into the air.

Orbs paused momentarily, motioning Chastity to join in. "Try this one," she suggested, pointing to another Crockozilla Fruit plant.

Chastity gently touched the stem and two nuts of the different plant. She then began giving the banana *'head'* too. She sucked and sucked and sucked, then stopped for a second. She turned to Orbs, wide eyed.

"Mmm, delicious! My mouth is all tingly," gasped Chastity.

Orbs, deep throating the shaft of her banana, pulled her head off to reply. "Yes, and the *nuts* are lickable too." The leader held her banana and tickled its two green nuts. Her tongue flickered and 'painted' each *ball* with warm saliva.

Seeing what Orbs was doing, Chastity repeated the same naughty thing on her Crockozilla plant. She leaned down and licked the two green nuts like a hungry animal.

From the look on his delirious face, horny-as-hell Ronaldo finally *did* explode in the front of his pants!

Orbs pulled her mouth off her banana's long shaft, and faced Chastity again. "The Crockozilla Fruit gives me my *super-powers.*"

Chastity lifted her bobbing head off her own banana.

"Super-powers? The nutrients and vitamins that potent?" she asked.

"I shall demonstrate."

Orbs moved to a huge boulder, and effortlessly picked it up, lifting it high into the air! She held the giant rock, which was about half her size, proudly over her head. Chastity was so amazed seeing the display of super-human strength, she was speechless for a few seconds.

"That must weigh *tons* . . . I see what you mean Orbs . . . " she muttered.

Suddenly, the jungle around Chastity began to spin. She was getting dizzy and everything was going black! The Crockozilla Fruit's miracle healing was starting to get to work on Chastity's sick body. She let out a sigh, and her eyes began to close.

"Aaaahhh . . ."

Chastity collapsed to the ground, and Orbs and Ronaldo instantly dashed to her aid. The drunken Mexican grabbed one of Chastity's ballooning balloons and tried to shake her back to consciousness.

"Miss Chastity! Miss Chastity! Wake up!" he exclaimed. She didn't respond. Only her big boobs shook.

"She will be all right," Orbs reassured him. "Healing is taking place in her body, and she will awaken in a few hours. She can then return to her home in America."

Ronaldo let out a sigh of relief, and rested his drunken head on Chastity's rotund globularity.

When she returned home, Chastity felt like a million bucks! However, she soon began to notice *strange side effects.* All of a sudden, she had *super-human strength* just like Orbs, but had difficulty controlling it. For example, she accidentally crushed a telephone in one hand, and bent a metal spoon with a couple of her fingers.

When she had her follow-up appointment with Dr. Della-Kwak, the physician confirmed Chastity was *miraculously cured* of her terminal illness. The wacky doctor didn't know what else to say . . . it was a *medical miracle!*

CHAPTER EIGHTEEN

Chastity, as Mona Lot, continued to fight Monty Jaybird's brainwashing, by recalling amazing events from her recent past!

As remarkable as the Crockozilla Fruit expedition was, Chastity's transformation into her alter-ego, *the Double-D Avenger* - busty costumed crime-fighter - was even more amazing. It all started when villainous bikini bar owner Al Purplewood of Al Purplewood's Gentleman's Club, was losing a ton of money to Chastity's pub. All the men in town were hanging out there, instead of in Al's bikini bar.

Purplewood was in his mid-fifties, he was overweight, and spoke with a New York accent. He realized 'drastic measures' had to be taken, or else he and his club were finished. Therefore, the crazy club owner ordered his three murderous strippers to *kill* Chastity!

Ooga Boobies was a blond bimbo with a *cave woman* themed costume. She had a hot body and big protuberant melons. Being a 'method stripper,' she'd only say *'Ooga-Boobies'* when communicating in costume.

Pirate Juggs was an Italian sex pot, with two extra-large, pizza-sized breasts. She had a curvaceous, voluptuous figure, and wore a sexy *pirate* costume and hat. She also held a pirate telescope, which she used to get close-up views of the front of men's crotches.

Hydra Heffer was slightly older than Ooga Boobies and Pirate Juggs. She was an exotic stripper, in a purple *gypsy dancer* costume that was light and airy. Her pretty face had glitter, which sparkled as she hissed. She also wore a special belly button gem, which lit up and flashed to hypnotize male customers. Once hypnotized, Hydra would steal their wallets, turning her private dances into *robberies.*

A mad scientist gave Al Purplewood special hand-held weapons in exchange for free lap dances with his strippers, so Al had the girls use the guns to shoot Chastity. When the strippers ambushed her in the pub's back parking lot one night, Hydra Heffer, Ooga Boobies and Pirate Juggs goofed. They accidentally shot and *killed* Chastity's cowboy boyfriend Bubba instead!

Devastated by the loss of Bubba, and furious the Driftwood Valley Sheriff was blowing the murder investigation, Chastity decided to take matters into her own hands. She'd use her new super-powers she got from the Crockozilla Fruit, but had to hide her true double-d identity. She then had a brainstorm . . . she'd become *the Double-D Avenger!*

Having taken sewing in junior high school, Chastity sewed her own superhero costume and bra mask. It was a blue leotard with red gloves, red boots, and a red cape. Her brassiere mask was also red, with 'eye slits' cut out of the lacy material where two nipples would have rested. Completing her costume was a red stretchable belt with two capital letter 'D's' on the round buckle. The big letter 'D's' had white trim around each letter, making her superhero initials truly stand out.

As the Double-D Avenger, Chastity vowed to give the villains a little *'Tit for Tat!'* She courageously hunted down . . . and fought . . . Al Purplewood and his evil strippers Ooga Boobies, Pirate Juggs and Hydra Heffer. There was dynamic action, spectacular battles of gigantic proportions, mile-a-minute car chases, and hair-raising escapes! Even Chastity was amazed by her new super powers. She discovered she could leap tall buildings in a single *'Booby-Bounce,'* and her giant breasts were indestructible! Nothing could harm them, including bullets and swords.

Only Chastity's cousin Billy knew her true identity. He ran the pub while she was out fighting Al Purplewood and his girls. Dr. Della-Kwak had known about Chastity's miraculous recovery and super strength, but she had no idea Chastity was the Double-D Avenger.

Chastity's only weakness, she strangely discovered, was *lemonade.* This happened when she used a clever British Beefeater disguise to flush out the villains, who were hiding from the law. In the Beefeater costume and hat, she resembled a soldier who guarded the Tower of London's crown jewels. Chastity used a terrible British accent to *trick*

Al and his strippers into showing themselves at the gentleman's club. When she transformed into the Double-D Avenger, and fought Ooga Boobies and Hydra Heffer, Al threw a booby mug filled with lemonade at her. This occurred after the Double-D Avenger finished an unusual sword fight. She and Hydra Heffer dueled using with two long, *buzzing vibrators. Zzzzzzzzzz-zzzzzzzzz-zzzzzzzzz!*

The lemonade's acid made Chastity weak, and she collapsed to the floor, powerless! Lemon juice curdles milk, and when it entered the pores of her face, it also curdled her super blood. She had a *toxic allergic reaction!*

Thinking she was done for, Al and his girls escaped . . . but luckily Chastity, a.k.a. the Double-D Avenger, had enough strength left to crawl over Al's bar and grab a carton of *milk.* Al had used milk to fix White Russian cocktails for some of his customers. After chugging down a few cups, the milk *neutralized* the lemonade's acid, and the Double-D Avenger was good as new again.

When Double-D chased Al and his girls in their topless jeep, 'the Booby-Buggy,' she discovered another one of her many super-powers. Getting down on her hands and feet, she began doing push-ups in the middle of the street. Her super boobies *smashed against* the street's asphalt each time she pumped up and down. This 'jack-hammering with breasts' caused a *'Booby-Quake!'*

Ba-Boing! Ba-Boing! Ba-Boing! Ba-Boing!

The busty crime-fighter created a *powerful earthquake* that spread over a few blocks, forcing the Booby-Buggy to crash.

Double-D then got back up on her feet, and chased the bad guys into the foothills of Driftwood Valley. She finally clobbered the fleeing strippers, and trapped Al Purplewood in her *'Booby-Trap.'* She did this by pushing Al's head between her two giant knockers and furiously jiggling them sideways, knocking the crook out cold! Al and his girls would spend many years behind bars, and the Sheriff thanked the

Double-D Avenger for her fine work. As the lawman shook her hand, he couldn't help but notice her delightful cleavage shaking along.

Chastity missed her moronic boyfriend Bubba, but at least she managed to give the villains *'Tit for Tat!'* She confessed to Billy that the next time there was trouble in town, the Double-D Avenger would give those new villains *'Tit for Tat'* too. That 'next time' would come sooner than she expected.

Months later, when werewolves appeared all over Driftwood Valley and attacked beautiful women, the Double-D Avenger was the only one who could stop them! Our superhero with super-breasts uncovered a diabolical extortion plot hatched by a 1970's style street pimp named King Hoochi. Why did guys transform into lustful wolf-men after making whoopee with Hoochi's prostitutes? Did the werewolf antidote the cunning pimp offered actually work? Double-D had a hell of a time solving the riddles, stopping the monsters, and bringing Hoochi and his Hoes to justice (read *The Double-D Avenger Meets the Horny Howlers*).

Our hero also recalled another unbelievable case she had to solve as the Double-D Avenger! Adult movie sites mysteriously shut down in Driftwood Valley! Triple-X video stores were then zapped to brick-and-mortar bits! From out of nowhere, a new X-rated movie house, the Tuchus Theater, opened to the public and raked in millions of dollars! Was it all a coincidence? Chastity, a.k.a. the Double-D Avenger, didn't think so! She investigated and was nearly crushed by the claws of a sinister, sabotaging robot! Our hero had to solve the dirty movie house mystery and stop the crooks responsible for the ingenious scheme (read *The Double-D Avenger and the Dirty Movie House Mystery*).

The Crockozilla Fruit's most amazing side effect was it turned Chastity Knott into a *young, twenty-five year old girl again!* After the ordeal with Al Purplewood and his murderous strippers, Billy noticed changes in Chastity's gorgeous face and body. He was truly shocked by what he was seeing! All he could think of was *how different* his cousin looked.

Chastity agreed, telling him, "I figure it must be a side effect of the Crockozilla Fruit I originally sucked. Besides giving me superhuman powers and strength, the Crockozilla Fruit's vitamins, minerals and magical nutrients must have acted like a *'youth elixir.'* That banana shaped miracle plant was a *'Fountain of Youth.'*"

Billy nodded, saying, "Right! When I first came to work for you, you were fifty-three years old. I'm now thirty-five, and you look *younger* than *me*. I'd say you look like you're twenty-five years old. It's a *miracle* . . . an absolute miracle!" He was completely flabbergasted.

Chastity concurred and was convinced that just like her super-powers, she'd retain her youthful looks for a long, long time to come.

Suddenly, our hero's mind *snapped back to the present* . . . back to Monty Jaybird holding her in the hydrotherapy pool's hot water! He was finishing his mesmerizing instructions.

" . . . again, you will faithfully follow your leader Monty Jaybird's every command. You may open your eyes now."

Chastity/Mona opened her eyes, and nodded to him in agreement, pretending to be successfully hypnotized.

I did it, she thought to herself. *I beat his brainwashing! My wig's still on too . . . thank God!*

Jaybird smiled, and reached over to the edge of the pool. He snatched the remote for the hypnotic lights, pushed the red button, and the colorful psychedelic show was over. The weird electronic music stopped too. Only a dozen white lights remained on to illuminate the room.

Dong and Delight snapped out of their trances too.

"Come everyone, it's time to introduce our newest Super Nudist to the team!"

"Right, sir!" replied Dong.

"Please lead the way Monty," mumbled Mona, still pretending.

The group stepped out of the giant Jacuzzi and quickly dried off using their towels. Jaybird then walked up to a Greek statue of a large breasted woman. He twisted the nipple on the statue's left breast . . . it was actually *a knob* . . . and a back wall automatically rotated open! The entire wall was sitting on a turntable base or revolving platform, similar to a record player.

Mona was stunned.

"Step this way," ordered Jaybird.

The four of them walked through the open passageway, and a second later, the false wall rotated back into position, closing behind them. The hydrotherapy pool room was now empty.

Inside, our awestruck hero found herself in the Super Nudists *secret hideout!* The room was brightly lit and huge! It looked like a cross between a mad scientist's laboratory, a karate studio, and a gym locker. Everything seemed ultramodern, clean and neat, and like the hydrotherapy pool room, there were no windows.

Mona looked around and noticed a strange *lotion* being made on a table's chemistry set. Glass beakers and flasks held the weird substance.

Bunk beds resembling those in army barracks, lined one wall. The other side of the room had floor mats, wall mirrors, and free standing punching bags for martial arts training. There were also bodybuilding weights displayed on racks, and a whole assortment of handheld weapons and bombs stored in sizable cubby holes.

Next to the weapons display was a clothes rack with the Super Nudists minimal wardrobe . . . the light-green and yellow colored helmets with black goggles, gloves, boots, utility belts, capes and metallic green *fig leaf* jockstraps and Jillstraps.

A few tables had chairs, phones and desktop computers on them, along with large maps of Driftwood Valley.

Mona noticed a back door, which was the second exit out of the secret headquarters. However, this rear portal didn't have any doorknob or handle.

Jaybird moved to his desk and pushed an intercom button.

"Attention team, assemble immediately!" he commanded into a small microphone.

In a flash, the eight remaining Super Nudists all walked in through the sliding back door. Mona saw, once again, that these nudists were clearly specimens of physical perfection . . . the men were handsome, tanned and muscular, and the women were spectacularly gorgeous, with marvelous bodies featuring perky, oversized breasts! They instantly put on their minimal costumes, and Dong and Delight joined them.

Our hero tried to hide her excitement as she thought to herself!

I did it! I hit the jackpot! There they are, this is their hideout! I knew my detective work would finally pay off! Oh, I better calm down, I've got to pretend that I'm still hypnotized!

She was heartbroken watching Oscar Dong put on his Super Nudist outfit, but couldn't show her sad emotions openly, as more thoughts raced through her mind.

. . . Oh Oscar, why? Why did you have to be a Super Nudist? I was hoping I was mistaken. I guess you have no real control over your actions or thoughts . . . . it's all Monty's doing.

Moments later, the Super Nudists were dressed in their minimal attire that exposed most of their bodies, including their bare asses and tits. The black goggles on their helmets were not lowered, and this fully revealed everyone's true face and eyes.

"Mona, allow me to introduce you to your fellow Super Nudists," explained the enthusiastic Jaybird. He pointed to each one of them as he said their Super Nudist name, and then their real name. He began with the stunningly attractive women first.

"Super Nudist Lemon, also known as Topsey Cyn . . . our office manager and bookkeeper."

Lemon nodded her 'hello,' and Mona nodded back.

"Super Nudist Guava, a.k.a. Candy Delight. You've met her already. Candy's our new membership and hospitality director."

"Yes," nodded Mona.

She did not nod back, and Mona realized Delight was jealous of her.

"Super Nudist Papaya, a.k.a. Rosey Bare . . . our activities/program director," continued Jaybird.

"Hi," smiled beautiful, black Papaya.

"Nice to meet you," replied Mona.

"Super Nudist Coconut, a.k.a. Babette Doll . . . our smoothie and juice bartender."

"Hi."

"Hello."

"Super Nudist Kiwi, a.k.a. Muffy Bell . . . marketing and advertising director. She also runs our nudist library."

Korean Kiwi and Mona nodded to one another.

"Now for our male Super Nudists," said Jaybird. "You've already met Banana, a.k.a. Oscar Dong, my assistant manager and captain of the team."

"Surprised Mona?" asked Dong.

"Yes," she half smiled back.

"This is Pecan," cut in Jaybird. " . . . a.k.a. Willy Piston . . . executive chef."

"Hi Pecan."

"Nice to see you Mona," Pecan grinned.

"Super Nudist Walnut, a.k.a. Dick Sharp, our in-house attorney. He also takes care of our horses. You wouldn't believe how much work *piles up* in that barn."

"Hi Walnut."

"Delighted to meet you."

"Super Nudist Peanut, a.k.a. Hans Allover . . . gardening and housekeeping."

"Howdy, Mona."

"Howdy."

" . . . and Super Nudist Macadamia, a.k.a. Taquito Tongueman . . . pool, hot tub, and miniature golf course maintenance."

Mona and Hispanic Macadamia nodded to each other.

"Hola," said the hunky 'Latin Lover,' as he gently kissed her hand.

"Hola," she replied back, blushing.

Mona relished Macadamia/Tongueman's South American charm and good looks! Oscar Dong noticed their pleasant exchange, and he wasn't too happy about it.

Jaybird strolled over to the costume rack and removed Mona's Super Nudist attire; her light-green and yellow colored gloves, boots, utility belt, cape and metallic green *fig leaf* Jillstrap.

"Mona, this will be your Super Nudist uniform," he explained.

"Thanks, Monty."

He handed it to her, and then grabbed her light-green and yellow colored helmet with black goggles. On the helmet's front forehead area was an illustration of two big watermelons.

"You'll notice the symbol of two watermelons on the front. You'll be known as Super Nudist Watermelons."

"Watermelons, huh? Has a nice ring to it," she fibbed.

Our hero examined the little chains hanging from her metallic green Jillstrap.

"What are these?" she asked.

"Every Super Nudist wears a fig leaf jockstrap or Jillstrap to protect their 'private parts' during battle. You attach those chains to your utility belt."

"Battle?"

"Yes, self-defense is vital in a world hostile to public nudity."

"I see."

Jaybird then moved to the chemistry set table.

"Now over here is where I make our Super Sunscreen lotion," exclaimed Jaybird with widened eyes. "I order you to put some on each and every day. Apply a liberal amount! It's a special formula I developed years back."

He held up a glass flask that contained what looked like normal, cream-colored, body lotion.

"It was originally an anti-skin cancer treatment, addressing the problem from the inside too . . . not like typical sunscreen ointments and creams which only affect the upper layers of the skin. This stuff will actually penetrate into your bloodstream! Years ago, when I added certain vegetables from South America to my formula . . . vegetables I discovered near the famous Ta-Ta Tribe's territory . . . something miraculous happened! The lotion gave anyone who used it super-human powers and strength!"

"It did?" exclaimed Mona/Watermelons. "Super human powers and strength?"

"Yes, but these powers are only temporary. As I said, the sunscreen must be applied *daily* in order for you to reap the full super benefits, otherwise it wears off."

"I see," she muttered.

Our hero's mind raced again.

I wonder if those certain vegetables could be related to the Crockozilla Fruit? But the Crockzilla Fruit's vitamins, minerals, and nutrients gave me permanent *super powers and abilities. This stuff's only temporary.*

Jaybird interrupted her train of thought.

"Let's put some on now," he suggested, as he uncorked the flask.

"Now?"

"Yes, now."

CHAPTER NINETEEN

Monty Jaybird tilted the flask and poured some of the sunscreen lotion out onto his open palm. He quickly rubbed and spread the magical cream all over Mona's delectable nude body . . . her back, arms, shoulders, and legs. He then spent a little more time carefully polishing her gorgeous, bubbly butt and enormous booby balloons. When he was done, our hero's sparkling nude body was erotically wet and shiny! Every male Super Nudist watching the sexy show was quickly aroused! The men's metallic green fig leaves all rose up in the air on their little chains, as if they were *saluting* her!

Mona/Watermelons did a bug-eyed double-take, noticing the boys levitating fig leaves! A few seconds later, she began blinking.

"My skin's all tingly . . . I feel funny," she stuttered, as a strange, invigorating feeling spread throughout her body.

"That's my magic formula going right to work!" Jaybird proudly boasted, as he recorked the flask. "You'll soon have super human powers, speed, and strength!"

"Bless my over-the-shoulder boulder holder!"

She then thought for a second.

"Do you use it too?"

"Of course I do, I lather it on every day, religiously!" he exclaimed. "Now go ahead and try on your Super Nudist costume."

"Yes, sir," she obediently said.

She quickly put on her minimal attire, but had a little trouble hooking the fig leaf Jillstrap chain onto her utility belt. Mona was also careful slipping the helmet over her wig. When she finally got it, she looked sensational. Like the rest of the team, she didn't lower her helmet's black goggles, but kept them up, so her eyes and face could be fully seen.

Our hero, now a sexy, topless and bottomless Super Nudist, modelled for Jaybird. She sauntered forward in her boots, waving her short light-green and yellow cape . . . like a runway model.

"That uniform's just dandy," eagerly cried Jaybird, looking her over from head to toe. "Mona, you're now remade as one of my Super Nudists! You'll have a new Super Nudist body, with vibrant health, physical fitness, and a new outlook on life!"

"It's really working . . . I can feel it," she gasped.

"You feel a different already? More alive? Free as a Jaybird? Of course you do!" he exuberantly cheered. "This is the new 'nude you!' Watermelons, I'm going to show you how much fun and how easy it is to be a Super Nudist!"

"Thanks Monty," smiled the helmeted Mona/Watermelons. "Thank you from the bottom of my Super Nudist heart."

"Don't mention it. By the way, your new Super Nudist abilities will give you sexual virility too!"

"Bless my boobies!" she replied with a red face. "Say Monty, where's your uniform?"

"Right there on the rack," he pointed.

Hanging on the end of the clothes rack was Jaybird's own Super Nudist Leader outfit. It was just like the other male Super Nudists minimal attire. On the shelf above it was his light-green and yellow colored helmet. It had the ornamental identification symbol of a gold *fig leaf* painted on the front . . . just above the black goggles.

"Your helmet has a gold fig leaf on it?" asked Mona/Watermelons.

"Yes, since I'm 'Boss Nudie' around here," he boasted.

Jaybird turned to the rest of the team.

"Team, let's show Watermelons how we train."

"Yes, sir!" they simultaneously declared.

Banana, Pecan, and Lemon lowered their black goggles, and then began practicing their martial arts skills in the 'karate studio' section of the hideout. They quickly punched, chopped, kicked, and flipped each other on the padded floor mats!

"*Hi-Yah!*"

"*Ho!*"

"*See-Yah!*"

"What type of martial arts are they doing?" asked Mona/Watermelons.

"Nude-jitsu, a nudist version of Jiu-jitsu!" explained Jaybird. "In ancient Greece, the athletes all worked out and competed in their birthday suits!"

"They did?"

"Why of course . . . they were all naked . . . disrobed most of the time! Our objective, remember, is to bring back the superb, ancient civilization of the Greeks to today's modern world! The Greeks held the naked body in the highest esteem! They did everything au naturel, imitating their undressed gods!"

As this was going on, Guava, Papaya and Peanut quickly exited out the sliding rear door. Mona/Watermelons caught a quick glimpse of them leaving.

Meanwhile, Macadamia, Kiwi and Coconut, cartwheeled to a corner and stood on their helmeted heads!

"What are Macadamia, Kiwi and Coconut doing?"

"Just what it looks like . . . standing on their heads," replied Jaybird. "Their blood, infused with the Super Sunscreen, is rushing to their brains. It's flushing away the cobwebs, making them intellectually superior, and giving them each a spectacular beauty treatment to their hair and eyes."

Jaybird turned to her.

"Try it."

"Okay."

Our hero waltzed over to the corner of the mat to join Macadamia, Kiwi and Coconut, but the second she tried standing on her head, she fell over! *Ba-Boing!*

"It's a little tricky with this helmet on," she nervously grinned.

After a few tries, she finally got it, and successfully stood on her head. The only problem was she couldn't see a thing . . . not because she lowered her helmet's black goggles . . . but because her monumental honkers were now covering her face and eyes! *Blooop! Blooop!*

"*Errgh! Mmm! Aaarghh!*" she gasped.

Mona/Watermelons *couldn't breathe* . . . she was being suffocated by her colossal boobies! Thinking fast, she rolled out of the headstand, and bounced back onto her feet.

Ba-boing-oing-oing!

"I seem to be a little too top-heavy."

"Don't worry, with practice you'll get the hang of it. I'll mold you like a clay doll into a Super Nudist of physical perfection . . . just like I did with the others!"

"I see," she nodded. "Monty, where did Guava, Papaya and Peanut go?"

"To the running track! Come over here and I'll show you," smiled Jaybird.

He moved to a wall's security monitor and turned it on. A live video stream suddenly appeared on the screen. It was a wide shot of the nudist resort's track.

"Watch them."

Mona/Watermelons moved closer to the screen. She could see the three goggled Super Nudists Guava, Papaya and Peanut, streaking around the track . . . at over fifty miles per hour! Their shiny helmets reflected the track's outdoor lighting, as their light-green and yellow colored capes waved vigorously behind them! *Za-Zooom!*

"Oh my gosh . . . I've heard of streaking, but that's ridiculous! It's like watching a video in fast-forward!"

"They're reaching speeds of close to sixty miles per hour! You'll be able to do that too, after you've had enough Super Sunscreen treatments."

"I will?"

"Of course."

Jaybird switched the screen off, and then walked over to his desk's intercom. He pushed a button and spoke into the microphone again.

"Attention team, return immediately."

Moments later, all the Super Nudists reassembled, including Mona as Watermelons. They raised their helmets black goggles, so all faces could be seen, and stood at military attention in front of nude Jaybird.

"Now, let's have a rundown on our upcoming schedule," Jaybird told them, as he paced back and forth. "Next week, the Driftwood Valley Wax Museum will be unveiling their nude figure of me, your glorious undressed leader, Monty Jaybird, to the public."

"Congratulations, sir," nodded Banana.

"Will your wax dummy be anatomically correct?" asked Guava.

"Yes, Romeo, the museum's caretaker, has assured me it will be . . . and don't call it a dummy. It's a life-like, life-sized *facsimile.*"

"Sorry, sir," muttered Guava.

"Is this unveiling part of the 'Monty Jaybird Day' the city council has announced?" wondered Coconut.

"Yes, it is. Wasn't that thoughtful of them?"

"It sure was!"

Mona, as Watermelons, was surprised to hear this news, but kept her mouth shut.

"Awesome sir!" chimed in happy Walnut.

"Yeah," added delighted Kiwi. "Just imagine . . . an official 'Monty Jaybird Day' . . . in Driftwood Valley!"

Jaybird continued pacing back and forth.

"Thank you. We'll run a front page story all about it, in our nudist newspaper *The Bare Behind Bugle*. However, there's something bigger and much more important to do before then."

"What's that?" asked Macadamia.

"We will be infiltrating tomorrow's parade."

"The annual Driftwood Valley Founder's Day Parade?" questioned our hero.

"Yes."

"Tomorrow?!" sputtered Guava.

"But why?" added Banana.

"To kidnap the state Governor and gently *persuade him* into becoming a devout nudist," revealed Jaybird with a sinister smile.

Mona, as Watermelons, went bug-eyed again!

"The state Governor?" spat Peanut. "Governor Sudsey Nightcap?"

"That senile, old drunk?" grinned Papaya.

"Yes, Governor Sudsey Nightcap, the senile, old drunk! With Governor Nightcap on our side, the *entire state* will go nudist!"

Jaybird spun around.

"Everyone take a look at this," he ordered, while pointing to a map laid out on a table. It covered the entire Driftwood Valley parade route.

The Super Nudists crowded around him.

"I've already entered our vintage van as one of the classic vehicles participating in the parade. The Governor's convertible car will be right behind us. As we approach the end of the parade route, all Super Nudists, except Watermelons, will jump out and nab the Governor. You'll then race back to the hideout with him. I'll drive the van back to the institute, using our secret back road. We have nothing to worry about, since the law is on our side now. In fact, our friendly Sheriff and Deputy will be spending the whole day here at the institute tomorrow . . . *not* at the parade. *Ha, ha, ha, ha, ha!*"

The Super Nudists, except Mona/Watermelons, joined in Jaybird's laughter.

"Ha, ha, ha, ha, ha, ha, ha, ha, ha!"

"Hey, what happens if that busty, costumed crime-fighter shows up . . . the Double-D Avenger?" asked Lemon. "She really clobbered us last time we were downtown!"

Our hero was shocked to hear the name of her alter-ego, and struggled not to react.

"Lemon's right," chimed in Peanut. "The Double-D Avenger is just as strong as we are, and she's got indestructible tits!"

"You can say that again," added Kiwi. "My butt's still bruised from when she blew us into that tiki bar's outdoor fountain!"

"If the Double-D Avenger sticks her super sweater-stretchers into our business again, just let her have it," barked Jaybird. " . . . only this time, no stark-naked snafus! To make sure, I want all of you to use your Super Streaker roller skates."

"Yes, sir," nodded the Super Nudists simultaneously.

"Super-Streaker roller skates?" asked puzzled Mona.

"Yes, the roller skates will give each Super Nudist increased speed as they streak off with the Governor. The Double-D Avenger will never catch'em!"

"I see," she nodded. " . . . and I won't be joining them?"

"No, Watermelons," replied Jaybird, putting a hand on her shoulder. "You still need Super Nudist training, and besides, someone must stay here to monitor the institute when it opens tomorrow. You're it. We'll only be gone a few hours, and once our doors are open, the resort can basically run itself, except for the café, the smoothie bar and library."

"Okay," said Mona/Watermelons. "Will I be sleeping here tonight?"

"Of course," stated Jaybird. "Eventually, you'll live here along with the rest of the Super Nudists. In fact, there's your bunk bed, right over there."

He pointed to top bed, and she glance over.

"Like it?"

"Yes, sir," she nodded, faking her approval.

Jaybird looked at the clock on the wall.

"It's getting late. Time for some late night 'recreational activity,' and then it's nudist night-night."

"Right sir," said Banana.

The Super Nudists removed their minimal uniforms and hung them back up on the clothes racks. Their goggled helmets were put away too. The hideout wall in front of them rotated, revealing the open passageway to the hydrotherapy pool room, and everyone exited . . . fully nude.

Naked Mona and Dong slowly walked out together.

"What type of late night 'recreational activity' is Monty talking about?" asked Mona.

"You'll see" said smiling Dong.

A worried look flashed over her face!

Our couple exited the redwood bungalow housing the hydrotherapy pool, and they pleasantly strolled along, hand-in-hand, onto the main lawn and pool area. It was a beautiful, warm night and the full moon illuminated the grounds. Crickets chirped, as the flames of a dozen tiki torches danced around, helping to light up the main patio. The pool itself was lit by underwater lights.

Mona and Dong stopped suddenly. Chastity, as Mona, couldn't believe what she was seeing . . . the Super Nudists and Jaybird were already 'hooking up' and going at it! They were fast! A *nighttime orgy* was taking place at the closed nudist resort, with everyone tongue wrestling, getting lucky, fornicating, and making whoopee! Couples were nuzzling, squirming, sucking, stroking, kneading, pulling, jerking, lustfully thrusting, bouncing, gyrating, grinding and co-climaxing! Cries of ecstasy and plenty of passionate moans and groans filled the air!

"Holy Hooters!" declared Mona. "I didn't think . . . "

"Mona, we're not a bunch of sun-worshipping eunuchs!" laughed Dong. "There's nothing wrong with this kind of recreational activity . . . the human body has certain biological needs and wants. We must fulfill those needs and wants! Back in the day, it was the Puritan ethic and Victorianism which interpreted the human body as impure and sinful. Body guilt and shame became the 'law of the land' when the Mayflower arrived."

"Is that so . . . ?" pondered our shocked hero.

"It sure is! Do you remember what Monty told you yesterday . . . about our Jaybird Growth Institute's Credo?"

"Yes."

"It states . . . there is an essential wholesomeness in the human body and all of its functions . . . and that man and his sexuality are part and parcel of our living, and no separation or division is possible without denying what man is and what he was created for."

Mona was all confused, as she stared out at the wild orgy.

CHAPTER TWENTY

Taquito Tongueman, a.k.a. Macademia, was burying his head in the crotch of Topsey Cyn, a.k.a. Lemon. They were getting frisky on the main pool's lower diving board! She was lying on her back, with her arms over her head. Her knees were bent, with her legs spread wide open. Tongueman tongued her beaver, shaking his face into the whole thing, while sucking and wildly licking all over the place! *Lick! Lick! Lick!* He used his fingers too!

"*Mmmm . . . oooohh! Oooooh! Eegh! Eeh! Mmmm . . . oooh,*" she cried, while breathing heavily and gasping for breath.

Tongueman/Macademia lifted his face out of Cyn/Lemon's deliciousness, in order to tell her something.

"I was gonna tell you a dick joke, but it's too long!"

She started to giggle.

"I love it when you tell jokes Taquito . . . you're such a cunning linguist!"

"You mean cunnilingus!"

"That too!"

When he dug his fingers, palms up, deep into her flower and hitting her G-spot, she shouted in ecstasy!

"*Yes! Yes! Yes! You nailed it! Aaaahh!*"

The diving board they were on started bouncing up and down, as Cyn/Lemon shook and climaxed!

Giving her a quick break, Tongueman/Macademia then licked her creamy thighs, as her enormous chi-chis trembled.

Hans Allover, a.k.a. Peanut, was getting his vagee-gee miner sucked by Rosey Bare, a.k.a. Papaya. They were having a romp on a gigantic inflatable raft, floating around in the pool! Her head nodded up and down on his rod, and he loved every second of it, throwing his face back in total pleasure. Up and down she bobbed, like she was bobbing for apples to win a prize or something!

Mmmm! Mmmm! Mmmm!

The ebony cutie stopped momentarily.

"Vegans like me give better head," she said.

"Really?" he replied.

"Yeah, cause we're used to eating nuts!"

Allover/Peanut rolled his eyes! He then pulled his hot rod out of her mouth and climbed on top of her! The big raft rocked back and forth in the pool as he did this, and both of them got their arms and feet splashed a little! He then rubbed the head of his long carrot against her Bermuda Triangle.

"*Ooo . . . yes!*" she cooed.

"I'm not a weatherman, but you can expect a few more inches tonight!" he grinned.

Before she could moan a second time, he shoved it all the way in and began humping away! *Za-zoom!* He boned her royally, as his tight buns flashed and pounded her faster and faster! *Ka-boom! Boom! Boom! Boom! Boom! Bang!*

"*Oooooo . . . . oooo . . . . ooo!*"

He nuzzled her neck while facing her, and then started kissing and licking. She was in heaven! Sweat appeared on his forehead, and a grimace flashed over his face! He was struggling not to 'blast-off' too soon inside her. In and out, in and out, he slammed and banged away at her! *Bang! Bang! Bang! Boom!* Her shaking tatas were starting to sweat too!

"*Aaaahh . . . egh . . . oh . . . eh! Ah! Ah! Oooh . . . argh!*" they both lustfully cried.

Wavy light rays from the moving, rippling, illuminated pool water, reflected and glowed all over their perfect nude bodies.

Dick Sharp, a.k.a. Walnut, was banging Babette Doll, a.k.a. Coconut, from behind. They were pounding away on the cabana's large swinging couch! *Thwack! Whack! Whomp!* She was on all fours as he did her 'doggy style!' The young man was practically 'stabbing' her love box with his sizeable tool! *Pop! Bang! Clap!* She loved it! The creaking couch swung back and forth, back and forth, as they were getting laid!

"*Yep! Yep! Yep!*" she squealed, like a female canine in heat. "*Oh, that's real good!*" she added, while biting the lovely fingernail of her right hand's pinky.

"You're like a cross between an owl and a rooster!" she happily cried.

"What's that?" he asked.

"A cock that stays up all night!"

He boinked her faster and faster, then his greedy hands reached down under to grab her swaying honkers! *Boom . . . boom . . . boom . . .* he went, practically shagging her to death! It looked as if her gorgeous behind was permanently 'attached' or 'connected' to his long tallywacker! A lot of heavy breathing followed!

Willy Piston, a.k.a. Pecan, was hovering over Candy Delight, a.k.a. Guava, 'titty balling' her! Their booty call was happening on towels next to the outdoor Jacuzzi! The hot tub's bright underwater light illuminated their sizzling bodies. Piston/Pecan rubbed his giant sausage between her two white chest balloons, quickly sliding it in and out, in and out, in and out! *Za-zoop! Za-zoop! Za-zip! Ka-bobble! Ka-bobble!* As he did this, the head of his bang stick kept taping her neck. *Boop! Boop! Boop!* She loved the exhilarating sensation between her overly-inflated pumkins!

"*Oh! Yes! Yes! Titty boom me!*" she declared.

"You see, boobs prove men can focus on two things at once," he panted.

"You can say *that* again!" she replied. "Willy, do you smoke after sex?"

"I never looked."

Muffy Bell/Kiwi strolled over to the couple to join them! In a flash, the lucky young man was standing, while the two lovely ladies sucked his jackhammer. *Slurp! Slurp! Lickety-lickety!* Bell was licking and kissing one side of it, while Delight did the same to the other side. Their flickering tongues worked their way from his bulky ball sack, and all the way up to the very tip of his baseball bat! *Lickety-lickety-lickety-lickety-lick!*

"*Mmmm! Mmmmm! Mmmmm!*"

When Bell/Kiwi grabbed his trouser monkey and impressively swallowed the entire thing down her throat, Delight/Guava got mad!

"Hey, don't hog the whole damn thing for yourself! Leave some for me!"

"Sorry Candy," replied the Asian beauty. "You know, I took dick sucking class in college and got an F."

"You did?" asked Delight/Guava.

"Yeah, I *sucked* so hard at it."

Delight/Guava rolled her eyes, and stormed off.

Nearby, Babette Doll/Coconut found a convenient place to sit . . . on top of Monty Jaybird's eager face . . . while she hunched over and sucked his erect rocket. *Sssswwoooooopppp!* They were 'getting it on' *sixty-nine style* on a long, umbrellaed lounge chair! He relished the lovely taste of her furburger, as she rubbed his nuts and slurped his huffing bone! Her long hair flew all over the place, as her head bobbed right and left, and up and down. The little minx then tickled the underside of his magic wand with her tongue!

"*Mmmmmm!*"

When her mouth got tired, she used her hand to stroke his slippery joystick! Not wanting to *ka-boom* just yet, Jaybird got up. It was time to switch positions. He sat on the lounge chair, and then she slowly sat down too . . . on top of his one-eyed monster . . . with her back facing him! Jaybird's hairy meat whistle was so plentiful, he couldn't put it all the way in . . . her love box was too little and tight. The garmentless guru closed his eyes and massaged her coconuts as she bounced away on top of him as best she could! *Boing! Boing! Boing!*

"*Oh! Oh! Yes! Yes!* Monty, you're so . . . *overgrown!*"

"I know," he boasted.

"I'm happy as a clam . . . . and my clam is happy too!" she joyously confessed.

"Babette, you remind me of a nurse I once knew who had dirty knees."

"You knew a nurse who had dirty knees? Who was she?"

"The *head* nurse!" chuckled Jaybird.

Chastity, as Mona, was spellbound . . . as she held Oscar Dong's hand! Her eyes had popped out and her jaw remained wide open! She just couldn't believe what she was witnessing. She'd never seen so many uninhibited, unrestrained people out in the open, brazenly thrashing the gash, planting the parsnip, burying the weasel and 'knocking boots' without any boots on!

Now I understand what Adrianna was talking about! thought Mona. *She was right all along!*

Dong moved closer to our hero and gave her a kiss on the neck. *Mmm-wah!*

"Why don't we do some of that?" he smiled. "I'll find us a nice, private spot where we can be alone."

"Oh Oscar, it's too soon for us . . . besides, I'm not that kind of girl," she nervously replied.

"But there's amazing health benefits to recreational sexual activity," he gently said. "It keeps your immune system in top shape, it lowers your blood pressure, and it counts as exercise . . . burning five calories per minute!"

"It does?"

"Yeah, and it also increases your heart rate and uses various muscles, it lowers heart attack risk, it lessens pain, it may make prostate cancer less likely, it improves sleep, it eases stress, and it extends your life."

"Is that so? Man, you're an expert on the subject."

"Thanks. Monty's always telling us, *'if it feels good, do it!'* We're clean as whistles too, disease free, and the Super Sunscreen on the guys' tools acts as a natural contraceptive. I can wrap my banana up too, if you like. We've got rubbers back in the hideout. So, what do you say?"

Our hero realized she'd better come up with a good excuse, or else she might blow her cover.

"Banana . . . and I mean, Oscar, I like you . . . I do . . . but I'm sorry . . . I've suddenly got a terrible headache."

"I see . . . must be from the hydrotherapy pool," he suggested. "Those ceiling lights are intense."

"Yes," she nodded. "They gave me a headache."

"Okay. Well, don't worry, I'll take you back to your bunk, and you can get a little rest. Our romantic activities can wait for another night. I'm a bit tired myself . . . I think I'll take a shower and hit the sack early tonight too."

"Thanks . . . you're such a gentleman."

They turned to walk back to the secret hideout.

"Oh, I better get my purse and bag . . . they're back in my car. There's aspirin in my purse."

"Great, I'll go with you."

Off they disappeared, as orgasmic moans and groans echoed throughout the warm night air.

After they fetched Mona's bags from her parked, metallic blue, 1970's Corvette Stingray, our undercover hero and Oscar Dong strolled back to the Super Nudists secret hideout. They passed the wild orgy still going full blast in the main pool area between Jaybird and the other Super Nudists. Cries and squeals of ecstatic, blissful ecstasy . . . and co-climaxing . . . continued just as before!

"Ooooo!"

"Aaaaahhhh!"

"My treasure box!"

"Mmmmmm!"

"My love muffin!"

"I'm getting all wet . . . and not just from the pool water!"

"Yes! Yes! Do it!"

"Aaaaarrrghhh!"

"That's the wrong hole!"

"My family jewels!"

"Mmmmmmm!"

"If it feels good, do it!"

"Oh Monty, this is a marvelous sex position!"

"Thanks honey! I invented it!"

Our couple entered the redwood bungalow housing the hydrotherapy pool. Inside, Dong moved to the special Greek statue of the large breasted woman. He twisted the nipple on the statue's left breast . . . the *knob* to the secret door . . . and the back wall automatically rotated open! The entire wall revolved around on its turntable base, just like a record player. The couple then walked through the open passageway, and a second later, the false wall rotated back into position, closing behind them.

Back inside the secret hideout, Mona turned to Dong.

"Oscar, I just want to take a quick shower before I go to bed."

"No problem. The showers are back in the hydrotherapy pool room. You know how to activate the secret door?"

"Yes, I got it."

"I'll join you in a minute . . . I just need to check our equipment for tomorrow."

"Okay."

Off she went to take her hot shower, as Dong moved to the Super Nudists weapons rack. He had to make sure they were ready for tomorrow's kidnapping of Governor Nightcap, so he carefully examined each special weapon; his banana boomerang, the pecan slingshot, the walnut smoke bomb, the macadamia whip, the lemonade squirt gun, the guava gas spray can, the coconut bolas, the kiwi dagger, and Jaybird's fig leaf shooting stars and telescopic fig leaf sword.

Back in the hydrotherapy pool room, Mona took her shower in the tiled 'group shower' section. She was careful not to get her brunette wig wet. As hot water rained down on her delicious nude body, massaging it, her mind raced.

I'll nail them all tomorrow . . . at that parade . . . as the Double-D Avenger! I'm so sorry about Oscar, but I don't have a choice here. I'll try not to hurt him! They'll all be legally caught in the act of trying to kidnap the Governor! I just wish there was some way to even the odds of ten against one . . .

Our hero thought for a moment, and then a fantastic idea popped into her head!

That's it! I've got it! If this works, I better move fast!

Chastity/Mona snatched a fresh white towel from an alcove, and quickly dried herself off. She then headed to the secret door. As she approached it, the turntable floor rotated around and Dong strolled out, heading towards the shower area.

"Going out as I'm coming in?" joked Mona.

"Yep!" smiled Dong. "See you in a few minutes. By the way, my bunk bed is right below yours!"

"It is?" she grinned. "Well, we've got a big day tomorrow, so no midnight climbs to visit me!"

"Okay," he chuckled.

Mona dashed through the open passageway, and a second later, the false wall rotated back into position, closing behind her.

She was now *all alone* in the Super Nudists hideout! This was her chance!

In a flash, she tossed her towel in an open hamper, and then snatched her bottle of normal, everyday sunscreen from her travel bag. Dashing over to the chemistry set table, Mona grabbed all the flasks containing the Super Nudist Sunscreen lotion. She uncorked them, and moved to a stainless steel sink in the corner. Turning on the hot water, she dumped all of Jaybird's magic formula into the sink, completely *emptying* each glass flask! To make sure all of it was out, she thoroughly rinsed the flasks with hot water.

Once that was done, Mona refilled each one with her own, store-bought sunscreen lotion! In order to 'stretch it out,' she added a little lukewarm water to each flask, and then recorked them. Our hero shook them furiously. After a few seconds, her phony Super Nudist Sunscreen looked identical to the real stuff!

Not wasting anymore time, Mona carefully put the flasks back on the chemistry set table, and everything looked exactly as it was originally. She then threw her empty sunscreen bottle into her bag, and hurried to her bunk bed. She placed the bag near the foot of her tall bed, and climbed the metal ladder to her top bunk. Pulling off the covers, she scrambled under them and covered herself. The sheets were clean and comfortable, and so were the pillows! Mona then closed her eyes . . . pretending to be fast asleep.

At that very second, Dong walked in, all fresh and showered. He sauntered over to their shared bunk and looked up at 'sleeping Mona' with his blue eyes. A smile appeared on his happy face.

"Out like a light," he quietly chuckled. "Pleasant dreams Mona."

CHAPTER TWENTY-ONE

Early the next morning, Chastity as Mona, was awakened by loud, angry growls and cries! She blinked, rubbing the sleep out of her eyes, and looked down from her top bunk. A strange looking man in old miner's clothes was wiggling around on the hideout floor! He was wearing an old cowboy hat, a long-sleeved, button-down, red flannel shirt and a pair of old, western blue jeans. A black neckerchief was around his neck, and on his feet were a pair of used cowboy boots.

"*Huh?!*" she cried.

The other Super Nudists were also awakened out of their bunk beds by the same strange fellow!

"*I can't stand it! I can't stand it!*" howled the man, as he frantically tossed and turned all over the floor.

The kooky cowboy pulled off his boots, whipped off his shirt and pants, and threw away his hat. As he untied his neckerchief, Mona finally realized who it was!

"*Monty!*" she exclaimed. "I didn't recognize you *with your clothes on!*"

"I can't stand the itchy feeling of that cowboy garb rubbing up against my delicate, uncontaminated, 'devote nudist' skin!" he hollered.

"Well, why did you put it on in the first place?" snorted Candy Delight/Guava.

"I thought it'd make a good disguise as I drove in the Founder's Day parade today, that's why!" grumbled Jaybird. "I'm not doing it . . . I can't . . . I won't . . . it's impossible! I'll just drive our bus in my minimal Super Nudist uniform, as usual!"

When he finally calmed down and composed himself, Jaybird addressed the team.

"Okay, everyone put on plenty of our Super Sunscreen! Lay the lotion on thick . . . you'll need all the super powers and strength you can muster today! We've got to get over to the parade route immediately."

"Yes, sir!" the ten of them simultaneously declared.

"Once you're lathered up, get into your Super Nudist costumes and meet me at the bus!" He then added, " . . . and remember, *teamwork* makes the Super Nudist *dream work!*"

"Yes, sir!" they all replied.

"What about me?" asked Mona.

"As I told you last night, just open the front gate at nine o'clock," he instructed. "You can tell our visitors the café, smoothie bar and library will be open a little later today. The team and I will be back as soon as we can . . . with Governor Nightcap."

"Understood," nodded Mona.

"Hey, this Super Sunscreen doesn't feel tingly!" revealed Babette Doll/Coconut, as she rubbed some of it all over her bare boobs.

"Didn't you get enough *tingly feelings* last night?!" joked Dick Sharp/Walnut.

"Very funny!" she snapped back.

Chastity, as Mona, panicked! She worried her trick might have been discovered! *Oh-oh!* she thought.

"Listen, we use so much of my formula day in and day out, our skin's gotten used to it by now," rationalized Jaybird. "Don't worry about it."

"Right, sir," replied Doll/Coconut.

Jaybird then rubbed a lot of the Super Sunscreen all over his nude body too.

Our hero breathed a sigh of relief!

The ten Super Nudists, and Jaybird, were quickly dressed in their minimal costumes, capes and helmets.

"We're off!" announced Jaybird. "See you soon, Watermelons!"

"Yes, sir!"

As they exited out the revolving front door, our hero mumbled under her breath.

"You'll see me a lot *sooner* than you think!"

The citizens of Driftwood Valley all turned out that morning to watch the annual Founder's Day Parade. The valley itself was established during the gold rush days of the 1850's, and Founder's Day commemorated the historic event. The parade route ran from one end of Driftwood Valley to the other, down the main highway. It was a bright, warm, sunny day, and excited people crowded the sidewalks. Some sat on folding lawn chairs, or on the edges of sidewalks, while other spectators remained standing.

Remarkably, most folks were not nude . . . they were fully dressed. The legalization of public nudity hadn't fully taken effect yet in the minds of most of Driftwood Valley's respectable residents. In fact, the majority flat-out rejected the crazy new law!

Vendors selling popcorn, cotton candy, ice cream and balloons strolled up and down the street, making a pretty penny.

The parade began with patriotic riders on horseback holding waving flags. Floats with young beauty queens rolled by, sexy pom-pom girls marched along, and college bands followed, performing rousing John Philip Sousa marching scores! Goofy clowns driving miniature go-carts scrambled down the parade route, followed by gold rush reenactors dressed in vintage cowboy and gold prospector costumes. One miner reenactor struggled, pulling a rope attached to a stubborn, live mule behind him!

Farm tractors, both vintage and new, rolled past the crowds, followed by an old fire truck with its flashing red lights on. Everyone was startled the moment the fire truck blew its loud siren! *Woooooo-ooooooo-ooooo!*

Spectators ate it all up, cheering and applauding. Many took photos and selfies.

Colorful Native American dancers dressed in buckskins and feathers, skipped by, beating tom-toms and shaking rattles. *Ah-yah-yah-yah! Ah-yah-yah-yah!* Right behind them were more floats, including a giant figure of a gold miner.

A vintage stagecoach with more cowboy and cowgirl reenactors onboard, rolled past the clapping throngs. The stagecoach was pulled by a team of four spirited horses.

Pretty baton twirlers marched by next, followed by a group of a dozen people holding guide ropes tied to a gigantic inflatable balloon in the sky. The enormous balloon was in the shape of an old, bearded prospector panning for gold! The giant figure floated around, high in the air! It drifted from one side of the parade route to the other, controlled by its human puppeteers below.

Next came the vintage automobiles! Dozens of gorgeous classic cars drove past the awestruck crowds! Nearly all the vehicles were in mint condition; Ford Model T's, Duesenbergs, 1950's hot rods, military jeeps, Cadillac Eldorados, muscle cars, Corvettes, Mustangs, Cameros, Trans Ams, VW bugs . . . and *a VW bus!*

Spectators noticed the classic VW bus was a light-green and yellow-colored vehicle . . . a 1960's 'Samba.' Twenty-three windows wrapped around the sausage-shaped 'hippy bus,' with bi-parting side doors, a sunroof, and a sloping split windshield in front. Monty Jaybird was driving, and seated in back, were the ten Super Nudists, ready to spring into action! The black goggles on everyone's helmets were lowered, covering their eyes and disguising their faces!

Behind the nudist villains hippy bus was a convertible Eldorado carrying the parade's 'Grand Marshall' . . . the senile, old drunk . . . Governor Sudsey Nightcap! Governor Nightcap was a jolly little man, with a bald head, a big round nose and squinting eyes. He was seated all alone in the back seat, in a loud business suit and tie, while a sexy lady chauffeur drove in front. The rich old geezer held a large beer bottle secretly wrapped in a brown paper bag! It was obviously no secret! He occasionally took a swig from the bag, as he waved to his applauding constituents on both sides of the car.

"*Hello! Hi there! Ha, ha!*" he cheered. "Thanks for the votes folks!"

Nightcap then turned to his driver.

"*Ha, ha*, I've got my next election in the bag!"

Meanwhile, back at the Jaybird Growth Institute, Mona . . . running out in her birthday suit . . . opened the front gates for the public. A line of cars had already formed! The crowd of enthusiastic nudists, uninterested in seeing the parade, raced their vehicles in to park. Once the resort's own parking lot was full, latecomers would have to find spots on the neighboring residential streets. Among the dozens of the autos driving in, our undercover hero recognized several drivers and passengers; Doctor Della-Kwak, Mayor Artie Phishel, and City Council members Helga Hoodwink, Max Phuckter, Harry Bottoms, Soupy Phishel, and intern Rod Long! Old wax museum caretaker Romeo drove in next, followed by the Sheriff and the Deputy in their squad car!

Mona nervously turned her brunette-wigged head away, so Della-Kwak, Mayor Phishel, Romeo, the Sheriff and the Deputy wouldn't recognize her as Chastity Knott. At that exact moment, a nude lady strolled past . . . Adrianna Azzhat!

"Good morning!" smiled Azzhat.

"Morning," Mona mumbled back, totally surprised.

Our worried hero quickly rotated her head to face the cars again, and luckily, Azzhat was none the wiser! The screwy lady made no connection between brunette Mona Lot and the blond Double-D Avenger.

Mona breathed a sigh of relief, as Azzhat casually strolled by! Our hero then looked around suspiciously. She noticed no more cars were driving in . . . there was a temporary 'break' in arriving visitors.

"Good! Time to get over to that parade!" she told herself.

Mona/Chastity discreetly dashed to her car . . . her classic, metallic blue, 1970's Corvette Stingray . . . still parked in the Jaybird Institute's parking lot. The nudists who had driven in, had already parked and walked off to other parts of the resort. Everyone was gone. Seeing the coast was clear, she opened her car's door and reached for a hidden zipper on the side of her driver's seat. She unzipped it! *Zzzzzzzzzzzziiiiipppppp!* Tucked away inside the large, secret seat compartment were her Double-D Avenger costume, mask, cape, gloves, belt and boots!

Mona/Chastity pulled the full costume out, and whipped off her brunette wig. She stuffed the wig into the secret seat compartment, shut the door, and then took a few steps back, away from her Corvette. Chastity quickly spun around in a circle . . . creating a dizzying blur of red, blue and yellow . . . and instantly changed into her Double-D Avenger superhero outfit! Within seconds, she was dressed as *the Double-D Avenger,* in her complete blue leotard costume and red bra-mask, her red gloves, red boots, red cape and red belt with two upper-case white letter 'D's' on its buckle.

Once her transformation was completed, our busty, costumed crime-fighter took a running leap, and bounced up into the air!

"Booby-Bounce!" she cried, as she soared away, up into the bright sunny sky.

Boi-oing-oing-oing-oing-oing!

This *dynamic momentum* of her super breasts *catapulted* the rest of her body thousands of feet *into the air!* High in sky, Double-D quickly surveyed everything down below through the two eye-slits of her brassier mask! She flew out of Toupee Canyon and glided towards downtown Driftwood Valley.

Back at the parade route, Monty Jaybird, in his helmet and costume, went bug-eyed behind the wheel of the hippy bus.

"We're reaching the end of the parade route! Everyone get your Super Streaker roller skates on and commence the operation!"

"Yes, sir!" they all replied.

In a flash, the side passenger door of the light-green and yellow-colored 'Samba' bus slid open! Out hopped all ten Super Nudists, with their roller skates on; Lemon, Banana, Walnut, Papaya, Peanut, Coconut, Kiwi, Macadamia, Guava, and Pecan!

Shocked spectators caught glimpses of their black goggles and light-green and yellow colored helmets with fruit or nut symbols painted on the front forehead areas! They also noticed the team's minimal uniforms of light-green and yellow colored gloves, boots, utility belts, waving capes and metallic green *fig leaf* jockstraps and Jillstraps!

Many bystanders thought the bizarre group was a bunch of insane, naked, roller skating performers . . . the parade's craziest participants!

The Super Nudists zoomed down the street on their roller skates and quickly surrounded the Governor's convertible Eldorado! The sexy lady chauffeur hit the brakes, stopping the car. *Screeeccchh!* Before she could yell at them to stop blocking her vehicle, Super Nudist Guava pulled her guava gas weapon . . . her spray can in the shape of a guava fruit . . . from her utility belt! She then shot the chauffeur in the face! *Ssssssss!* The lady driver was knocked out instantly!

"Say, what's going on here? The parade over already?" asked drunken, senile old Nightcap.

Guava reached over and put the car in park, as male Super Nudists Banana and Pecan grabbed the plastered politician in the open back seat. Banana held Governor Nightcap's arms, while Pecan held his legs.

"Oh, how nice of you fellas to help me to my limo!" chuckled Nightcap, oblivious to what was happening. He then noticed his unconscious chauffeur slumped over behind the wheel. "Thanks for the ride, miss," he giggled. "Oh, she must have had a few drinky-poo's! *Ha, ha!*"

Nightcap looked up at Banana, and then to Pecan, and joked, "She's got a nice pair of knockers, ay boys?"

"Yep," smiled Pecan.

"*Egads!*" cried Nightcap. "You're going to *carry me* over to my limo? *Ha, ha,* what service! What service! How kind of you boys! You know, I did have a *little something* to drink myself . . . *ha, ha!*"

The Super Nudists skated off down a side road with the Governor in their clutches, before anyone could do a thing about it. The four wheels on each of their skates buzzed away at top speed, as the Super Nudists 'shook a leg' or 'two,' literally! They were all lightning fast on roller skates, as their capes waved, and their legs and bare behinds pumped away . . . swaying right and left, and right and left! The female Super Nudists big bare breasts swayed right and left too!

Jaybird, in the hippy bus, drove off, following his team of birthday suit kidnappers. He struggled to keep up with them.

"Roller skates? How novel! *Ha, ha!*" commented the loaded Nightcap, looking down at Banana and Pecan's wheeled feet.

The helmeted villains zipped away from the parade route and its crowds, passing many of Driftwood Valley's iconic mid-century modern buildings; the wax museum, the vintage drive-in movie theater, the bowling alley, Cactus Wilmington's Used Car Supermarket, the drive-thru car wash, and the permanently closed Al Purplewood's Gentleman's Club . . . which was the location of the Double-D Avenger's very first adventure!

Nightcap abruptly looked up at Banana, who was holding his arms. "Say, how far away did you park that damn limo, son?! I hate to pay for parking myself, but this is ridiculous!" He then took a closer look at the black goggles on Banana's helmet. "By the way, nice sunglasses fella! Where'd ya get'em?" he slurred.

Suddenly, the Double-D Avenger fell out of the sky from her last powerful Booby Bounce! Down, down, down she descended, in her blue leotard costume and red bra-mask, her red gloves, red boots, waving red cape and red belt with two upper-case white letter 'D's' on its buckle! She landed right in front of the Super Nudists! *Za-Zap!*

The unclad abductors skidded to halt on their skates, as Double-D's powerful super boobs absorbed the impact of her landing!

"Stop right where you are, and hand over the Governor!" demanded the Double-D Avenger. She heroically stood in the middle of the street, with her hands defiantly on her hips!

"It's the Double-D Avenger!" exclaimed Guava.

"Not again!" snarled Kiwi.

"But how?!" sputtered Walnut.

"I knew this would happen!" snorted Lemon.

"Super Nudists attack!" ordered Banana.

Banana and Pecan released Nightcap, rolling him onto the sidewalk! *Wa-Boom!*

"Whoa! Ha, ha! I see we're getting the party *rolling . . .* literally!" chuckled the blitzed doofus.

The two male Super Nudists shook their heads, and quickly joined the rest of their team in battle!

As another street brawl was about to begin . . . between our hero and the ten Super Nudists, Jaybird screeched the hippy bus to a stop! *Eeeeeeeeeee!*

"The Double-D Avenger!" he snarled, looking out his driver's window. "She's stuck her troublesome, tom-toms into our business again!"

Jaybird put the bus in park, and opened his driver's side door. Out he ran, not to join the fight, but to grab the Governor!

Nightcap did a double-take, as Jaybird approached him in his helmet, cape, and minimal Super Nudist attire.

"Another parade clown?!" exploded the bombed Nightcap. He glanced at the gold *fig leaf* painted on the front of Jaybird's helmet. "Where's my limo? Where's my driver?"

"Here I am, come right this way Governor," Jaybird reassured him.

He lifted Nightcap and scrambled over to the bus. He then slid open the side passenger door, and literally threw the wasted Governor onto the cushioned bench in front! Jaybird slid the passenger door shut again, and ran around to the front of the bus.

"What kind of limo is this?" mumbled Nightcap from inside.

Ignoring him, Jaybird climbed back in, and once he was settled in his driver's seat, he hit the gas pedal and drove off at top speed! *Raa-Roooommmm!*

CHAPTER TWENTY-TWO

Back in the middle of the street, the earth-shattering fight was on! The Super Nudists, wearing their roller skates, attacked the Double-D Avenger, with plenty of punches, chops, and flips!

"You can't trick these ta-tas a second time!" boasted Double-D, while pointing to her overinflated blimps.

Our hero brilliantly blocked and kicked each of their moves, as the villains rolled around her on skates.

"Aaahh!"

"Yaahh!"

"Key-Yah!"

"Ho!"

"Waaa!"

Macadamia pulled the whip out of his utility belt and attacked Double-D! Before he could lash her with it, she grabbed his arm holding the weapon and flipped him away! *Ka-Voom!*

"Ooohh!!!"

Kiwi then charged with her sharp dagger, but Double-D jumped out of the way!

"Holy Hooters!" gasped our hero.

Coconut tried to assault our hero next, using her bolas! Before the villainess could spin and throw them, Double-D lifted her up and tossed her bodily into Peanut and Walnut! *Crash! Bang! Boom!*

"Aaaahh!"

"Errgghhh!"

"Ooohh!!"

"How's *that* for some Kalamazoo Karate?!" joked Double-D.

Banana threw his banana boomerang, not realizing the Double-D Avenger was actually his new love, Mona Lot!

Whoosh-whoosh-whoosh-whoosh-whoosh!

Seeing it flying at her, Double-D ducked, and the boomerang clobbered Papaya's helmet instead! *Klang!*

"*Ouch!*" Papaya cried, dazed from the sudden concussion.

Banana did a double-take, gazing at the gorgeous Double-D Avenger! She was just as hot and sexy as he remembered her from their first battle! Oscar Dong, as Banana, really didn't want to fight her . . . he wanted to kiss and make love to her! The handsome young man was truly enamored by her breathtaking beauty . . . so much so, he forgot all about Mona Lot!

The shifting battle moved in front of the Atomic Age Beauty Parlor . . . a mid-century, 1960's style futuristic hair salon. A dozen ladies drying their hair in enormous 'astronaut helmet' looking dryers, observed the skirmish from the salon's front windows! They couldn't believe what they were seeing!

Papaya pulled the papaya grenade from her utility belt, and was about to throw it . . . but she wasn't fast enough! Double-D zapped her in the nick of time with a *Booby-Lightning Bolt!* Our hero did this by quickly massaging her twin peaks and generating *static electricity* between her big bra and costume. Once the powerful static electricity built up, she *threw out* her arms and a bright lightning bolt *shot off* her giant Bra Buddies! *Za-Zapp!!* There was an instant *thunderclap* that sounded like '*Va-Voom!*'

"*Booby-Bolt!*" hollered Double-D, as the lightning fired off her chest.

The electrical bolt *nailed* Papaya's grenade in midair as she tossed it! *Bang!*

"*Waaaaahhh!*" cried stunned Papaya. Luckily, her Super Nudist helmet and goggles saved her from the explosion.

On the opposite side of the street, in front of the Driftwood Valley Magic Shop, sidewalk pedestrians stopped and gawked at the clash! They were bewildered, just like the beauty shop ladies under the 'astronaut helmet' dryers! The old store had magic tricks, wands, floating tables, playing cards, top hats, books, and rubber masks displayed in the front windows. Painted below the shop's neon sign were the words; magic tricks, gags, novelties, jokes, fireworks, and juggling.

Lemon whipped out her lemonade squirt gun and started firing at Double-D! *Squirt! Squirt! Squirt!*

"Oh, my boobies are tingling . . . they sense danger!" our hero told herself.

She did a quick cartwheel to dodge the spray of acidic lemonade! Clearing the stream, Double-D turned and glanced down at the yellow puddle on the ground.

"Lemonade!" she declared. "If that stuff had hit me, I would have been a double-d goner! Lemon juice is my vulnerable Achilles heel! It curdles milk and it also curdles my super blood!"

When Lemon tried to zap her a second time, Double-D swooped in and kicked the plastic squirt gun out of her hand! *Pop!* The pistol broke when it hit the asphalt, cracking and losing all its lemonade!

"You broke my squirt gun!" bellowed Lemon.

"You can get another!" laughed Double-D. "I buy my guns from a fellow named T-Rex."

"T-Rex?"

"Yes. He's a *small arms* dealer," she joked.

While she was laughing, Pecan and Walnut abruptly rushed Double-D again! Pecan had his pecan slingshot ready to fire and Walnut had his smoke bomb. However, our hero was too quick and smart!

"Time for a little *tit for tat!*" exclaimed Double-D.

She charged them, doing a flying kick in the air! She spread her legs . . . not for sex . . . but for kicks! Double-D's right boot smacked Pecan in his face, and her left boot struck Walnut's kisser! *Bang! Boom!* Down the bad boys went!

"Waaaaahhh!"

"Oooopphhfff!"

Macadamia attacked a second time too, using the best of his Nude-jitsu! Double-D blocked his chops and punches, and then gave him a couple punches of her own . . . Booby-Punches! These consisted of Chastity turning, twisting and throwing one powerful breast at her opponent after another.

"Booby-Punch!" she declared.

Ba-Bap! Ba-Bap!

"Waaaahhh!" hollered Macadamia, as he was clobbered. The mighty booby-punch sent him rolling backwards on his skates! The Super Nudist wheeled out of control, finally crashing into the front doors of a German restaurant called The Cuckoo Clock!

Thwack!

"Ouch!"

The German eatery actually resembled a huge, old-fashioned cuckoo clock! It was a two-story wooden chalet, with fancy carved windows and a balcony. The front doors had white trim, and a huge clock face was right above them. A wooden cuckoo bird was also displayed near the top of the A-frame roof, popping out of an open window.

Customers dining inside could see the street altercation! They stared out the dining room windows, with their jaws dropped and their forks and knives in midair!

Double-D rushed over and grabbed Macadamia's left arm and his left leg. She then began spinning him around! Around and around she went . . . like an out of control merry-go-round ride . . . taking Macadamia with her!

"Waaaahhh! Aaaaahahhh!" he yelled. *"Let go!"*

"Certainly," she politely replied. "Happy landing!"

Our hero released Macadamia's arm and leg, and off he flew . . . right into Guava, Papaya, and Peanut! *Crash! Ka-Pow! Whamm!*

"Aaahh!"

"*Ooophhff!*"

"*Waaa!*"

Mad as hell, Peanut whipped out his machine gun peanut shooter! He then fired at Double-D, really letting her have it!

Rat-tat-tat-tat-tat-tat-tat-tat-tat-tat-tat-tat-tat-tat-tat!!!

Dozens of rock-hard peanut 'bullets' hit our hero's chest! She cried out in fear, more than in pain!

"*Ahhhh! Booby-Bumpers!*"

Double-D's indestructible melons protected her once again, acting like the rubber bumpers in a pinball machine! The peanut bullets simply ricocheted off! *Boing-boing-boing-boing-boing-boing-boing-boing-boing!*

Seeing this only made Peanut angrier! He aimed his peanut machine gun at her *head* this time and fired again!

Rat-tat-tat-tat-tat-tat-tat-tat-tat-tat-tat-tat-tat-tat-tat!!!

Double-D booby-bounced away just in time!

"*Booby-Bounce!*"

Up our hero flew into the air . . . *Ba-Boing* . . . dodging the second spray of peanuts!

A few seconds later, she was back on the ground. *Za-Zap!* Our hero landed right in front of another one of Driftwood Valley's novelty architecture businesses . . . a taco stand in the shape of a giant taco called Josefina Jumpingbeans!

"Thank goodness for my indestructible tits!" said Double-D, congratulating herself. She grabbed one blue costumed boob of hers at a time and kissed them. "*Mmm-waah! Mmm-wah!*"

Customers couldn't believe what they were seeing, as they ate their delicious, crispy tacos in front of the whimsical stand!

Stunned, dazed, and aching in pain, the ten Super Nudists quickly huddled.

"*Something's wrong!*" snarled Guava.

"*She's kicking our naked asses!*" cut in Walnut.

"I feel like I've lost my Super Nudist powers!" confessed Papaya.

"Me too!" added Pecan.

"You're right . . . we're all 'off' today. Like our power's been zapped," thought Banana.

"We gotta get out of here!" exploded Coconut.

"Right! Everyone follow me! We'll retreat over there!" ordered Banana.

He pointed to a massive factory with a vintage neon sign on its roof. The sign read, *T & A ROOT BEER.*

"The T & A Root Beer Factory?!" spat Peanut.

"Yes . . . we can ditch her in there! Hurry! *Super Nudists, retreat!"* declared Banana.

Off they streaked on their roller skates! *Za-zooooommm!*

Double-D noticed the Super Nudists rolling away and smiled. "Looks like my little sunscreen switcheroo worked! They're not as strong or as powerful as before! *Ha, ha!* They can't escape from me now!"

Our hero sprinted after them, as sidewalk lookie-loos continued to gawk!

Rolling into the T & A Root Beer factory, the ten Super Nudists were immediately spotted by a couple of workers in white garments and hair nets.

"Hey, what are you doing in here!?" shouted one of the assembly line workers.

"Them gals don't have no tops on!" exclaimed another, excited, male worker.

Before they could say or do anything else, Kiwi and Coconut rolled over and used a little Nude-jitsu on them. The Super Nudist gals knocked the surprised workers out cold! *Chop! Chop!*

The devilish group then glided on their skates to the opposite end of the factory. The entire place was about three stories high, with industrial lighting on the ceiling, metal pipes and tubes running everywhere, and conveyer belts carrying bottles of root beer across the enormous space. Stainless steel vats were mixing the sugary brown drink, and a control panel with a couple of rolling chairs was positioned right next to these containers. Flashing buttons and lights lit up the computerized control board. On the opposite side of the vats were stacks and stacks of wooden barrels. These old-fashioned root beer barrels were for restaurant and other commercial customers.

The Double-D Avenger burst into the factory, looking for naughty nudnik fannies!

"Come out, come out, wherever you are!" taunted our hero. "There's no escaping the Double-D Avenger!"

Female Super Nudists Guava, Coconut and Kiwi suddenly popped out from behind a huge stainless steel vat! They closed in to attack on their roller skates!

Skating faster and faster, Guava and Kiwi raced ahead of Coconut! They then reached back and grabbed Coconut's right and left arms! The two of them used all their strength to slingshot Coconut ahead of them, throwing their arms forward like whips! *Za-Zoom!* Coconut was flung onwards like a rocket on roller skates, passing Guava and Kiwi, and plowing right into the Double-D Avenger!

Ka-Pow!

"Oh!" sputtered our startled hero, as she flew and fell down.

Thinking fast, Double-D quickly rolled back up onto her boots! She grabbed a couple root beer bottles passing by on a moving conveyer belt! Shaking the two bottles up, she then flipped off the caps using her thumbs!

"Here . . . have some T & A Root Beer!"

Our hero held the two bottles up to her big tits and sprayed Guava, Kiwi and Coconut with powerful blasts of carbonated root beer!

Sploooossshhh!!!

"Waaaaaahhhhh!" cried the trio.

The root beer's sticky white foam dripped all over the women's bare breasts, and their helmets, goggles and lips!

"What are you crying about?!" joked Double-D. "Root beer is a *tree's* favorite drink! *Ha, ha!*"

"Oh, she's a *real* comedian," sneered Coconut.

"It's also a mathematician's favorite drink?" added Double-D.

"A mathematician's favorite drink?" snorted Guava.

"Yes, after all, it's *root* beer!"

"*Very funny!*" growled Kiwi.

Banana turned to them and shouted, "Super Nudists huddle!"

In a flash, Guava, Coconut and Kiwi skated back to the rest of their group.

"We'll have to jump her and knock her out with Guava's gas . . . all of us, at the same time! It's the only way! Take off your skates! Hurry! *Super Nudists Pyramid Formation!*"

The Super Nudists quickly followed Banana's order, and tossed off their roller skates! Like amazing Chinese acrobats, they instantly took up their positions to form another human pyramid! The men . . . Banana, Pecan, Walnut, Peanut and Macadamia . . . lined up side by side, throwing their arms over each other's shoulders, to form the pyramid's strong base. They stood still in a perfectly straight line. Next, three of the women . . . Lemon, Guava, and Papaya . . . super jumped up into the air, to stand on top of the men's shoulders! *Zoop! Zoop! Zoop!* The near naked ladies did it, and then threw their arms over each other's shoulders to form the pyramid's second level.

Finally, the last two female Super Nudists . . . Coconut and Kiwi . . . super hopped up, to stand on top of the ladies shoulders forming the third and final level of the human tower! *Zoop! Zoop!* The two placed an arm over each other's shoulders for support, just like the others below them had done.

The Super Nudists now had another one of their incredible, three-storied human pyramids!

"Here she comes, get ready to attack . . . on my signal!" declared Banana. "I don't want her hurt . . . don't injure her when you grab her! Guava, just give her some of your gas."

"What do you mean, *don't hurt or injure her!?*" snapped Guava. "She just beat the crap out of all of us!"

"That's a good trick!" interrupted Double-D, as she neared them. She admired their acrobatic balancing skills to form the human pyramid. "I've got a good one too . . . a real trick up my brassiere! Watch this maracas magic!"

In a flash, our hero pulled out two little red tassels from her belt, and attached them to the tips of her big super boobies! She then began to gyrate her blue costumed tits around and around, causing the tassels to spin faster and faster!

"What the hell is she doing?!" cried Guava from the pyramid.

The Double-D Avenger's nipple tassels were soon spinning like two airplane propellers! The powerful whirling wind this caused was incredible . . . like a *mini hurricane!*

Whoooooosssssshhhhhh!!!!

The Super Nudists hair, metallic fig leaves, and capes blew around like crazy!

"*Titty-Tassel Hurricane!*" cried Double-D, announcing her secret weapon.

"*Titty-Tassel Hurricane?!*" yelled Walnut.

"*I'm losing my balance!*" cried Coconut.

"*That wind . . . it's so strong . . . it's gonna knock us over!*" added frantic Kiwi.

"*That's right!*" laughed Double-D. "My Titty-Tassel Hurricane is much more powerful than my super double-d breath! *Ha, ha, ha!*"

"*Stop her!*" demanded Macadamia.

"*Let's jump her now!*" howled Pecan.

"*Ahhh!*"

"*Waaahh!*"

"Super Nudists Pyramid, disassemble!" shouted Banana.

Too late! The Double-D Avenger's Titty-Tassel Hurricane smashed the Super Nudists pyramid apart! Her severe cyclone winds reached seventy-four miles per hour! This hurricane force struck the villains down, like a mighty bowling ball knocking over a line of tenpins! The villains flew all over the place, crashing to the hard factory floor! *Bang! Boom! Oof! Bop! Thunk! Bam! Crunch! Whack! Zok! Splatt!*

When Double-D stopped gyrating, her Titty-Tassel Hurricane ceased and the wind died down. Our hero then sprung over to unconscious Guava and removed the can of knock-out gas from her utility belt.

"Nighty-night everyone!"

Double-D held her breath, as she shot each and every dazed Super Nudist in the face with it! They ended up getting the gas instead! *Sssssss! Sssssssss! Sssssss! Sssssssss! Sssssssss! Sssssss! Sssssss! Sssssssss! Sssssssss! Ssss!*

Sentimental thoughts ran through Double-D's head, as she stared down at sleeping Banana . . . who she just blasted with knock-out gas.

Oh Oscar, I hope I didn't hurt you! I tried to pull my Booby-Punches!

Spotting the old-fashioned root beer barrels in a corner, our hero got an idea. She carefully lined up ten of the big empty barrels, and gently plopped each Super Nudist inside one!

"Roll out the barrels, we'll have a barrel of fun!" she sang to herself.

In order to make sure the Super Nudists wouldn't go anyplace when they came to, Double-D used some shipping rope to lock each nudist inside their own barrel. She snagged the packing material from a shipping counter.

By the time she was done, all ten Super Nudists looked like they were wearing *'bankruptcy barrels!'* Each sleeping streaker wore a suit consisting of a wooden barrel, held on by rope suspenders. Back in the old days, bankruptcy barrels indicated that someone was so poor, they couldn't afford clothes!

"That's great honkers handiwork, if I do say so myself!" she boasted. "I'm double-dee-lighted! Those bankruptcy barrels are the perfect outfits for those Not-So-Super Nudists!"

Double-D smiled, admiring her fine job. She then pulled out her slim, tiny red cell phone secretly clipped behind her Double-D Avenger belt buckle. The phone was in the shape of a small brassiere, with a figure-eight screen in both bra cups. She quickly dialed the police.

"Hello, Officer Peaks? This is the Double-D Avenger. Listen, I caught the kidnappers . . . they tried to nab Governor Nightcap this time. The Governor was released on a sidewalk . . . near the Atomic Age Beauty Parlor. I've got all ten of the culprits tied up here, at the T & A Root Beer factory. Come and get'em!"

There was a pause at the other end.

"Yes, that's right," replied Double-D. *"What?!* The Governor was seen in the back of a speeding hippy bus? A classic VW bus . . . light-green and yellow in color . . . a 1960's 'Samba?' I'll call you back!"

She ended the call, clipping her Double-D cell phone back behind her belt buckle.

"Monty has him! I've got to get over to the Institute at once! Time for my two big zoomers to zoom!"

Spotting an exit, our hero rocketed out the door . . . and a few seconds later, her loud, echoing cry was heard outside the root beer factory.

"Booby-Bounce!"

CHAPTER TWENTY-THREE

Back at the Jaybird Growth Institute, the hippy bus was seen parked behind the redwood bungalow housing the hydrotherapy pool. The front doors were locked, with a sign hanging over them reading, *'Hydrotherapy Pool temporarily Out of Service. Sorry.'* Nothing could have been further from the truth! Inside, Monty Jaybird was struggling with the drunken, senile old Governor, trying to take off his loud suit and tie!

"I see you've redecorated the Governor's mansion," slurred Nightcap.

"Yes sir," nodded Jaybird, playing along. "Now just take off your clothes and enjoy the warm water."

"Beg your pardon?"

The inebriated politician gazed at the huge indoor Jacuzzi . . . the rectangular pool big enough to hold at least fifty people!

"Bath time already? But it ain't Saturday night . . . is it?!"

Nightcap's boozy eyes nearly popped out, when he saw the attractive Greek statues of naked men and women, all life-sized and carved in white marble!

"Don't tell me you planned an orgy for me!"

"Orgy?" stuttered Jaybird, while lifting off his Super Nudist helmet.

"I love it!" declared happy Nightcap. "I'd like those two lovely ladies on the right! Talk about hot, sexy mamas! *Ha, ha!"*

Jaybird rolled his eyes, as he whipped off the Governor's clothes, and carried him into the hydrotherapy pool. *Ker-Plunk! Splash!* The two of them were all alone in the spacious indoor pool. Although Jaybird removed his helmet, he still wore his minimal, waterproof, Super Nudist costume.

The water was nice and hot! Surrounding them were the Greek statues and columns, the benches, running fountains and the stunning assortment of indoor tropical plants. The windowless space was illuminated by the 'normal' recessed ceiling lights . . . for the moment.

"Governor . . . take a look up at the ceiling," Jaybird coolly said, while floating near him. "Watch the lights."

"Lights?!" wondered Nightcap.

Jaybird moved to the pool's edge and grabbed the control box resembling a TV remote. He pressed the red button. *Click!*

Suddenly, hundreds of other recessed ceiling lights turned on, and began flashing in every color of the rainbow! The entire room was transformed into a colorful, psychedelic light show . . . which cast weird, twinkling globs of moving colors all over the place! Weird electronic music was also heard through hidden speakers. The bizarre tune was slow, soft and soothing.

"Don't tell me you put the Christmas tree lights up already?!" barked Nightcap. "Why it's only July! You're too early son!"

Jaybird grabbed the Governor and tried to rock him in his arms.

"Just relax, sir," purred Jaybird.

The hammered nincompoop shot him a strange look.

"Get me a wine bottle!"

"A wine bottle?"

"Yeah!" shouted Nightcap, while gazing up at the mesmerizing light show.

"But we can't drink in here."

"I don't want it to drink, I wanna use the cork to plug my hairy donut hole, in case you try any monkey business!"

"Don't worry Governor, they'll be none of that in here, I can assure you," Jaybird explained in his English accent. The nudist guru's eyes were solely on Nightcap . . . he never looked up at the lights on the ceiling. "Just relax . . . look into your subconscious and discard any fears and doubts. Avoid emotional fog through clear, organized thinking."

Jaybird continued rocking the Governor in his arms, while speaking softly.

"You are being relaxed into a deep meditative state, where I will reach into your unconscious mind and rewire your mind patterns."

"I am?"

Nightcap suddenly let out a huge burp.

"Bbbuuuuurrrraaaaappp!"

Jaybird ignored the rude belch and continued.

"Your brain frequencies are being lowered, equalizing the left and right hemispheres, so my subliminal suggestions can be firmly planted into your unconscious mind. You will follow my every order from now on. You're going to be a devout nudist!"

"Devout nudist?! *Hiccup!*"

"Yes, indeed! You love the sun's rays . . . and a slight breeze . . . all over your nude body! You don't want to wear a hot, sticky, confining pair of pants, or an itchy button down polyester shirt! It's a thrilling feeling of exposure without the bondage of your business suit . . . yes, an exhilarating sensation being freely exposed to the tingly air and warm sunlight."

"You suggesting every day be *Casual Friday? Hiccup!*"

"Yes, you could put it that way."

"I like that!"

"I knew you would! Governor, you're going to love being a nudist so much, that you're going to pass laws allowing public nudity throughout the entire state! Social nudity is a civil liberty . . . never forget that! You're going to insure this happens, and I'll be there to instruct and direct you every step of the way. You will listen to my every word and obediently do as you're told."

"No he won't!" exploded an echoing voice from across the room.

Jaybird whipped his head towards the front doors and there stood the Double-D Avenger.

"The Double-D Avenger!"

"That's right," our hero confidentially declared. "Get the Governor out of that pool at once! You're coming with me back to the Sheriff's station."

"Never!" spat Jaybird.

He released the Governor in the shallow water, and leapt out of the pool quicker than a speeding fart! Jaybird scrambled to the special Greek statue of the lady with the giant knockers. He twisted the nipple on the statue's left breast . . . *a knob* . . . and the back wall automatically rotated open! The entire wall opened on its turntable base/revolving platform, similar to a record player. Jaybird bolted through the open passageway, and a second later, the false wall rotated back into position, closing behind him.

Our hero dashed over to Nightcap to fish him out of the water before he'd drown!

"Come on, Governor Nightcap," urged Double-D, as she helped him out of the pool.

"Thanks, honey!" Nightcap then did a double-take at her big boobies! *"Great Scott!* What wondrously ripe, up thrust bazooms you've got there darling! That's quite a rib rack! You here for the orgy?"

"No, sir."

She managed to get the bombed ignoramus out, and sat him down on one of the marble benches.

"Don't look up at those lights . . . they're hypnotic! Just stay put for now . . . I'll come get you in a second."

"Whatever you say, my love!" he happily slurred.

Nightcap then looked around at the group of the life-size statues surrounding him.

"Thanks for your votes folks!"

Double-D didn't bother using the statue's nipple knob to open the revolving door to the secret hideout . . . she just used her super boobs to *smash* right into the place!

Ka-Boom! Crash! Ba-Bang! Crunch! Thunk!

As the dust settled inside the Super Nudists hidden headquarters, our hero's sharp eyes caught Jaybird exiting out the sliding back door.

"Stop! You can't escape from the Double-D Avenger!"

Outside the bungalow, Monty Jaybird streaked away! He quickly ducked behind the trunk of a eucalyptus tree, ready to ambush our hero! As Double-D bounded through the sliding exit, Jaybird reached into his utility belt and grabbed a half-dozen fig leaf shooting stars! These handheld fig leaf daggers were throwing weapons . . . thin, flat plates of shiny, metallic green metal with razor sharp edges! Jaybird fanned the flying stars at our hero with lightning speed!

Zip! Zip! Zip! Zip! Zip! Zip! Zip! Zip!

Off the propelling fig leaves flew . . . spinning around . . . straight for the Double-D Avenger's extravagant breastworks!

"Holy Hooters!" she cried.

Our hero cartwheeled out of the way, just in the nick of time! The twirling projectiles missed her, hitting the redwood bungalow wall instead!

Thunk! Thunk! Thunk! Thunk! Thunk! Thunk!

They stuck in the wood, like thrown darts!

"Drat!" snapped Jaybird. "She was too fast!"

A sinister smile then flashed over his face.

"Well, she won't be fast enough for this!"

He pulled another handheld weapon from the side of his utility belt. This time it was a sword handle, with a decorative, metallic green fig leaf on it. There was no long blade on the sword, until Jaybird squeezed its handle!

Snap-snap-snap-snap-snap-snap-snap-snap!

The fig leaf sword was *telescopic!* Jaybird held the weapon's handle near his crotch's own fig leaf, pointing it upwards. All of a sudden, sharp blade sections sprung out, one piece at a time, until the sword reached its full four foot length! It looked as if Jaybird had sprung an enormous metallic erection, the way he was holding it!

"Bless my over-the-shoulder boulder holder!" cried Double-D, seeing the expanding sword!

"On guard!" yelled Jaybird.

He lunged out to strike her, but the second the long blade hit our hero's unbreakable tatas, it crumpled and shattered! *Ka-Chink! Ding! Klink! Klang! Ping!*

"I . . . I don't believe it!" hissed Jaybird, looking down at the broken blade pieces and coiled springs scattered all over the grass. "Your indestructible boobies broke my telescopic sword!"

"Of course they did! *Ha, ha!* Now, give up Monty! The odds are stacked against you . . . literally!" she declared, while proudly sticking out her colossal chest. *Boi-ing!*

"Never!" he roared.

The bare-assed outlaw dashed away, but our hero kept on his cotton tail! Jaybird still had some Super Sunscreen energy left in him, so he was able to run away at close to fifty miles an hour!

"Time for a Booby-Quake!" thought our hero.

Double-D dropped to her hands and knees, and began doing *push-ups*! The ground started shaking! Our hero's super breasts actually caused a minor *earthquake*, each time her jiggly puffs hit the grass. *Ba-Boing! Ba-Boing! Ba-Boing! Ba-Boing!*

"Waaaahh-aaaahh!" cried Jaybird, as he fell down. "I get so nervous during earthquakes, I start shaking uncontrollably!"

Nudist guests at the resort also felt the strange, sudden tremors! Our hero didn't want to harm them, so she stopped her push-ups and sprung back onto her feet!

Snarling Jaybird got up too, and spotted his parked yellow bulldozer! It gave him idea! He'd use it to run over . . . and squash . . . the Double-D Avenger! Off he streaked!

He leapt into the driver's cage, turned the ignition key, and started up the forty-three thousand pound tank with metal treads!

Our hero's eyes widened behind her red bra-mask! The noisy bulldozer was rushing straight at her . . . its wide metal shovel ready to push and crush her! Double-D reflexively stuck out her arms and chest, as the bulldozer's shovel hit her!

Ka-Bang!

The Double-D Avenger and the bulldozer were now in a wrestling match! The mighty tank pushed her backwards with its shovel, but our hero summoned all her super strength to shove it away! Clouds of dust rose in the air, during the deadly game of tug-of-war!

"Eerrrr!" grunted Double-D.

"I'll pulverize your prodigious pompoms!" hissed Jaybird through gritted teeth.

"We'll see about that!" she snapped back. "I wish this bull<u>dozer</u> was just a bull *falling asleep!"*

Double-D let go of the metal shovel for a second, hopping backwards. She then threw the most powerful 'Booby-Punch' she could muster!

"Booby-Punch!" she heroically cried.

Ka-Boom!

Jaybird was rattled in his driver's seat! He suffered whiplash and lost control of the bulldozer! The heavy tank was pushed to the side by our hero's mighty melons! Double-D jumped out of the way, as the racing tank sped right past her. Some engine parts were left on the ground . . . damage from her devastating wallop!

"Waaahhhh!" hollered Jaybird. "I can't stop . . . can't steer! She busted something!"

The one-hundred and sixty-eight horsepower engine drove the bulldozer straight into the bungalow housing the hydrotherapy pool and the Super Nudists secret headquarters! Jaybird struggled at the controls, but something was wrong. Double-D's Booby-Punch compromised the steering and brakes.

"Oh-oh!" gulped Double-D, seeing what was about to happen.

The out of control bulldozer, with Jaybird at the wheel, crashed into the building, smashing it into thousands of pieces!

"Aaaaaahhhh!" screamed Jaybird.

Ka-Krash! Boom! Va-Voom!

Smoke and debris flew everywhere . . . wood pieces, drywall particles, electrical wiring, shingles, marble fragments, and other rubble!

Nudist visitors quickly gathered around to see what all the commotion was about! They were shocked by what they saw . . . a huge, smoking hole in the hydrotherapy pool bungalow! A flash of flame suddenly erupted from the opening, and everyone panicked! A crackling fire had started inside, and soon the entire building was ablaze!

"Fire!" exploded our hero.

Double-D ran off to save Governor Nightcap and Jaybird!

Inside, smoke was everywhere! Double-D had trouble seeing! The ceiling lights were off and so was the weird electronic music. The only sound she noticed, besides the cracking noise of the fire, was the sound of 'crunching' under her boots. Double-D realized many of the hypnotic light bulbs had fallen and shattered. Glass was all over the floor.

"Governor Nightcap?! Are you okay?" she called out.

"Why, yes, my dear!" he responded back. "I must have dozed off!"

Following the sound of his voice, our hero inched towards a bench. She could now see him! There he was, still sitting, happy as a clam.

"There you are!" she cried.

"Yep," replied the senile old drunk. "I have to say, I don't like this new steam room. The heater starts off with a loud bang, and instead of steam, it shoots off black smoke!"

"We're not in a steam room, Governor. There's been an accident! I've got to get you out of here! The bungalow's on fire!"

"A fire?! Oh no! Get me a phone, I've got to call my insurance company!" cried Nightcap. He then thought for a moment. "Madam, do you realize I'm nude?"

"I won't look."

"Where'd that new butler put my laundry?"

"Butler?"

"Yeah . . . the one who looked a little like my new chauffeur. They must be related."

"Don't worry about that now! Let's go!"

"Don't rush me! Where's my cigar lighter?!"

Nightcap felt around his bare chest, searching for a cigar and his lighter.

"Governor, I'm going to carry you out, because you'll cut up your bare feet. There's glass on the floor!"

"Glass on the floor?! Why I've told the help a thousand times to only use *plastic* wine glasses in the pool area!"

Double-D, using her super strength, carried Governor Nightcap out of the burning building. The sweltering heat was getting worse, and both of them were now sweating like pigs.

Our hero passed the disabled, wrecked bulldozer, but Jaybird wasn't in the driver's seat! Some smoke had cleared, and she noticed the open rotating passageway leading to the Super Nudists hideout! The revolving wall remained half-open. When Double-D took a closer look, she could see frantic Jaybird throwing a fit.

"My Super Sunscreen formula! It's burning!" he screamed.

Double-D could see the flaming papers on a burning table! The entire Super Nudist headquarters was on fire! Jaybird tried to save his secret written documents, but they burned to a crisp before he could reach them. The Super Sunscreen formula . . . which gave the villains their super-human powers, strength and speed . . . was incinerated! It went up in smoke!

"Noo!"

"Monty, get out of there! You'll burn to death! Come out and give yourself up!" she yelled.

"Never!" he shouted back.

The boiling heat was too much for him! Jaybird quickly retreated out the hideout's sliding back door . . . and not a moment too soon!

A falling wall of fire blocked Double-D and Nightcap from exiting out the same way.

"Take shelter under my shielding shakers!" urged Double-D.

"Gladly! *Ha, ha!*"

Nightcap happily did as he was told, and ducked his head under her monumental knockers.

Avoiding the scorching wall of fire, Double-D turned around and retreated out the big hole the bulldozer had made.

When they were safely outside, our hero sat Nightcap down on the grass. She took in some deep breaths of fresh air to clear out her lungs. Her giant boobs expanded and contracted as she did this! *Ba-Boom! Ba-Boom!*

"Just stay put Governor. Breath in some of this fresh air."

"Okey dokey," he smiled. "My, you sure are big balconied! I love your conical, super cantilevered charms! They're quite chestworthy!"

"Thanks!" she replied.

Nightcap suddenly had a puzzled look on his face.

"That's funny," he stuttered.

"What's wrong?"

"I suddenly have this strange desire to become a nudist! *Ha, ha!* Well, at least I'll get the nudist vote!"

Double-D rolled her eyes, and then zoomed off after Jaybird.

A red firetruck drove onto the property and screeched to stop in front of the burning bungalow. Its lights were flashing and its siren blaring! A group of handsome, *nude* firemen jumped off the truck and whipped out their fire hoses . . . not the hoses between their legs, those were already out! The firetruck's hoses were used! Moving fast, the men began putting out the fire.

Tipsy Nightcap looked at the naked firefighters and called out to them.

"Hey fellas, the men's locker room is over there!" he pointed. "Put something on before the ladies see ya!" He then added, " . . . and don't stand too close to that fire, or you'll have a weenie roast!"

CHAPTER TWENTY-FOUR

On the other side of the resort, the Double-D Avenger caught sight of naughty nudist Monty Jaybird, streaking off towards the miniature golf course. He ran past the sweat lodge, some busty ladies bouncing on trampolines, a naked couple playing leap frog, a nude photography class, and a group of nudists having an outdoor wine tasting event. As he zoomed past the display of wines on a draped table, he grabbed a glass for himself!

"To your health!" toasted Monty to the group.

He instantly gulped down the glass of red wine . . . all of it! *Gulp! Gulp! Gulp!* A second later, he put the glass down and sped off! *Burp!*

A giant, ten-foot tall fiberglass *golf ball* was standing in front of the miniature golf course, like a big statue. Groups of nudists were playing on putting holes, scattered around the little windmills, castles and other funny, toy-like fantasy buildings. The course had beautiful grounds filled with evergreen bushes, freshly cut grass, and gorgeous, blooming flowers of all shapes and colors.

As Jaybird raced around the man-made pond and flowing waterfall, the Double-D Avenger approached a couple of surprised nude golfers.

"Excuse me, may I borrow your putter and ball for a second?" she asked.

"Okay," stuttered the dumfounded, naked player.

He handed his iron and red golf ball to her.

"Thank you."

"By the way, who are you?" the man's nude girlfriend asked.

"The Double-D Avenger."

"The Double-D Avenger?!" they both joyously replied, suddenly recognizing her.

Our hero put down the golf ball, she carefully lined up her putting iron, and then looked across the course to where Jaybird was running.

He was slowing down now, unable to streak as fast as before, because his Super Sunscreen powers were wearing off.

Double-D glanced back down at her golf ball, she lifted her iron way up behind her caped shoulder, and then took a careful swing! *Swooossh! Boom!*

She hit the ball perfectly, with all of her super strength!

"Four!" she bellowed.

The red golf ball flew like a rocketing meteorite, straight for Jaybird! It flew up in a high curve, and then headed back down to Earth! Jaybird shouldn't have taken off his helmet earlier! As he scurried past the thirteenth hole, the speeding ball hit him right in the back of the head! *Pop!*

"Waaahhh!" he howled.

The Super Nudists guru leader was instantly knocked unconscious, and collapsed onto a mound of soft grass. *Ka-Plop! Zzzzzzzzzzzzzz!*

"A hole in one!" shouted happy Double-D.

Our hero turned and noticed white smoke rising from the bungalow housing what was left of the hydrotherapy pool and the Super Nudists headquarters.

"I see the fire's out, thank goodness!" she said in relief. "Those naked firemen did a splendid job! I think I'll go over there and thank them myself, after I get Officer Peaks here to cuff Monty!" A huge smile appeared on Double-D's horny face!

Several days later, Monty Jaybird's nudist brainwashing started to wear off on everyone. All the kidnapped victims 'sobered up,' returning to their 'normal selves.'

At the Driftwood Valley City Hall building, Mayor Artie Phishel called councilmembers Max Phuckter, Harry Bottoms, Soupy Phishel, and Helga Hoodwink to an emergency meeting. Hoodwink's young male intern, Rod Long, was present too.

" . . . so in conclusion, I motion that we *rescind* our recent law permitting public nudity throughout all of Driftwood Valley. It shall be annulled, and the city's original nudity laws will be reinstated. All those in favor say 'aye.'"

"*Aye,*" replied Phuckter, Bottoms, Soupy Phishel, and Hoodwink.

"All those opposed?" asked the mayor.

There was silence.

"The 'ayes' have it, the motion passes!" smiled Mayor Phishel.

"Ah, Mayor, now that we've finished that important bit of business, I'd like to motion that my intern Rod Long step in as our new city treasurer," suggested Hoodwink.

"Are you nuts? That ding-a-ling 'boy toy' of yours . . . our new city treasurer?! You've got to be kidding! Never! It's preposterous! He's a moron! Just look at him! He couldn't add up to two without taking off *your* blouse!" snapped the mayor.

Hoodwink turned red in the face, struggling to bite her tongue.

"You mean I've been screwin' this old bag for nothin'?!" remarked Long.

Hoodwink went ballistic and turned to her young gigolo! Grabbing her purse, she started belting him with it! *Bop! Boop! Bang!*

"*Old Bag?! Who the hell are you calling an old bag?! How dare you! You no good, ungrateful, son-of-a-bitch!*"

Nearby, at the Men's Central Jail, Chastity in her disguise as Mona Lot, paid a visit to her inmate boyfriend Oscar Dong. A thick glass window separated the seated couple as they talked using speakers and mics. Chastity/Mona tried to subtly adjust the back of her brunette wig, as they chatted.

"I'm so sorry Mona," muttered Dong. "I didn't know what I was doing . . . it was all Monty's fault . . . his brainwashing made me do it."

"I know Oscar," she reassured him. "That hypnotic hydrotherapy pool was diabolical!"

"You ain't kidding! My lawyer says the judge will probably let me off easy. Same for the others; Topsey, Candy, Rosey, Babette, Muffy, Willie, Dick, Hans and Taquito."

"I'm glad to hear that," she smiled. "It's funny, Monty's ideas and philosophies were very nice . . . the only problem was when he started using force! Brainwashing! Kidnapping! He should have let people *freely decide* if they wanted public nudity or not. Everyone must have the right to think and decide things for themselves . . . *the freedom to choose.*"

"I agree one-hundred percent!" he nodded. "Ah, Mona . . . there's something else I must tell you."

"What's that?"

She noticed an unhappy look on his face.

"Oscar, what's wrong?"

"Mona, you're a nice girl and I really like you . . . but . . ."

"But what?"

"There's another woman in my life."

Mona's eyes bugged out.

"Another woman?!"

"Yes."

"Who?"

"I only met her a couple of times . . . but I can't get her out of my mind! I'm obsessed with her! I think about her all the time . . . day and night! I dream about her constantly! She's captured my heart."

"She has?"

"Yes! There's something magical about her."

"Magical? Who is she?"

"The Double-D Avenger."

"The Double-D Avenger?!" gasped shocked Mona.

"Yes, the Double-D Avenger."

"I see," mumbled our hurt hero.

"I'm sorry Mona. We only had two dates . . . sort of . . . and I wanted to be honest with you before our relationship really took off. I'm sure you'll find the right guy someday. I'm just not him."

"Are you sure about this Oscar?"

"Yes."

" . . . but the Double-D Avenger is a total mystery. Nobody knows who she is, or where she comes from, not even the Sheriff. All we know is that whenever there's trouble in town, she shows up to give villains a little tit for tat."

"I know all that, but I'm still obsessed with her! Sorry Mona."

"Okay," she replied, as a little tear ran down her check.

"Goodbye, Oscar. Good luck."

"Thanks," he waved.

Mona waved back, then slowly got up and shuffled unhappily out the visitor doors.

As she stepped out of the Men's Central Jail, into the bright sunshine and fresh air, she thought carefully to herself.

Well, don't be too sad Chastity! Maybe this is all for the best. Carrying on a long charade as Mona Lot with Oscar would have been impossible to pull off. It wouldn't have been fair to Oscar. Eventually he would have found out I was Chastity Knott, and the Double-D Avenger! He's right, we only dated a few times, and maybe he isn't my 'Mr. Right.' True, we were physically attracted to each other . . . but did I really want to marry a devout nudist? I don't know. I can't answer that question. I might find the right guy someday, and when we marry, he'll know I'm the Double-D Avenger and keep my secret. I just have to be one-hundred percent sure he's 'the one' before I do it! Man, being a superhero sure is tough on dating and relationships . . . if your true identity is revealed, you're finished. Leading a double life as the Double-D Avenger can be protuberantly problematic!

Back at Chastity Knott's English Pub, afternoon business was booming as usual. Customers could be seen walking into the white, one story restaurant and bar, as British and American flags waved above the front entrance.

Inside, Chastity and Cousin Billy took a quick break from assisting customers. The two of them huddled at the end of the bar, so no one could hear them talk. Our hero didn't bother mentioning her brief love affair with Oscar Dong, since it was over now anyway.

"So, all's well that ends well," summarized Chastity. "Everyone's back to normal . . . all the brainwashing wore off . . . on the Super Nudists, the Sheriff, the Deputy, Doctor Della-Kwak, Romeo at the wax museum, Mayor Phishel, and the rest of those wacky politicians, including Governor Nightcap. I also saw a new TV commercial for Cactus Wilmington's Used Car Supermarket."

"Was he dressed?"

"Yep, and wearing his white cowboy hat."

"Wow! What an amazing story! It's unbelievable!" whispered Billy. "This was the Double-D Avenger's most incredible case!"

"I agree. Monty will be taking a nude vacation behind bars, but the rest of the Super Nudists will be out sooner."

"Because they were brainwashed?"

"Yes."

"Well, that's the end of them."

" . . . and the valley's original public nudity laws are back."

"That so? Guess we won't have to put towels on the bar stools anymore."

"No, we won't."

Billy suddenly looked puzzled.

"Chastity, what will happen to the Jaybird Growth Institute?"

"Adamite Acres purchased the property!"

"Adamite Acres? Oh, that other, competing nudist colony bought the place?"

"Yes! Monty had huge legal bills and fines to pay, so he was forced to sell off his valuable property. Adamite Acres needed a larger location, so now they've got *three* resorts open and running . . . Adamite Acres East, Adamite Acres West, and their location in Alaska."

"They have a nudist resort in Alaska?"

"Yes."

"What's it called?"

"Frosted Tips."

"So Jaybird's place will remain a nudist colony?"

"Yep. Good thing I cashed the five-thousand dollar check I got for winning that silly talent contest! Monty didn't want his institute turned into a subdivision of new homes. Now, at least, the property will remain a nudist, or shall I say, naturist resort."

"I see."

"Thinking about that gives me an idea," she smiled.

"Oh-oh!"

"I might just pay *another* visit there someday! It was kind of fun!"

"You will?!" asked surprised Billy. "As Mona Lot?"

"No, as Chastity Knott!" she laughed.

Cousin Billy eyes nearly popped out!

Meanwhile across town, at Adamite Acres West . . . formerly the Jaybird Growth Institute . . . business was booming, just like at Chastity's pub! The busy nudist resort was mobbed with naked visitors and the parking lot was full! This led to a spillover of cars forced to park on the neighboring residential streets.

Adrianna Azzhat, standing on the roof of her house, was livid! *She was mad as hell!* There she stood, holding her binoculars in one hand, while nervously rattling her house keys in her other. Her blue eyes were frantically scanning the area, above her pointed nose and pouting mouth. She quickly darted around from one corner of her roof to the other, in her conservative dark pants and purple turtleneck top. From her rooftop, she had a bird's-eye view of the nudist colony and the surrounding neighborhood streets.

"Nudists! Those confounded nudists! They're illegally parked! They're parading around in their birthday suits! Look at that obscene pose! Is that man flaunting an erection?! It's outrageous! I'm living next-door to a recreational sexual playground! It's the nightmare that never ends!" she howled. "So shameful and immodest! Untidy too!

Curse those motley throngs . . . those buck naked perverts . . . causing endless traffic and noise at all hours of the day and night! I need peace and quiet around here!"

Through the telescopic lenses of her binoculars, she could see peaceful, fun-loving nudists flying kites, having a picnic, and playing volleyball, horseshoes, and shuffleboard. One naked couple, relaxing on a big beach towel, had fallen asleep in each other's arms.

Azzhat's jaw dropped, as she lowered her binoculars.

"*Ooo!* Those unclad keisters make me sick to my stomach! How could anyone in their right mind, frolic around *naked* like that?!"

Just then, a car full of nudists . . . dressed, but soon to be nude . . . passed by, searching for a place to park! They quickly found a spot all right, *right in front of her house!* Furious Azzhat went absolutely *bonkers* seeing this, and rattled her keys at them like an angry rattlesnake!

"*Go away, you . . . you . . . no-good nudniks!*" she screamed, from the top of her roof.

ABOUT THE AUTHOR

WILLIAM WINCKLER was born in Van Nuys, California. During his prolific career, he has written, produced, and directed nearly fifty feature films, several TV series, pilots and English language Japanese movies and anime. Select credits include; *Tekkaman the Space Knight, Gaiking, Danguard Ace, Starzinger, The Double-D Avenger* (reuniting the Russ Meyer film stars), the award-winning *Frankenstein vs. the Creature From Blood Cove*, Capcom's *Zombrex: Dead Rising Sun* based on the famous zombie video game *Dead Rising, Ultraman X the Movie* (the 50th Anniversary film of the iconic Japanese *Ultraman* superhero character/brand), *Ultraman Ginga S the Movie,* and *Mega Monster Battle: Ultra Galaxy* (a Warner Bros. Japan release). Winckler has also authored several works of fiction, including the western-horror novel *Demon Head of Tucson*, and the humorous erotica titles *The Double-D Avenger Meets the Horny Howlers, The Double-D Avenger and the Dirty Movie House Mystery* and *The Double-D Avenger vs. the Super Nudists* based on his cult film classic *The Double-D Avenger*. He currently resides on the east coast of the U.S., after spending most of his life in Southern California.

Correspondence for the author should be e-mailed to: williamwincklerproductions@gmail.com

Milton Keynes UK
Ingram Content Group UK Ltd.
UKHW030824181124
451360UK00001B/161

9 798227 935540